Venero Armanno was born in ⌐___ at the University of Queensland, the AFTRS (Australian Film, Television and Radio School, Sydney), Queensland University of Technology and the Tisch School of the Arts, New York University, New York City. The son of Sicilian migrants, he has travelled and worked widely throughout the world. In 1995, 1997 and 1999 he lived and worked in the Cité Internationale des Arts, Paris.

Venero Armanno is the author of one book of short stories (*Jumping at the Moon*, equal runner-up in the prestigious Steele Rudd Award) and six critically acclaimed novels. These are *The Lonely Hunter*, *Romeo of the Underworld*, *My Beautiful Friend*, *Strange Rain*, *The Volcano* and *Firehead*. Following several successful residencies and speaking tours in Spain, France and Germany, *Strange Rain* and *Firehead* have been published internationally. He is also the author of two short books for younger readers, *The Ghost of Love Street* and *The Ghost of Deadman's Beach*, which have been recognised by the Children's Book Council as recommended texts, and his play, *Blood and Pasta*, was shortlisted in the 1996 George Landen Dann Award.

Also a screenwriter, he is currently working on the film production of *Firehead*.

Why do lovely faces haunt us so?
Do extraordinary flowers have evil roots?

Sexus, Henry Miller

'An Angel is here from the heavenly climes,
Or again does return the golden times;
Her eyes outshine every brilliant ray,
She opens her lips—'tis the Month of May.'

Mary, William Blake

'Oh, it was all such a lark . . . '
(dying words) of Ian Fleming

A Vintage Book
Published by
Random House Australia Pty Ltd
20 Alfred Street, Milsons Point, NSW 2061
http://www.randomhouse.com.au

Sydney New York Toronto
London Auckland Johannesburg

First published in Australia by Pan Macmillan Publishers Australia 1994
This Vintage edition first published 2001

National Library of Australia
Cataloguing-in-Publication Entry

Armanno, Venero, 1959– .
Romeo of the underworld.

ISBN 1 74051 074 7.

I. Title.

A823.3

Cover design by Greendot Design
Typeset in 12/16 pt Perpetua by Midland Typesetters, Maryborough, Victoria
Printed and bound by Griffin Press, Netley, South Australia

10 9 8 7 6 5 4 3 2 1

This book was written with the assistance
of the Queensland Office of Arts and
Cultural Development

Contents

ONE

Stronzo in a *Stronzo* Land

Stronzo is a seriously Italian, Italian type of word. More so when used in one of the southern dialects, preferably Sicilian. Look the word up in the Collins paperback *Italian Dictionary* and you will be told it means 'turd'. But take the word in the Sicilian dialect, pronounce it the right way—gutturally, *shtroonzoo*—and a world-weary grubbiness just can't help but ooze from your soul. It's best to have too much to drink before you utter the word, it's best to ache to the very core of your bones and, if you can manage it, to have not slept well for longer than you can remember. Then the word takes on its legitimate meaning and, when applied inwardly, with great personal insight, describes that gut-queasy sensation of realising you've made a mess of not only your own life but of the lives of those who have been luckless enough to become intimate with you.

Still, I get the feeling no translation can do justice to the Sicilian *stronzo*. You just have to live it.

Well.

To tell the truth of my story, Romeo's story, this lover's story, I'd felt that way long enough that I'd forgotten how to feel any other way. So I thought, and so said those who make an art of pointing out my shortcomings, of whom there are many. How I twisted and turned, apologised and deflected, obfuscated and bared my rotten soul to empathetic lovers and ferocious ex-lovers, to incensed friends and baffled family. Exhaustion made me pull myself together. What, in the end, were the multitude of sins I was guilty of, and better yet, who even cared? Whatever those sins might have been it was time to apply a psychic diuretic and just get rid of them. I found the yellow pages and I found myself a therapist and I spent a fortune on American self-help books. I developed a new vocabulary centred around the affirmation, 'I'm all right, Jack, so *fuck you*'. With my paid professional's professional support I repeated my dirty affirmation to nearly everyone I came into contact with. I stopped feeling sorry for myself and I sought out a new beginning and I made peace with my inner child. I addressed my higher power, I had a holiday with myself, and I declared the first day of the rest of my life. And ended up running screaming from my great city of Sydney as if all the devils of all the circles of hell had crawled up my *culo*.

Well, all right.

So even while checking in at Mascot airport on a stormy Sydney morning, there were mutterings and misgivings

amongst the passengers of impending doom. My antennae
should have been out; I should have realised these were signs
from the very beginning, for we Silicians like to believe
this—there are always signs.

More storms were predicted, turbulence, the types of
things we prepare ourselves for by entering that tiny yet well-
visited room in the traveller's soul and locking the door
against the discord the traveller's world will throw up at us.
There were a few shakes of the aircraft as we tilted toward
the sky over Sydney's rain-obscured bays and shoalwaters, a
significant dip that made me grab my armrest in one hand
and my copy of *The Comedians* in the other, there was a
rattling of the right wing, then as we levelled and stretched
out toward the blue forever we were above the ranges of
tumbling alabaster clouds and I knew my traveller's world
would experience no more discord.

My antennae were now worth as much as my extensive
library of self-help books.

Breakfast came. The two men in the row beside me made
as if the scrambled egg and fried sausage and grilled tomato
would make them throw up. One asked for a can of beer
and the other asked in a whisky-hoarse voice for whisky. The
steward obliged them though it was 7:10 in the morning;
she seemed to understand. My companions seemed terribly
hungover and terribly depressed. There was a contingent of
them spread throughout the aircraft, all joined by the umbil-
ical cord of maroon football jerseys with similar logos and
mottos. None of the contingent seemed likely to have actually
stood on a football field for twenty or thirty years. Good old
boys with potato-sack bellies and thinning hair, they called
out to each other loudly, made forced jokes, wallowed in
despair. For Queensland had lost the State of Origin series

to New South Wales the night before. I buried myself in the breakfast in front of me and watched a big old bank of breathless clouds.

We were on our way to the city of my new beginning, Brisbane.

The first hint of escape came as a telephone call late one night while I sat watching the ocean's black from the window of my apartment. Little Pepita and her brood were mysteriously quiet as angels, all curled together on the rug in front of the television. Bondi's night traffic hummed with car engines and radios. Drunks swayed under neon lights. The scent of salt air was like the sweat of an honest day's labour. Moonlight reflected in the moving swells of the sea, and the glass in my hand held the last squeezed-out dregs of a two-litre wine cask. I turned from the window and tried to focus on the ringing telephone. With only one or two more glasses of red I might have punctuated the night by hurling that telephone into a wall, as I sometimes liked to do with the odd piece of furniture. Wooden chairs are best. Still, I was drunk, but for that night at least, not sick-drunk.

It was a long-distance call from an old friend. Johnny Armstrong—now Doctor John, to his patients—lived in Brisbane and he wanted someone to mind his house while he was off on his extended overseas leave. He didn't want his house in the hands of strangers. Doctor John got it into his head to ring me. We'd had some times together, Johnny and me, all of those times back in our teenage past. I hadn't laid eyes on him in eighteen years. *Eighteen years*. But we talked about once a year, and one companionable year, twice.

Still, a few weeks after his call I was organised, Johnny was organised, and I was on flight 161 out of Sydney.

'Not eatin' the snag?' the first man in the maroon jersey

asked, turning his appropriately football-shaped head toward me. He was a huge old fellow, ruddy in the face, doing his best not to be spread over two airline seats and not succeeding. I was cramped against the window yet it was no less uncomfortable for him. I didn't really care. Fifty-five minutes air-time to Brisbane, what's a little awkwardness against the promise of spiritual emancipation?

'No, been off meat for a while,' I replied, which was true. The new me, a vegetarian of love. I'd grown sick of my stocky frame, I'd grown sick of a lifetime of being mistaken for a human version of a donkey. About a year earlier it occurred to me that if I could affect the pale and weedy aspect of an intellectual bookworm, maybe, just maybe, someone might actually take me seriously. Oh, I munched lettuce leaves and carrots and endives and radish sprouts until all I could shit was garden mulch, and it had the desired effect. It was a miracle of weight loss, a miracle of stupidity. I was no longer a donkey, I was a good head of broccoli. Puny for the first time in my life, thanks to which I had a constant head cold. A condition not helped by the cabin's pressurisation as we'd taken off from Mascot. My eardrums had ached like crazy and took ages to settle down.

The big fellow's big laugh rocked five rows of seats in front of us. He said, 'You think there's meat in *that*?' He was over his nausea. He scooped the lonely snag out of my tray and fed himself on it like a corpulent magpie with a juicy worm. 'Sinneysider?'

'Not for much longer.'

'Betcha crowed with the result, eh? But she's enemy territory you goin' inta now, matey. We eat Sinneysiders alive.'

He stared at me and I blew my nose and wiped my eyes until he left me alone.

'How long ya plannen stoppen in Brissey?' my neighbour asked, back again.

'About six months.'

I took air, facing away. His breath was equal parts new whisky and the rotten dregs of an older bottle. I concentrated on the open pages of my book until he fucked off. Which he did. My neighbour turned to his companion and grumbled loudly, but within a half-minute they'd forgotten about the snub and were calling for more drinks and I could stare, peaceful again, at the tumult of white clouds.

There were no storms and none of the pitching and yawing the captain's Yankee voice told us to expect. That little safe house inside my traveller's soul was vacant. I could enjoy the sunshine and ignore the familiar desire to hide and be afraid. As my therapist liked to say, with his Viennese-via-New York-come-to-Sydney-for-the-sun accent, 'Zo, Romeo, you zee, ze universe iz indeed *ze benign place*, und ze future iz zo *bright* for you.'

We passed the mendacious Vision Splendid of Gold Coast beaches. The outskirts of Brisbane approached. I craned this way and that for I was keen to lay eyes on the city. Way back in the past—1976 to be exact—I spent six months there. Six months, when I had been sixteen turning sixty. But for a while it had been an oasis made perfect by its very distance from the living hell of Marrickville. No wonder Johnny Armstrong's new idea that I mind his house while he spent half a year in Switzerland had seemed such a gift from God, so right, so very, very, me.

My two fat and cramped companions also craned to get a look out the window but they conspicuously avoided eye

contact with me. That was fine, I didn't care. *Fuck you both*,
I thought. Doctor Martin Kolner was justifiably proud of my
new ability to not give a shit what strangers think of me.
What might have disconcerted him still were my neverending
thoughts of taking one of the stewardesses from behind while
the 727 ploughed through marshmallow clouds.

So who's perfect?

The aircraft descended through those puffy clouds and
the closest stewardess was perfectly safe from me. As the
landing gear locked down—a reassuring pneumatic wheez-
ing and clicking—I glimpsed the edges of a brown city,
a brown river. Travellers chatted and pointed through their
little porthole windows. I remember checking my watch.
Eight a.m. on what was supposed to have been a breezy,
stormy Tuesday morning. The skies had stayed blue and
the winds had stayed away. The cabin crew were strapped
into their jump seats, our hand luggage was securely
stowed under our chairs or in overhead lockers, our stom-
achs were warm with eggs and hot drinks and juice and
rolls and marmalade.

And there was our destination.

And here was an explosion.

It rippled like a wave from the back of the aircraft to
the front, its forward motion passing like a living thing
beneath my feet. The *blatt!* was something more felt than
heard, though there was a lot to hear. People shouted as the
727 jerked and dipped sideways. Then down. More shouting,
not screams, just garbled words. I grabbed the armrests of
my seat as if that could make a difference. Out the window
I was treated to an unwelcome, awfully angled spectacle of
the entire waking city of Brisbane.

Hurtling toward me, personally.

No red roofs, I thought. We were going to drop out of
the sky onto an absence of red roofs. *A winding brown river,* I
also thought, *it's like some mythological snake. And our flaming
sky detritus will be swallowed whole by the gaping maw of a shit-
coloured serpent.*

The aircraft righted itself and the view of a hurtling land
mass disappeared from my window, to be replaced by blue
sky and, yes, breathless clouds again. I knew then we would
live. It was okay. We were still flying, not dropping like a
stone, flying. I wanted to laugh out loud. *This* had happened
to *me*? Then the urge to laugh died for from the rear of the
aircraft to the front, just as the dull explosion had moved,
the word fanned along that we were on fire. Those in the
back rows saw a long streak of flame trailing one of the great
engines. And when the trailing flame caught up with that
great engine?

All for just the price of a budget one-way fare.

I looked at my hungover buddies but they were engrossed
in each other. Why had I been rude to them? I wanted to
look into the eyes of a fellow being and be told I wasn't
about to die. And if I was to die, I at least didn't want to
die alone. I needed them, Jesus, I really *needed* them. As if
they cared. So what good was a 'Fuck you!' now, Doctor
Kolner?

The intercom speakers spat five words 'Purser to the
flight cabin!' and clicked off. Where was the captain's steady
Yankee voice? Where was the dreamy new age music of
television advertisements? The captain sounded exactly the
way I felt. The purser and every other flight attendant into
the bargain blundered up the aisles into the front cabin. We
all watched them go as if they were leaving us to fry alone.
What was happening? Where were the answers? Where was

the clear-eyed strength and security that made us buy tickets from *this* godforsaken airline?

But this is Australia, we just *don't* have air disasters— didn't anyone realise? Apparently not. Oh how those flight attendants bolted like short-distance sprinters!

Amongst the now half-hearted cries that we were on fire, some started to call out that we were going to die. Except they were doing it as a joke. The football jersey contingent, verbatim:

'We're gonna crash! Woo-hoo!'

'And we're gonna die! Woo-hoo-hoo-hoo-hoo!'

'Woo-oo-oo-oo-oo!'

Like the chant of a revved-up television talk-show audience, or a stadium crowd who have seen their team score a miraculous try. Maybe these football fans really did want to die, their state had just lost the series after all. They could have been sincere—who could tell?

I prayed like I'd never prayed before, I looked into my *stronzo* soul and tried to make peace with the Author of my existence, but somehow the Author had gone missing.

When the crew came out of the front cabin I stopped looking for Him/Her. The crew rushed down the aisles. The strangest thing, nobody tried to ask what was happening. You didn't need to because the answer was in the faces—it takes a lot to turn faces that shade of white. Our crew were scared and showing it. That was at least some relief. No room for lies, we were in deep shit, and it shut the good old boys right up.

The purser spoke through the speaker system. If the captain's voice was strained, his was nothing compared to the wretchedness of this voice.

'We are approaching the airport.'

(Breathless, lungs starved of air.)

'We have to attempt an emergency landing.'

(*Attempt? Attempt?*)

'Check for your nearest emergency door. The emergency slides will be activated.'

(Now the purser became authoritative, maybe barking orders made her feel better about the whole thing.)

'Check the emergency procedures as described on the card in the pocket of the seat in front of you! Once we're down everyone must exit the aircraft as quickly as possible! Leave all hand luggage! Newspapers, magazines! Flowers if you have them! Anything at all, leave it behind! Once you are down the evacuation slide—*run from the aircraft.*'

Click.

Did the purser's nerve run out? Who could blame her? The aircraft plummeted from the sky in the way of bad dreams. It was obvious what was happening. We had an engine on fire and if we were really, terrifically, superbly unlucky, we would explode in mid-air. Run away from the aircraft once we're down the slides? Try and put a shine on that one!

Sweet and sunshiny Brisbane.

Any minute we could be so much scattering ash to cultivate Brisbane gardens. I hadn't seen the city in nearly twenty years. It should have been a hundred. At this time on a normal Tuesday morning I should have been in bed with a cheap wine hangover and Pepita curled over the blankets. Oh, my absent God, *such* is my reward for not facing my problems like a *mensch*—Doctor Kolner's favourite word. He had warned me of consequences for running away. I'd accused him, loudly, vociferously, of being hungry for more of my money. A house extension, a new BMW, an apartment for some mistress—how sadly he had shaken his head!

The far and wide spread of Brisbane kept me occupied as a coolness descended over the craft. Silence. Maybe all passengers were studying their emergency cards, or maybe every one of us was in a not-so-successful monologue with our Maker. Below, the city was peaceful and quiet, a whole metropolis of folk so gentle they barely raised a sound. And on this aircraft, a world of ninety or a hundred folk similarly hushed.

The terrain was familiar—at least I wasn't to die in a completely alien place. And I would make history by dying in Australia's first commercial aircraft crash. If I'd ever wished for fame I must have done it on a monkey's paw. Anyway, now I saw the television towers on top of Mt Coot-tha. When I was sixteen, in some friend's car, usually Johnny's, we'd go parking. Friday night, Saturday night, smooching in the dark hills, rubbing secret bits of growing bodies. How many times in six months had I been there; with how many bad-breathed and badly-perfumed companions; what could we have possibly spoken about in those days?

We were past Mt Coot-tha and then there was the green sweep of Brisbane's western suburbs. First though the vast grounds of the Toowong cemetery. I stared and stared down at it. Would they have room for another ninety or a hundred?

The 727 was screaming down and no one said a word.

There was one more landmark coming. I pressed myself to the perspex passenger window. Where was it, where was it? I looked hard, as if that gem from my memory could save me from this hunk of fatiguing metal. The aircraft wailed over and I saw clearly the gem was no longer there. We were low enough and there was just enough time to get a glimpse of some kind of housing development, apartments or something, townhouse terraces, FOR SALE signs.

Fuckin' fuckin' fuckin' (if I said it enough I could almost forget where I was) stupid bastards.

For once upon a time at the peak of Bowen Hills' hillock there was a place we'd go for music and dancing and beer, and for girls. A huge and ornate structure from a bygone era, that Cloudland Ballroom, and never was a place so properly named. You saw it from all over Brisbane, perched on its hill with its neon lights more colourful than anything in the evening sky. The ballroom always seemed so kind of nice, so magical. It must have burned to the ground, a Brisbane tragedy, for no one would knock such a place down for anything as crass as commercial housing. The red lights of Cloudland's central dome always made me think of the silhouette of a volcano—the active Mt Etna, of course. Its sprung wooden dance floors used to always make me think of the canvas floor of a wrestling ring, bouncing up and down, up and down, ready for sparring, skirmishing, for the beery-dreamy love match that would start when you latched onto some new Friday night girl.

The craft was over the river again. The river wound into my memory. The river, the river, it *was* a river of memory, all right, and I was back at the Cloudland Ballroom. I just couldn't help myself. The aircraft might have been about to explode but somewhere in that winding, shit-coloured snake my eyes saw the lights of 1976.

Friday night and I've already put a few away back at Johnny's parents' house. They let him drink at home, the lucky prick. They go away every second weekend to a piss-weak little wood cabin on Cylinder Beach at Stradbroke Island. Johnny gets the family home to himself, every second Friday night

to Sunday night. Born under a lucky star. His good point is
that he lets most of us in on his good fortune. His bad point
is that he has so much good fortune. Makes me sick. Well,
fuck it anyway.

Tonight Johnny and I have been drinking Fourex cans so
we're pretty juiced as he parks his old Holden ute in that
football field of a car park behind the ballroom. Ushers guide
the streams of cars in. Their torches tell you where to go
but Johnny's not the type to be guided at all. He sticks his
car where he likes and one of the ushers, a tall skinny guy
in a white shirt and black bow tie, gives us a look but no
trouble. Johnny's glare is enough. Tonight it's just me and
Johnny because we're going to do well, that's what he promised with the superior knowledge that comes from being
older by a year.

How could Johnny have known?

For that's the night I met her, my treasure.

She happens to be with us in the front row. The crowd
has shoved we intrepid front-rowers right up against the
stage. Every now and then a roadie with long greasy hair
throws a couple of buckets of cold water over us so we won't
expire from the heat a lot of excited little bodies generate.
A rhythm and blues band with a new recording contract are
playing loud, amps up to eleven, drummer flaying, harp
soaring like heaven's own instrument. We're hot and sweaty,
Johnny bobbing and rubbing up against her and her friend,
and me stupid and shy and scared.

Because she's got black mascara eyes and bottle-blonde
hair, because she's small and delicate, because when she looks
at me it's like a stab, a scary mortal stab.

So I dance like a loony because I'm too nervous to do
anything else.

The sweat pours. Everyone around is just as drunk and just as excited. But her eyes, God they sober me up. Will I ever be as happy as I am standing close beside this tiny stranger in front of this raucous band? They're sweating too, lined muso faces dripping with exertion and love. When they finish their first bracket Johnny has the one girl by the elbow and me by a bicep. He's going to make sure things turn out just fine for all of us—that's his way. He's got sharp blue Paul Newman eyes and thick black Elvis Presley hair and he can bowl a spin ball at cricket. With credentials like that Johnny can do just about whatever he wants.

I look around and black eyes has to follow us because Johnny's got her friend, but there's an insolent look on her face. She's pissed off. I can't even smile at her. Taped music echoes loud and hollow in the cavernous ballroom as Johnny leads us across a floor slick with sweat and beer and a bit of blood. We head to the crowded bar.

And somehow Johnny's got black eyes' friend buying *him* drinks. We go out into the fresh night of the car park with double Scotch whiskies and ice smuggled with us. I haven't said a word yet. Black eyes isn't drinking her drink and I'm not drinking mine. We stand awkwardly together, looking this way and that—anywhere but at each other—then with a shared thought we both toss the booze into the grass and can't help but share a grin. So I ask her her name and she says Monica. Her voice is soft and husky but she's going to stay as aloof as an ice princess. She doesn't ask me my name but tilts her head back to where Johnny and her friend tongue-kiss against the side of a dented panel van.

'And *who's* that?'

'That's Johnny.'

'God.'

We watch the two of them some more. They're supposed to be in the dark but the moon is full and it's clear
enough to see Johnny working his hand up Monica's friend's
shirt. I wish I could count how many nights I'd spent with
Johnny that ended with his hand up someone's shirt. Monica
looks away.

'*Jesus.*'

'Well,' I say, worldly-wise. 'Two to tango, huh?'

'She's drunk. Anyone can tango.'

Monica folds her arms and looks pissed off. It's like she
practices this look in her mirror to get it just right. Maybe
she wants to go home or maybe she wants to go dance. The
rhythm and blues band strike up again, and even out here
it's good and raw and kind of grungy. But maybe more than
anything else Monica doesn't want to leave her friend alone
with Johnny. Monica leans against a shiny canary-coloured
Torana XU-1 with mags as fat as hell, and sighs at the sky.
Then she looks at me, waiting.

So I say, 'Come and dance.'

'*I'm* staying right here.' Monica flashes her eyes at me to
let me know that if there's a dickhead amongst us, it's definitely me. Somehow that makes me grin at her.

'I mean dance here.'

'You're kidding.'

I take Monica in my arms as if I've known her all my
life. I can't dance to save that life, and I've never been more
scared, but sometimes there's this bold little part of me that's
maybe the greatest actor in the world. As we do a waltz in
the dirt and sand I see something in Monica she would never
have wanted anyone to see. And it's this: she's as scared as
me. It's just that we're both good actors, that's what you
learn if you want to get through Friday night. *Oh Monica,*

your eyes back then, your hair, the way your hand was so warm in
mine. You felt like magic and pain all wrapped up into one. Who'd
ever seen an Italian girl with dyed-blonde hair?

She barely comes to my chest, she's graceful, she's light
as a feather, and stone silent. Monica looks up at me once
then she looks up at me again, and it makes me like her
more. Over her shoulder I can see the famous neon-lit two-
storey Cloudland arch. My heart is lifting and I have this idea
that everything in life from now on might just border on the
fantastic. Under the moon Monica's hair is snow white.
Under the stars Monica's lips are moist. I know I want to
kiss her.

So I blurt, 'Will you go out with me?' because that's the
way you ask in 1976.

Monica looks at me again and we're still dancing a bad
waltz that has nothing to do with the drifting, booming
music. She gets this look in her face like she's one up on
me. 'Why?' Monica says with the inflection of a little bitch
queen.

And right then there's a falling star, bright and big across
the black sky. We see it at the same time. From the Cloudland hill it's as if we can reach out and snatch it from the
jet. Monica's hand clutches mine and we make our wishes.
I'm giddy both with her and that trace of fire in the sky.
Monica's breath is on my face.

She's excited, and she asks, 'What did you wish?' Her
voice is husky and low again, lower.

I'm eating her up with my eyes. I can't help myself at
all. 'I wished I was on that star.'

Monica punches my arm, then she pauses as if she needs
to catch herself and think. Very evenly, looking straight at
me, she says, 'I wonder why you would make a wish like

that?' Her lips curl at the corners and she stands away from
me. 'What was your name again?'

I don't even have a chance to tell her because Johnny's
behind me and he snaps us out of our rigmarole. Monica goes
over to her very dazed-looking friend.

'What?' I just about spit at Johnny while staring at
Monica and her friend and the missed opportunity. 'What?'

Johnny looks at me a minute. His expression says I've
gone loony. Then he gives me that crooked Elvis Presley grin
that goes too well with his Elvis Presley hair, and he takes
me by the arm, and Jesus Christ, I'm not pissed off any more.

The aircraft hummed and the atmosphere was icy. Fear
jangled in the very air we breathed. I blew my nose, which
only made things worse. The closer we came to the ground
the harder my ears hurt. Everything was closing up—I was
no longer conscious of sound, only of a subaural humming
that was my own blood. Shit! It felt like my eardrums would
explode. Which would go first, the aircraft or my ears?

Crashing in toward Brisbane airport.

The control tower, scurrying fire engines, it all happened
too fast and I was deaf as well. My neighbour stared bug-
eyed out my window and then his ever-more ruddy face
yammered at me. Spit gummed his lips. I couldn't hear a
thing but at least I wasn't alone any more. On the armrest
his pudgy hand went over mine. The bulge of his eyes looked
into the bulge of my eyes, then we were coming down. We
watched a fire-engine-red fire engine race alongside us as our
wheels bumped against planet earth. We saw the faces of the
men inside the unit's front cabin. One man had a heavy
moustache, the other wore a white helmet with black straps.
The fire engine was a vision of salvation. My ruddy neighbour

and I suddenly grinned at each other; we watched, transfixed
by an outside world we quite sincerely wanted to be a part
of again. Our hands gripped harder. Flight 161 screeched and
skidded and slewed across the tarmac.

We were far from the terminals, in fact at the very outskirts of the airport. Beyond were marshlands, swamps,
Moreton Bay. Some omniscient control tower being had
decided it was better we didn't explode all over Brisbane's
nice new terminals. The fire engine raced with us, that is
until it crashed into a hole in the ground twice its own size.
My neighbour and I exchanged a look—so much for our
salvation! Then the aircraft gave a jaw-breaking jerk and a
spine-cracking slew and the aisles were full of people. The
emergency doors were open and Brisbane air came flooding
in, carrying with it the stench of burning fuel, benzine, oil,
marshes, crap, who knows.

The agony in my head made me almost too nauseous to
stand. When I did I might as well not have bothered because
bodies jammed up the aisles and I wasn't about to be let in.
The cabin crew yelled as passengers jumped and slid down
the sloping yellow baby-cushion circus slides. Silence, all in
silence. This had happened to me once—the deafness, that
is—many, many years before on a Lufthansa flight into
Frankfurt while in the grips of a European influenza. Miserable, deaf, a sympathetic German stewardess had thrust a
polystyrene cup of water into my hand, had dropped a few
pellets of some concentrate into it, and I tried desperately to
drink it—nearly poisoning myself. You had to sniff it you
see, to open up your air passages. God knows what it would
have opened up if I'd ingested it.

Now a few passengers held cellular telephones—cellular
telephones at a time like this?—and spoke urgently into

them. An old man in a grey suit and with a yellow flower in his lapel wept as he was pushed forward. Many tried to heft out hand luggage. Were we *all* deaf, hadn't *anyone* understood the purser's instructions?

The attendant at the emergency door over the right wing was white-faced but efficient; her training hadn't been for nothing. I could see her mouthing words to people going out the aircraft. I felt sorry for her. How much would she have wished to be getting out of that aircraft sooner rather than later? And what were the urgent words she was speaking? I turned around. People went out each of the emergency doors, helped—pushed!—by attendants. My turn came closer, the line moved forward, and I focused on the words formed by my attendant's red lipstick mouth. I read, *jump and slide, jump and slide and then run*, and everyone did their best.

At the emergency door the attendant shoved passengers out like throwing sacks of potatoes from the back of a truck. That was how I was expelled. I slid and bounced for all I was worth, and tumbled too, completing the slapstick with a thunking forward roll onto the tarmac—hardly the best way to meet terra firma, but by then who was complaining?

I looked back at the aircraft.

The very next passenger after me had punctured the yellow ski slope with a high heel. She was stuck halfway up, her dark blue skirt up around her hips, stockings torn. I clambered back up and collected her as air gushed from the long diagonal rent in the fabric. The emergency slide was deflating like an old balloon. At the door over the wing the attendant dragged remaining passengers to another escape route. I helped the lady with the offending high heel onto the strangely greasy black tarmac, then a man with mournful

eyes elbowed me aside, took her by the forearms and half-
lifted, half-dragged her away.

The aircraft was being doused by three fire units. It
seemed to float in a sea of white foam. That was why the
tarmac was so slippery. To my right, the crashed fire engine
was upended like a toy. It stuck out of the ground perpen-
dicular to the sky. Most passengers were running but a few
of the more dazed wandered near the ditched fire unit as if
inspecting. A war zone wouldn't have looked much different.
The air was a mixture of pungent odours, mostly man-made,
yet also the farty primordial stench of the marshes. It was
then I noticed that in spite of the fire units and the many
men in heavy uniforms and the foam being poured over the
aircraft, what looked like a rich geyser bubbled from a rear
engine. Fuck! The marshlands were ahead and I ran like
buggery.

I lapped young and old, middle-aged men still with cellular telephones inexplicably jammed to their ears, the good
old boys puffing and wobbling their bellies toward safety, and
then there was a little blonde girl with braids who was mean-
dering. I snatched her up under one arm and sprinted on,
the absolute winner, lugging the little girl like a magnificent
melon.

Welcome to Brisbane.

So we were left in the marshes, in disconsolate groups,
for what seemed like hours. More hours followed inside the
private rooms of the terminal complex. There was what they
called a 'debriefing' for the passengers. What could they tell
me that I wanted to hear—now that I *could* hear again? My
ears unblocked sometime during the sprint from the aircraft.
Free flights in perpetuity would have made amends. So would
first class ticket upgrades whenever I travelled. But there

wasn't even a souvenir. They should have kept key rings in the shape of a burning flying kangaroo for occasions just like these.

Passengers with connecting flights were promised other connecting flights, and we were served breakfast again. Scrambled eggs and grilled tomatoes and sausages but not nearly as good as those we'd had on the flight. I draw no conclusions.

Outside the private rooms police and television camera crews interviewed anyone from flight 161 who had enough spit left to speak, and people really did want to speak, mainly about Trauma and Life. I wandered up and down in front of the media. No one wanted my story. The heroes of the day were the good old boys recently dejected by the State of Origin loss. The cameras couldn't seem to get enough pictures of their maroon jerseys and camaraderie. The second-tier heroes were those middle-aged men who had their mobile phones out from the time we hit the runway. As it transpired they were journalists themselves, all from the sports pages, also returning from Sydney's game. They'd been phoning the story to their editors *in situ*. There is no tragedy, or tragedy in the making, or tragedy averted, that isn't better first-hand.

Once reunited with our belongings, hand luggage from the aircraft cabin, heavier luggage from its bowels, I even found my copy of *The Comedians* again. I should have been elated but I was only tired. The business of survival had a sense of tedium to it; it just took too long. So I wandered off and went to look through the terminal lounges for Johnny, who had promised to meet me. All in vain.

I hefted my bags.

Outside there was a tremendous Brisbane sun that

wanted to sear the skin from my face. I could feel it burning away as I leaned on my baggage and waited for a taxi to appear. The pure light was dazzling. Everything seemed unfiltered. Where was a protective halo of smog? The Brisbane sun would achieve what flight 161 had failed to do; I would be burned to a crisp in two minutes. My shirt clung to my skin and everything about me felt oily and acrid.

Once upon a time I'd spent a few hours in the famous Mercan Oruculer Hamami bath-house in Istanbul. For several Australian dollars you are made to lie on a long slab amongst the marble pillars while one or two burly dark men with burly dark moustaches give you a muscular scrubbing with warm water and lye soap. Every bit of your skin is left raw-pink. That was exactly what I needed now. Something about the mugginess of this Brisbane day reminded me of those steamy bath-houses near the main gates of Istanbul's main bazaar, but it seemed strange to believe Brisbane was always like this. Why did I only remember the river and the frangipanis and Monica's kisses?

A yellow taxi took its time in arriving. The driver then wanted to talk about the trail of fire nearly all of Brisbane had seen in the sky. I wanted to find out if the car had air-conditioning.

'We were waiting for it to go up but it didn't. It was on the radio. They had journalists up there, you know that, on their way back from Sydney. They came *that* close. *That* close. The whole city stopped what it was doing and went outside and looked up at the sky and prayed like anything.'

He drove slowly, at Brisbane's pace.

'Didn't explode. Didn't explode and didn't bloody crash. Some very lucky individuals will be very happy to be home today. Where do you call home?' It was a good question; the driver waited for me to answer. When I didn't he said, 'Anyway matey, welcome to Brisbane.'

I watched passing suburbs, the faces of people in their cars, the kinds of clothes people wore in the streets.

'What happened to Cloudland?'

The driver turned in his seat and glanced at me, mouth twisted. Then he went back to his driving. 'Met my missus there in '66. National Party wanted it for the land developers in the mid-eighties. Worst kept secret in the world. Had the Deen Brothers raze it to the ground at 2 a.m. One day you woke up and the whole thing was gone. Took them years to get their new construction going up there, don't know why. It's still called Cloudland. Don't know why that is either.' The driver breathed heavily through nostrils sprouting tufts the colour of tobacco. Some disease, or maybe it was just too much drink, left him a blue-veined and very bulbous nose. 'Fuckin' bastards,' he said.

We drove the rest of the way without speaking.

Next I found a note and a mad dog. The note was outside, the mad dog was inside, and Johnny Armstrong's house was falling down. Johnny Armstrong himself was nowhere to be seen.

The long verandah at the front was shielded from the mid-afternoon sun by two large yellow awnings. All the same, the timber underfoot was split and spongy. The outside walls of the old wooden Queenslander peeled in the sunlight, patches showing where white paint had given up the ghost maybe ten years earlier. The gardens were overgrown and anything good, like the pale pink camellia in bloom by the front gate, seemed strangulated by thorny weeds. It was lucky to be alive at all.

Sometime many years ago someone had cultivated a
vast warm-climate garden for the weather-beaten old place,
but it certainly hadn't been Johnny Armstrong. The ragged
remnants of frangipani, gardenia and fuchsia struggled in
the suburban jungle. There were enough perennials, bulbs
and herbaceous plants to fill a nursery. All of it gone to
ruin and probably disease-ridden as well. Why had Doctor
John let things go so? What kind of life did he live? It
was like letting Eden disappear for lack of a motor mower.
I'd seen this kind of thing often enough in my Sydney
gardening rounds; that was how I made my living, after
all. Finding a job like this one would have made my
wallet's day.

And the house itself, I stared up and around it. Where
would you start if you wanted to recapture some of its
former glory?

I wiped my brow and put down my suitcases and
untacked the note from the front French doors. A dog yapped
inside the house. The sound was aggressive and desperate and
strained all at the same time. Peering through the little
squares of glass in the French doors, instead of a monstrous
hound from hell I saw a blue heeler cattle dog. There was a
surprisingly well-furnished lounge room in which the dog
turned quick circles. It was angry and it was alone. If *this*
was to be my companion for six months, how would I even
get through the front door? I needed all this like a hole in
the head. And where was Johnny? My flu and the events of
the day gave me a headache. I felt I was still falling into the
snaky river.

Dear Romeo,
You big dumb shit-for-brains, where have you been for the past

two days? I've been trying to ring you! Change of plans, had to leave early for Switzerland. Don't bother asking why, it's too long a story. All I can say is I'm glad to be the fuck out of here. Went this morning while you were no doubt arriving. If you're reading this then you're all right and Blue hasn't starved to death. He's a friendly little shit-for-brains himself, your only danger is he'll lick you to death. Unless you have a bad aura, in which case he'll eat you alive, starting with your plump little dick. A word of advice, don't make any sudden gestures. Two Dobermans laid into him once and tore an ear off. Since then he's been a little jumpy. The key's in the usual place. Too bad I couldn't be there to give you the grand tour and catch up. Make yourself at home for six months and don't worry about my mail, phone calls, all that bullshit. It'll catch up in the end. Where have you been the past two days?

And welcome to Brisbane, arsehole.

J.A.

I nearly turned around and went back to the airport. Just what I needed, Johnny's brand of sarcasm. Hilarious. But I wasn't a big dumb shit-for-brains any more. I was thin, bookish, wasted! But then I thought, *what am I really doing here?*

I sat on my largest suitcase and ate my hands up.

The mutt inside the house yapped and snapped away as if he longed to traumatise me in the same way two Dobermans traumatised him. A dog? There had been no talk of a dog. If that dog didn't shut up I'd tear his other ear off. What else could go wrong?

I reread the note and perspired. One thing about the note was unclear. *The key's in the usual place.* What usual place would that be, Johnny, seeing as how I've never been to this house before? Maybe it was all a joke, some long-forgotten ruse from 1976. Any second Johnny and a stack of now-lined, now-aged, now-unhappy faces from the past would jump around the corner. Surprise, Romeo!

Didn't happen.

I leaned my forehead against the glass of the front doors and stared at the barking cattle dog. It now gave little jumps in the air. At my jugular, I supposed. Where were the neighbours and what would they be thinking of this ruckus? But the answer was simple. In this inner-city suburb all the neighbours were where they should have been, at work. So what was I supposed to do, break a window to get in—then what?

And I still hadn't had the chance to tell anyone about my near-death experience.

It came back to me. 1976. Johnny Armstrong's parents going to their little Stradbroke Island beach shack every second Friday through Sunday. Johnny letting us all make use of their house while they were away. It had been a big home in Enoggera, with a vast empty space under the house where Johnny's father had progressively built a laundry, a workshop, a music room, and where a spare front door key was always kept in an unusual place. Johnny hadn't forgotten and he had faith that I wouldn't have forgotten. I left my baggage on the front verandah and went down the rickety wooden steps and around the side of the house.

The block of land accommodating Johnny's home was larger than it looked from the front. In Sydney it would have been worth a fortune, even if most of it sloped at a thirty and then a forty degree angle so that the front of the house was level with the road, but its rear was supported by twelve-metre iron struts. I stopped a minute and studied what I could see of the back part of the land. It was like Johnny

Armstrong's personal rainforest, but I knew these inner
suburbs of Auchenflower, Bardon, Milton, and Toowong
were still all part of the foothills of Mt Coot-tha's forest, no
matter how populated the areas had become.

Colours were everywhere, mostly pinks and greens. The
largest jacaranda tree I have ever seen dominated the level
part at the back of Johnny's land. And it wasn't alone. There
were palm trees even taller than that solid and ancient jacaranda, two of them side by side and with a canvas hammock
strung in between, swinging in the breeze.

There was so much space, nothing seemed crowded. In
Bondi I had an infinity of sea, here there was endless jungle.
I had to rack my brain for the names of all the other species
of trees and bushes. Many seemed native to tropical and
subtropical climates and I hadn't come across them before.
When I was settled I would take a closer look and maybe
consult a book or two, but the most obvious specimens were
a beautiful Australian wattle and a white honeysuckle with
lots of different birds in it—the rest were just well-shaded,
and in awesome colours. White and yellow, tall and with
sprayings of flame. I breathed deeply; a scent of peach, a
scent of eucalyptus and dew though it was well into the
afternoon.

Paradise.

I went under the house. From the floorboards above I
could hear the dog restlessly shadowing me. Its paws made
scuttling sounds over what was probably polished timber or
ceramic tiles. Now that the mutt couldn't see me it was
making a sort of high-pitched whining noise. Johnny must
have locked it into the house in the morning, expecting me
to arrive soon after, except that it was now about seven or
eight hours later than when I should have arrived. Poor mutt,

but I guessed that wouldn't stop it trying to tear my throat out. So what was the solution, clobber it with something?

This had possibilities.

I expected to find the key secreted somewhere near the third concrete post, just as in that Armstrong home from the past. I stopped. But there was the doll's house! I hadn't expected *that*, for it was the same doll's house where the Armstrongs used to hide their keys. It was like having something lost in the past suddenly pushed back into your face. It was as if no time at all had passed, I was still sixteen, Johnny was still my friend, Friday night was still a good place.

I squatted beside the balsa and pine doll's house and opened its little white-painted front door. There was a set of keys on a ring, as I expected, yet also a large business-sized envelope. I shoved it into my pocket. Searching around in the dirt beneath the house I found something that I thought might help me handle Blue——a hunk of wood, heavy and splintered, enough to do the trick. I carried it over my shoulder like a baseball bat and returned to the front verandah. The paradise of the back garden, and the little doll's house as well, lifted my spirits.

But the mutt was following my every step.

It waited, glowering, behind the French doors. Little bastard. I peered in through the squares of glass then moved my baggage aside from the door. The dog's eyes were on me, and now it took stock of itself and prepared to defend its home. I saw it tense the muscles of its shoulders. I'd stove its fucking head in before I'd let it bite me. I hadn't survived a near air disaster just to get my throat eaten by a dog. Hands hardly shaking, I slipped a key into the deadlock and turned. Wrong key. Try again. There were six wrong keys in a row.

How many deadlocks did the house have? There was a low growling. The dog leaned forward on its short front legs, poised. The dog's concentration somehow eroded my resolve. I gripped my stick of wood and found the right key.

I let the door open just a crack.

That was enough for Blue.

He burst the door wide with the hefty meat and muscle of a shoulder. The French door bounced against the bridge of my nose. Tears came into my eyes and I had to sit down. Blue wasn't interested in me at all—I would have been easy afternoon tea for him, that was for sure. Instead he was a blur across the verandah, claws scuttling frantically, then he was in the front garden, crouched low, already crapping the life out of himself. I stared at him and he stared into the sky with a very human look of heartfelt thanks. He whined as he crapped, and it went on and on. The poor bastard relieved himself for so long he probably thought it might never come to an end, then a constricted sigh escaped Blue's throat, like a sick man having a slow orgasm.

I had enough time to get a good look at him. As well as the one ear, one eye was missing, and a jagged lightning scar ran all the way across the side of his face. Blue cocked his head and that single black eye bored into me as he started to scrape dirt. Then he very slowly came up toward the verandah. I grabbed my suitcases and went into the house and slammed the front door in his wet little nose. He could keep the garden; the house was mine.

It was spacious inside, and cool. Winter was a month away and I was glad to see a combustion fireplace occupying one corner of the lounge room. What Johnny hadn't spent on anything outside the house he had spent on the interior decorating. The walls were a peaceful colour and the tongue

and groove of the timber were all properly sealed. The furniture, floor coverings, curtains and paintings were good
without being expensive. Every room was busy with potted
plants; the main bedroom had a lascivious four-poster
wooden bed.

I went into the bathroom and soaped my face and neck
with warm water, cold water, hot water. None of it made
me feel much better. That bed was the only place for me—
but not just yet.

There were many generously sized rooms but I was
always drawn to the windows at the back of the house, those
that overlooked the sloping jungle of trees and leftover rainforest. A scrub turkey picked its way beside the hammock
then ran off; a lizard long as my forearm and the colour of
granite made use of the sunshine coming through the lush
green canopy. And that scent of peaches again. I was starving.
As I went to have a look in the kitchen for whatever I could
rustle up, I passed the telephone and answer machine. The
message light was flashing, the numeral '10' registered.

Ten messages. I wondered if one was for me, maybe a
local newspaper wanting to interview me about the flight,
wanting to give me a medal for my actions. I pressed the
play button and leaned my elbows on a window sill. Down
below, the lizard's tongue flicked, its only activity.

There was a young woman's voice on the tape and it
came over and over again. There would be a message, a
burring, clicks, then the next message would be her again.
And again. It was like a joke, except the message didn't vary
significantly and it didn't seem a joking matter. The young
woman's voice moved from pleading to despair to anger and
to love; and back again. I replayed it.

What the fuck was Johnny up to?

But it was too obvious, really, the messages made it easy to figure out what went on in this big old empty home. Whoever this unnamed young woman was, she was, or had been, Johnny's girlfriend, and they were supposed to travel to Switzerland together. Only Johnny had absconded. I unfolded the note again—*change of plans, had to leave early*— and shook my head. Johnny had fucked off on her, just like that, and now he wouldn't be back for six months.

Johnny, please ring me, tell me everything's all right. You haven't gone without me, you wouldn't leave me here. Johnny?

And hadn't I also absconded from my life, just like him? My head ached. My guts crawled and the one-eyed one-eared cattle dog scratched at the front door. Johnny had abandoned the girl and gone to Switzerland and it was none of my business.

All right.

I found about six months worth of canned dog food in the kitchen's pantry, all of it stacked in exactingly neat super-market-type rows. Maybe Johnny thought man and animal could share the same diet. I looked around and found what I could. There were a few strips of fatty bacon wrapped in plastic, but I wasn't hungry enough to try meat after so long. As the sun sank behind the enormous jacaranda tree I was boiling tomatoes with the rotten bits cut out of them. Tomatoes boiled, peeled and unseeded, I then chopped the good bits of a brown onion. Cracked a lot of garlic, boiled whole-meal pasta. Fried the ingredients in a little oil, added dry oregano leaves and chilli seeds. The aroma made me long for a good bottle of wine. There was a third of a leftover bottle corked in the fridge so I took it out and let it stand, con-densation running down its sides. But for the kitchen all the house lights were out and I already felt enough at home to

leave it that way. I ate standing up, looking out the windows
at the living darkness of Johnny's jungle.

It was getting cold. Night-time winter-approaching cold.
Possums moved in branches and fruit bats flapped across the
white sliver of moon. Possums and fruit bats!

Winding down completely.

Standing, feeding, drinking bitter cabernet straight from
the bottle. That did the rest. Not enough time to take that
shower I'd dreamed of. Left everything where it was. Turned
out the kitchen light.

Johnny's bed. Under covers, pillow soft and flat.

Bedroom spinning and an aircraft crashing.

Stronzo in a stronzo land.

What time was it? Who cared. But some time in the
night I heard the Brisbane lullabies. Possums mating, growling, dragging across the tin roof, making their strange bleat-
ing-farting noises in the trees. Fruit bats screeching from their
high branches and flapping across the moon. A telephone
ringing, soft electronic buzzing, a beep, a voice coming softly
into the bedroom . . .

Johnny you won't leave without me will you Johnny you don't
know what that would do to me now . . .

. . . so sleep tight, strange angel.

TWO

Eating the Man

Rain drummed against the roof. Rain gushed through holes in the old guttering above the bedroom window. Rain came in torrents.

Smudgy light filtered through the bedroom but I stayed in bed listening and sleeping and waking again until the rain passed and sunlight crept across the foot of the bed. After the rain the sun warmed my feet. The arches ached. When I was a boy and I moved my feet under the covers my mother would try to catch them, crying, *Veddo una rana! I see a frog!* Sometimes she would sing quietly to herself as she stood in the doorway and waved my father off to work, that man who always wore long trousers and

a moth-eaten woollen cap and who was dusty even at five
in the morning; she would come into my room and her
hard palm would brush my hair and she would always smile
at me. Until later, of course.

I pushed myself out of Johnny Armstrong's bed.

Blue waited behind the verandah doors.

His one eye was big and expectant. I decided to approach
him with plenty of food to take his pea-brain off my own
pungent meatiness. Opening a big tin of dog food, I piled up
a blue feed bowl. Those neatly stacked cans in the pantry
were like a wailing wall of dead flesh. My stomach turned.
Blue waited, salivating, growling, agitated.

I scuttled the bowl across the outside verandah before
Blue could take off my hand. He snuffled and nuzzled at the
food like a wolf at a bleeding deer. The stump of his missing
ear twitched. I slammed the French door shut and went in
search of coffee. There was an old tin of instant and no milk
and the coffee turned bitter-black in a blue mug.

Johnny's clothes cupboards were mostly empty and I
hung my things in with the few of his that remained. I tried
on a very loud jacket and the fit was fine. In 1976, before
I'd developed into a donkey, I often used to wear his clothes.
In those days I'd run away from home. I'd run away from
my family's disappointments in me; Johnny, who befriended
me, let me wear his best stuff.

Now it didn't take long to get settled. Hang the clothes,
pile my books, put out my towels. I took a long shower and
washed my hair; when I stepped out and dried myself I realised the last bit of flu had taken care of itself. And I had
survived a near-death experience. The *stronzo* seediness of
Sydney was gone and that was something to celebrate. Even
if I was alone in this city, somehow I *would* celebrate. I felt

like popping a bottle of champagne. I pulled on clean trousers. The bathroom mirror showed a slighter frame, where there had been muscle there was sagging skin, and it made me smile. I was hungry but another cup of that coffee blunted my appetite.

The telephone started to ring as I rummaged around the kitchen.

'Hello?'

'Johnny! Johnny! Where have you been?'

I froze.

I didn't know what to say at all. I wasn't her Johnny. There was silence. Was it up to me to explain Johnny Armstrong? I listened to the heavy fall of breath—in, out, in, out, quickly—and was transfixed. I wanted to say something but the sound of her breathing stunned me.

She said, 'Johnny,' once more, sadly, and the receiver burred in my ear. I slammed it down. When would Johnny call her and tell her what he'd done? How could it be up to me, I who had never explained anything to anyone?

I quickly finished dressing.

My previous day's clothes had suffered with me and I dropped them into a wash basket. The business-sized envelope that had been waiting in the doll's house protruded from the back pocket of my dirty jeans. I sat on the side of the bed and tore open the seal and worried some more.

Twenties and fifties and hundreds, one five note and a two dollar coin, out they came, and they added up to $1767. What? What joke was I the straight man for? *Fuck Johnny*! I shoved the notes into the envelope and shoved the envelope under the king-sized mattress and shoved myself around the house, jumpy for the ring of the telephone.

Blue was curled on the verandah. The huge garden was

choking. Blue cocked his one ear as I edged by him.

He rose to his feet and was at my heel. I went down into the back and stood under the jacaranda, then under the wide fanning of the poincianas, then beside poinsettias cultivated in whites and yellows and oranges and deep red. Under the house I found secateurs, a small rusted shovel, and a wheelbarrow with a perished tyre.

The hardest part would be the strangling thorny vines. I started digging, pulling, cursing, the Brisbane sun over my shoulder. Blue waited. Maybe he'd never seen a human digging in the dirt; maybe he expected me to void myself the way he'd done the previous day. When that didn't happen he wandered off and returned with a tennis ball in his mouth. Blue dropped the saliva-baited ball beside me, waited, picked it up, tried again. He nudged my arm, my back, my leg. His breath reeked of dog food and I kicked him away, but maybe Blue had learned it's impossible for humans to say no forever.

Soon I was throwing the ball and Blue just kept coming back and back and back for more. In between I tried to keep weeding. Thorns tore at the skin of my hands and forearms, and Blue went on chasing, and from inside the telephone kept ringing. I didn't want to know. The answer machine would be getting it all, yet when I finally returned to the house the digital counter registered zero.

Fuck all that.

Night fell by 5:30; by six I'd escaped.

It was a Wednesday night. I didn't have a plan. But the number 10 came hurtling down Raintree Avenue and stopped for me and took me by the city centre. Something told me to stay aboard until Chinatown, and then I was wandering around the vaguely familiar, vaguely changed streets and malls of Fortitude Valley. The restaurants were busy. Kitchens billowed smoke and spices. The windows of grocery stores were a tableau of wizened, garrotted, beheaded, eyes-poked-out, feet-cut-off, upended, cadaver-coloured chickens, ducks, quails, denizens of the deep, and other things unrecognisable as once having lived.

Fervent and indecipherable shop-banter drove me further along.

A throng of coffee-fragrant and garlic-wafting enterprises showed that even Brisbane had discovered café society. Suits and beautiful people were everywhere. Yet somehow amongst all of them Gothics fitted in, greasy-haired hippies in sandals, tottering drunks, and lost tourists like me. Things had changed.

I looked for a free table amongst the spreading alfresco restaurants at the top of the mall. Waiters with cummerbunds and slicked-back hair carried out more tables and chairs. There was a regular chatter, a regular passing parade. A queue of Italian suits and portable telephones shimmied for one of the new tables. I wandered on, hungry, wanting to sit down. Every restaurant seemed a goldmine. I'd rarely felt so alienated. I found a bar and sat amongst solicitors, sales-men, stockbrokers, and listened to their conversations as I drank too much beer.

Then outside it seemed more crowded than ever, a like-able kaleidoscope of colour. I wasn't so alienated, my feet seemed to float, and I meandered around until a just-vacated table appeared in front of me. This restaurant did a bustling trade despite being on the footpath of the main road. Council buses passed and farted into patrons' faces and food at regular intervals. Across the teeming roadway was the Empire Hotel and from it Shirley Bassey bellowed; from inside the restau-rant/café the Pet Shop Boys thumped electro-beat. *Now let me get right to the point, I don't pop my cork for every man I see* entwined with *I've got the plan you've got the looks let's make lots of money.*

I drank a few more beers.

Two paddy-wagons pulled up and a gaggle of drunks were politely loaded aboard. Two baby-faced police officers did the rounds of the mall. Two transvestites in silver police uniforms playfully followed. Two prostitutes in black leotards and gold high heels strode along. They passed my table and ran golden fingernails over my shoulders. Across the way, outside the Empire Hotel, a young skinny urban black sat down on a step. He watched me watching him before a big guy in bum-and-crotch-hugging trousers, a short-sleeved white shirt, and a handlebar moustache shoved him on.

My cuisine nouveau came, little arty portions on a big white octagonal plate. Lots of coriander and parsley, no meat. The two prostitutes passed me again, smiled at me again, took two sprigs of coriander from my plate and went on, hips wiggling. I wished I wasn't alone. And then I wasn't for the lonely urban black from across the way pulled out the spare chair at my table.

'This free, mate?'

I said, 'Fuck off,' but he sat down and helped himself to the menu. His face was black as a cockroach's behind and his eyes had a wild smashed jaffa look to them. He was better dressed than me and smelled of an expensive aftershave.

With a cocked eyebrow that signified everything, a waiter set before my visitor a plate of exactly what I'd ordered. With a beer.

'I guess they're mind-readers here now,' he said with a funny grin.

'Well, I can vouch for that dish,' I said. 'It's pretty good.'

'There's not much to it but I guess I'll give it a go.' His teeth were big and white, like a newly painted picket fence. 'You know the service here is usually fucked.'

I was looking to get the waiter's attention for my bill. 'Come here a bit, huh?'

He kept grinning at me. 'No, I can tell the service is bad because when I sit over there I can see how shitty everyone gets.' He indicated over his shoulder, the steps of the Empire Hotel. 'But they won't show it because this is an ''in'' hang-out and everyone wants to suck up to the owners. They speak Armenian you know.'

'The menu looks French.'

'Course it does. Who'd come to an Armenian restaurant in the Valley?' He poked the coriander sprigs on his plate and moved the cherry tomatoes around. 'Jesus, where's the meat?'

The waiter caught my signal, nodded in my direction.

'You're not going?' my visitor said.

'Yes I am.'

'Mate, I can't pay for this.'

What I'd had to drink was only enough to give the world a rosy glow, not make me stupid. 'Then don't eat it. You didn't order it.'

He looked hurt, then for some reason he smiled and hurriedly stuffed coriander and big basil leaves into his mouth. 'Where you headed? I'll take you to a good place. Sixteen bucks for the two of us and we're in. You're a good-looking bloke, you'll do really well there.'

'What is it—a brothel?'

'For sixteen dollars? It's a nightclub. Come on, what else you got to do tonight?'

'I haven't got any money. I'm not working.'

'Me either, mate. But you can pay for this and I can't.
How about it? We'll trade: I'll introduce you to some
dancing partners of mine. You like to dance? You'll dance
your feet off. Nice girls—really—every single one of them.'

The waiter approached and I told him I would be staying
a little longer. He cocked his eyebrow again, it really was
his most expressive commodity. My friend's face lit up and
he chewed through the small portions on his plate.

'I said the magic word, huh? Once we're in you won't
spend another cent. The girls'll look after us once they see
you can dance. You *can* dance?'

When I paid the bill I saw an error had been made. A
different waiter—thick flat eyebrows that joined in the
middle, totally unexpressive—only charged for the one
dinner. Maybe my Sicilian predilection for omens was with
me. I looked at the kid. So what was there to lose? I hadn't
spent a cent on him but he didn't know that. He was all
gratitude. Taller and much, much skinnier than me, and
about eighteen years of age. I at least promised myself this:
if there was so much as a hint of trouble I'd break him in
half.

A crescent moon was low over the Chinatown arch.

I took him into a bar and while I had a few more beers
he drank water and watched the Sky station's nude mud-
wrestling show.

'You're a saint, mate,' he said, 'but I could have used
something a little more substantial than all that green stuff.'
He felt the thread of my shirt. His aftershave was like the
gardens of Johnny's house—brilliant and unexpected.
'Hmm,' he said. 'Kind of new-age-cum-swamp-black. More
Melbourne than Brisbane. A bit passé. Maybe you're just old,
brother. Like my attire?'

'Seventies pimp. Who'd have thought it'd come back?'

He grinned. 'Mate, it drives the ladies wild.'

The Underworld nightclub's red carpeted steps led down and down and down, and the neon lights of Fortitude Valley were left behind. A cashier and a bouncer were taking money and stamping wrists. The queue wasn't at all like the line of suits waiting to enter the mall's alfresco cafés; here teenagers jostled, abused, and put their arms around one another's cavalcade of styles, from torn fishnet stocking slut to crazy-eyed cyberpunk to sixties retro mixing badly with seventies heavy metal. And me.

The thump of music came from inside.

'Fuckwit Nigel,' the bouncer said as I paid my sixteen dollars to the cashier's long crossed legs. She flicked a heavy jade earring. 'Twenty-two dollars.'

Nigel said, 'Jesus, mate, inflation everywhere.'

The bouncer stamped our wrists and we walked into the nauseating scent and smoke and sweat of the nightclub. I went to find the toilets; when I returned, walking around the smoke haze and the obfuscated bodies of the dance floor, I saw Nigel amongst the drinkers, a smudgy tall exclamation mark in clothes two sizes too big for him. I hadn't already noticed that his trouser cuffs were rolled up, the waistband was gathered by a leather belt, and the shoulders of his shirt hung just a little too low. A glass of vodka and ice was waiting for me.

I said, 'What about you?'

'Me? I'm like Fred Astaire. Once I hit that dance floor the spirit moves me and the whole beautiful fucking universe comes into my soul. What do I need a drink for?' He winked. 'Join me when you feel like it.'

Nigel left for the smoky fog and spinning lights. A trio

of young women covered his face with kisses, then he shimmied and disappeared as if he himself was only a tendril of
that fog. I smiled and turned to the bar.

The barman said, 'Social worker?'

'What?'

'Youth worker?'

'Give me a vodka and ice.'

I tried to hand him money but he spoke low. 'Nigel's a
brother of mine. Drinks are on the house.'

'Yeah?'

So I ordered a double.

She's teaching me to dance. I'm all left feet while she's graceful as a ballerina.

'Costanzos are the pack mules of Sicily,' I try to explain.
'They bred us for carrying rock out of quarries. Any runts
in the family tree were sent to church choirs *in castratum*.' I
step on her foot again. This is hopeless. 'Sometimes the
padrones would just carry the weakling babies up to the mouth
of Mt Etna and toss them in.'

'Will you be quiet, Romeo?'

Monica is trying to explain the basics of two-four time
to me. It might as well be nuclear thermodynamics. As if I
can concentrate when we're standing so close. She looks at
me, displeased, but that can't spoil the peaches and cream of
her complexion. Does she know she is a gift to the world?

'You're not trying.'

'I am trying. It's not easy.'

'You're telling me.'

It's about five weeks after I met her.

That night at Cloudland she wouldn't give me her telephone number and Johnny disgraced us both by going ahead

and playing hide the salami with her paralytic best friend. He
says her friend lay in the back seat with her eyes rolling
around her head and when it was finished asked him if he
could buy her a cup of coffee and some hot chips. So we
weren't in Monica's good books. But I saw her one afternoon
at a bus stop. She was in her school uniform and so was I.
I forced myself to a standstill in front of her.

And started acting again.

It turned out we're both in grade twelve. Her eyes kind
of glazed over but I kept up what I thought was a pretty
funny monologue until her bus came. When the bus left I
felt as wrung-out as a tea-towel, but exhilarated as well: from
the back of the bus she and her friends had given me a glance.
That was enough. I made sure to see her again and again and
again at that bus stop, her stupid school friends giggling and
poking fun the whole time I talked and she listened without
seeming to.

Then one day she said, kind of suddenly: 'Do you like
jazz?'

I said: 'Yeah.' (A lie.)

She said: 'Swing?'

I said: 'Sure.' (*Swing?*)

She said: 'Can you dance?'

I said: 'We danced in the car park at Cloudland, remember?' (Dumb! Why remind her of that? And for the price of
coffee and chips my best friend copulated with your best
friend in the front seat of a ute. Dumb!)

But she said, 'Oh. That was dancing?' and smiled at me
as if she knew most of life's secrets. 'Well look,' she went
on, 'they're having a jazz night next Saturday and I want to
go. I better show you how to dance properly if you want to
come too.'

So it's Friday afternoon and we're in the rumpus room of her family home and she's got Glenn Miller on. Monica's trying to show me how to swing her little body elegantly but firmly. I like the way her fingers lock with mine, I like the way her white hair swishes around her face, I like her laugh when I start to get it right, but I am a slow learner.

'Now, around, around . . . *this* way.'

Instead I hoist her over my shoulder in a fireman's sling and give her an aeroplane—just like they do in world championship wrestling.

'Ah-ah!' she cries.

When I put Monica down the warm imprint of her is now a part of me. She's panting and there's pink in her cheeks. She shoves me in the chest, 'Jesus! What's the matter with you?' and pants some more. 'You don't know the first thing about jazz music, do you?'

'Well . . . '

'What about other music?'

'Well . . . '

'Come on.'

'I like Neil Diamond a lot.'

'Oh *God*.' Monica rolls her eyes and we sit down on the floor in front of the stereo. She flicks her hair behind one ear with this agitated sort of hand gesture, then shoves me again. There are hundreds of records in shelves, hundreds and hundreds.

'These are all yours?'

'Of course.' Monica looks at me as if I'm dense. 'Your education starts right now, Romeo. Music is changing and it's about time. Something new is happening. This year and in the past three or four years some incredible music has been made. Really incredible, and you missed the lot while you were listening to "Cracklin' Rosie". Maybe we'll see if you can learn.' She looks at me. 'What are your best subjects at school?'

I don't really have any, but I say, 'English and history.'

'English,' she says. 'What writers do you like?'

'Ahm. I actually really like adventure.'

'Like Robert Louis Stevenson?'

'Like Alistair Maclean and Desmond Bagley.'

Monica is exasperated. It seems anything I say will be wrong. So I decide to clam up. She's busy pulling records out of their places and making a little pile, then she stops and turns around and those black eyes of hers stab at me.

'Okay then,' she relents, patronising me so much I want to throw up on the spot. 'One step at a time.' Then she's arranging her records. But she's on her knees and her jeans curve in the most magical way. It's better now that I've decided to shut up. I can't out-think Monica, but I can concentrate on her. And I can't believe how petite she is. There's not a touch of make-up on her face and her dyed hair is a little lank and I've forgiven her for being so superior.

What will it matter if I touch her?

So I do and she slaps my hand away. Monica stares at me but I don't back down. As she watches me I reach out and touch the curve of her hip. She stares at my hand. For a moment it's as if her hip presses into my palm with a warm life of its own. My throat is very tight. Monica's eyes move down to the distended front of my canvas trousers. I want to die. My hand moves away from her hip.

'All right,' Monica says in a voice that's a little quieter. 'It's never too late to learn.' She shuffles the records around. 'Look.' And I don't know if it's her nerves or what, but she pushes record sleeves at me. '*Desire*, Bob Dylan. *Born to Run*,

Bruce Springsteen. *The Who By Numbers*. Patti Smith, *Horses*.
Blue Oyster Cult, *Agents of Fortune*. Iggy Pop and Nils Lofgren
and this new group from the UK called The Jam and look
at this one, a new Australian group called The Sports.
Stephen Cummings is a genius. Southside Johnny and the
Ashbury Dukes. There's so much. Haven't you heard of any
of them?'

I just stare at her now, uncomfortable in the loins but
too high-strung to move.

'I like opera and classical as well. But this is my first
love.'

I can see she's perfectly serious about all this, so I say,
to keep her interest, 'My parents play their Caruso 78s until
the neighbours go crazy.

'Uh huh,' Monica says absently. She's lifting the needle
onto the black vinyl of one of her treasures. 'The great
Enrico. Did you ever see that big Italian ham Mario Lanza
play him in a film?' I shake my head. 'You're lucky,' she
says. 'One day I'll play you Caruso singing some of my
favourite arias. He played your namesake once, you know.
In Bellini's *Romeo e Giulietta*.' Then she holds the needle away
from the record. Monica's eyes are half-closed, a lascivious
look straight out of the movies. 'You know what one of his
lovers once said about him?'

'About Caruso?'

'Her name was Billie Burke and people said she was the
most beautiful actress of 1910. Billie liked to tell people,
"Caruso made love and ate spaghetti with equal skill and no
inhibitions." What do you think about that?'

My arms are covered in gooseflesh. Monica sets the
needle down. Crackles from the speakers, then a piano and
harmonica introduction, a raspy voice. Monica says, 'A voice

like sand and glue,' and then she kneels in front of me.
Somehow she seems to fill the space of the room in the way
music does. She puts both her hands on my face and she
doesn't draw me to her, she only holds me and looks at me.
Why is it that Monica fills the very air? This must be the
first time I've felt such a heavy yearning, not in my cock but
in my heart. So I guess this is it and she knows it, this must
be where Monica's education of the donkey, Romeo Costanzo, starts.

Where is she now? What became of her? Who does she love?
     Oh, but God should never have invented free drinks,
they lead to these thoughts, and vodka is the worst. I didn't
want to think of Monica. I didn't want to see her in my
mind. Drunkenness was preferable, the kaleidoscope of
colours I'd started seeing in the mall now collided in the
Underworld, yet I still couldn't get Monica out of my mind.
     Nigel tried to drag me onto the floor with his friends
but reverie made me boring. I sloped around and staggered
around and kept an eye on the groups of kids smoking or
kissing or staring. We were not at all unlike the wailing wall
of dog food Johnny Armstrong had built in his pantry for
Blue; all you had to do for a choice cut was reach out.
Everyone was available, and in a minute I noticed one girl
more available than most. She wore a baseball cap and a slip
of a satin top and cut-off little shorts.
     The nightclub dark made her exquisite and I forgot
Monica.
     I was transfixed by her white legs; by the way her hair
gathered at the nape of her neck; by her come-fuck-me
mouth. I stood stone-still and felt that heavy yearning again.
It was the same old pain but in this lousy nightclub hardly

spiritual; I wanted to taste her flesh and run my tongue over her meat. Her arm was around a female companion and together they swayed a little but just enough to the music.

I went to the bar and got a vodka from Nigel's friend and when the young woman in her baseball cap and satin slip and cut-off shorts stood alone I offered her the glass. She looked at me like I was crazy. I said, 'What's your name?' and it was as if there were slugs behind her eyes. Or were they behind mine, is that why she took a step back? I drank the vodka myself and tried to say something but the expression on her face was that of a deer who has taken a wrong turn and has come across a wolf. She stepped further back and her arm found her friend's waist. The two of them looked defiantly past me.

Nigel came out of the dance floor mist and saved me from my own perdition. This time I let him take me inside the technobeat. Through swirling smoke and music I joined them, Nigel and his three consorts. The young women were maybe five or ten years older than him, high-heeled and nuked. Yet with them Nigel was so graceful and weedy he could spin and spin and spin as if on a coin, speeding up, slowing down, always spinning. He didn't look much like the Fred Astaire I knew, but the ecstasy in his face was real.

Through the smoke one of his friends came closer and put herself against me. First her perfumed wrists, then her sweaty forearms, then the cold backs of her arms slid over my shoulders. She plunged herself into my face and she tasted of too many menthol cigarettes and too many cheap dinners and not enough sleep.

'No wonder they call him Romeo,' Nigel laughed. 'Our Romeo of the Underworld.'

I took the drunk young woman's arms off me. There was

no hunger at all, the wolf had turned tail, it only seemed that I had gone such a long, long way from Monica—and then I cursed her for finding her way back into my thoughts. Nigel followed me to the bar.

'Do you like Julie? I think she likes you.'

'I'm going home,' I said, guzzling another free double, crunching ice. Nigel's face swayed in front of my eyes, another of his dance moves. 'Fuckin' stop it.'

'Stop what?'

I grumbled into my drink, 'How come all these drinks are free?'

'Ssh, you've had too much,' Nigel said, dragging me away from the bar. 'Count your blessings. You want my mate out on his arse? He was like me. No home. But he's got himself an honest job.'

'Why don't you get yourself an honest job? Where'd you get those bloody clothes?' I said, and slapped at Nigel's collar.

'Oh, you know.' That clean-faced grin of his must have got him out of a thousand scrapes. 'A flat on Bowen Terrace with a faulty kitchen latch.'

I swallowed more vodka. 'The fuck . . .' From the dance floor, out of the smoke, Julie smiled at me, enticing in the most unenticing manner. I was full of melancholy.

Oh, Monica.

Nigel rubbed my back with affection, as if I was a horse—or a donkey. I was already heading for the door. Nigel followed. 'Hey,' he called after me. I turned and he gave me a loopy smile. 'Brother, can you spare a dime?'

'Get the fuck away.'

Nigel grinned more.

I stopped. *Fuck it.* My wallet held a ten and a five. So I offered him the five but he took the ten, kissing it. 'Give a man a fish, and he'll eat for a day; teach him how to fish and he'll eat forever,' he said. I staggered at him for the note but he warded me off with that diamond smile. 'I won't be forgetting you, Romeo. Promise.'

I went up the steps toward the street, head down, sliding my shoulder along a wall, balancing on a rail so I wouldn't fall. Up, up, once more to the cars and wandering cops. The fresh air was invigorating. I was drunk. Thanks to Nigel I only had five bucks.

How far would that get me through *Stronzoland*?

At least to the start of the western suburbs but not all the way home. The driver wasn't about to give me a free ride. At least I'd had the presence of mind to tell him to stop when his meter hit five bucks, but when he dragged me out of the back seat and pointed me in the direction of Raintree Avenue I felt I had no presence of mind left at all. The footpath was unsteady and the night sky too low.

The way seemed all uphill and the sweat ran down my face and into my collar. I wasn't afraid of the cars that hurtled by, or of the footsteps or voices or odd dry cough I sometimes heard behind me. We were midnight ramblers, all of us, as one. A lonely ageless woman danced down the cracked and weedy footpaths toward me. What assignation had left her dancing down these dark streets? We passed each other with the exchange of secret smiles.

Oh, here in Brisbane we walk without any fear of each other at all. Why should I choose to call it *Stronzoland*? That name was only right for the terrain of my heart. The stranger was happy and she was gone, her strong perfume an exciting mist for me to walk through.

Now I was in Raintree Avenue.

A breeze coming down from Mt Coot-tha blew my hair

and dried the sweat from my brow. The lights of the television towers winked and called from up amongst the stars.
There was a song's verse I knew by heart:

> Somewhere up above the world tonight
> Far away from the stars
> Someone says, 'Are you all right?'
> And I think therefore I am . . .

I am, I finally thought.
I am, I finally believed.
I am.
In the far distance behind me the city glowed, an irregular
outline of office buildings. Those ghost-buildings shone with
all the lights of a paradise that has never known power
restrictions, and the Executive Building was the brightest of
all, a proud Tower of Babel. The weather spire on top of
the MLC building said there was no wind and no chance of
rain. A little of the freeway's fairground lights traversed the
brown river.
I walked up Raintree Avenue and felt for the key in my
pocket. There was only the faint glow of Johnny's lounge-
room lamp as it reflected in the glass panes of the front
doors. There was a car parked in the street, an ugly Volkswagen. When the little gate in the fairytale picket fence
creaked, Blue started his merciless bark from inside the
house. I bet the neighbours just loved his early morning
howls.
I hurried past the fragrant garden and jogged up the dark
front verandah steps. It was as if Blue was being murdered.
His unholy din made my fingers fumble the key in the deadlock. Through the little panes of glass I could see Blue, his

head was up and he bayed on and on as if some emotion I should have understood inspired him. It was almost as if he was yelling a warning.

And the glass panes reflected movement behind me, shadows. Blue went crazy. Footsteps came onto the verandah and shadows were over me before I could even turn.

A hand had me by the throat, choking, by the shirt, tearing. I struggled but my arms were weak as celery, then blows started in on my stomach and across the side of my head and all I could do was hold on for dear life, to the two of them. One broke free. Of the other I held hair and fabric. A cracking sound across my head made me drop to my knees. My fingernails scraped skin. Even as I was falling I knew Nigel and his tribe had followed me—he didn't need a faulty kitchen latch this time for the front door key fell right out of my palm.

Something crashed into my skull.

I was dropping backward but I still had one of my attackers by the hair. If only this one was Nigel! I dragged him with me, my nostrils filled with his gamy stench. Where was Nigel's fragrant aftershave? Whoever it was fell with me and the obscure face was down beside mine and I wasn't about to let him go.

The wolf was back; by the hair I pulled that unseen face to my mouth, and as more blows and kicks numbed me I bore down hard on the exposed meat of a stubbly cheek.

The man was screaming.

Juices flowed. I gripped his skull hard and he screamed louder but he wouldn't be going anywhere until they found a way to kill me.

Then a woman's voice was shouting. A final punch to the head freed the one I was biting—they didn't need to kill me after all. My face ran with blood and my arms were like jelly and I floundered on my backside. I heard the sounds of running feet. A face floated in the black above me, a woman's face, a succubus come to finish me off.

I tried to ward her away but she pinned my arms and said, 'It's all right, they've gone.' Then she found the deadlock key and opened the front door and picked me up in her own strong arms.

Blue was waiting. He was quiet now and his one eye was trained on us. My saviour laid me down onto the carpet and went into the bathroom, and when she returned she had hot wet towels and a blanket to cover me with. I tried to get up but couldn't find my feet. The bottomless well of vodka had anaesthetised me, yet while this woman knelt beside me and dabbed at my face a black pit cried out.

'Tell me if you've got any pain in your neck. Any paralysis, weakness, numbness or tingling in your arms and legs.'

I spat a mouthful of blood into the towel. 'What are you talking about? . . . ' I muttered.

She said, 'I can't believe you bit someone in this day and age. Don't you know anything? Is that your blood or his? Here, rinse your mouth as thoroughly as you can. Do you need to vomit?'

When the shakes started she lay on top of me and kept me warm but she was no weight at all. Pinpricks of light in her eyes and straggly hair falling down the sides of her face. Everything about her seemed to glow and then slowly-slowly she grew blurry.

Who are you? I dimly heard. *Are you a friend of Johnny's?*

Blue was over her shoulder. Around them was complete black. Blue seemed to be listening. My saviour put her lips close to my ear.

Tell me, please, who are you?

'. . . My name is Romeo . . .' Trying to grin. '. . . Romeo of the Underworld . . .'

Her gaze was intent. Her hair grazed my cheek. She said, *Romeo and his underwear?* and her sweet face went out of focus.

Goodnight, angel.

THREE

This is Not the Way Home

M onica leans toward me and a strand of her hair is on my cheek. Then her teeth touch my throat.

I do myself up.

Her hands are cold because we're out in the open dark by the river. I hold her hands to make them warm and a last ferry skates across the black glass of the Brisbane River. It heads away from us over toward the Norman Park bank, where a lonely jetty light glimmers.

We're half-sitting, half-lying beside a paint-blistered bench on the grass of the river bank. The silhouettes of dinosaur trees loom, but they protect us too. The river gives off a sour catfish odour that right now is the scent of heaven.

Behind us New Farm Park goes on forever, a wild Garden
of Eden beside the winding river. Branches hang low to the
ground and living creatures rustle amongst them; night-time,
and the park is as alive as a tropical jungle.

Monica puts her arms around my neck and squeezes me
tightly. Her lips are cold.

'Maybe we should get going?'

'No. I want to stay here.' The sound of her low husky
voice is thrilling. 'Do you like what I did?'

'I liked it all right.'

The grass is messing up her pretty silk and rayon dress
but she doesn't want to sit on the bench. Instead Monica lays
herself flat under the stars.

'Lie on top of me, Romeo.'

I look into those black eyes, into the pinpricks of light,
and she holds me hard to her tiny body.

'Do you want me to—'

'No. I want you to just stay here.'

It's a miracle to be with her.

For in spite of Monica's tuition we didn't cut a very
dazzling figure on the dance floor. We had to sit the music
out with a few drinks. She liked rum and cola. I had beer.
Johnny and a load of others had been hanging around. I
wished they'd fuck off.

'They're such a bunch of jerks,' Monica said to their hee-
hawing and gawking. Then Johnny came to our table. Only
the losers and the alcoholics and the infirm were sitting the
dancy jazz out.

'I think we could give this a try,' Johnny said with a grin
that gave him two dimples in one cheek. He put out his
hand. 'Do you think you'd like to try?'

Monica gave him that patented black-eyes stab of hers

but it was me who said, 'Yeah, go on, Monica, at least you can get one good dance in.'

Monica wouldn't take Johnny's hand.

Instead, after a sip of her rum and cola, she smoothed the lap of her silk and rayon dress and stood up. Johnny winked at me. Seventeen years of age and six feet two; parents who didn't admonish him for having to repeat his senior year so that he might have a better chance of getting into med; a ute to drive around in. I hated him right there and then. It was a wonder I hadn't hated him all along, but when I'd run away from my family in Sydney and landed in his class at school, Johnny was the only one to make friends with me.

So I knew he had a heart.

But he probably had a cock too.

Now I learned Johnny had rhythm. Plenty of professional lessons went into the way he did a proper jive. So much for hippy-trippy parents.

'Look at that,' cherubic Paul Chang said as he came over. Paul was another from school. With his slanty eyes and big gut he was as much a class misfit as me. He sat down and watched Johnny and Monica and couldn't hide his admiration. Or his envy. At my murderous glare he buried his jowls into a jug of beer and gulped like a guppy. With a knot in my guts I watched Johnny's sublime grace. Monica's dress billowed and her hair flew and her body melted into his. The others, all full of piss, came around as the band leader picked another up-tempo beat. Cloudland bounced to the type of swing music Monica had played me on her stereo, Johnny turned Monica the way she had tried to teach me, and I stood up from the table.

I looked back.

Johnny was wearing the thin speckled-grey tie his grandfather had left him. He had shown me that tie many times.
It was seventy-five years old, and for seventy-five years had
been a talisman to the opposite sex. For Johnny's grandfather
had been a cocksman of the old school, all the way to the
retirement home where he eventually fornicated his last.
Now Johnny held Monica close and that three-quarter
century old talisman was pressed against her breast.

So what chance did I have?

My black mood made the others sombre and quiet. I
couldn't resist another backward glance: for all the refine-
ment and all the lessons Johnny and Monica looked like they
were mud-painted naked, Johnny's dick jingle-jangling and
Monica's breasts bouncing to a throbbing jungle beat.

Outside, the Cloudland arch was so luminous, so ridic-
ulously full of hope. Kids in the open courtyards trailed
streamers and kicked coloured balloons. Music wafted in the
air. An old man in a grey suit was playing with the children,
every now and then he used his cigarette to pop one of their
precious balloons. Kids screamed and cried at the casual
cruelty of adults. Over at the car parks young men stood
drinking and smoking in groups. Young women stood drinking and smoking in their own groups. And they all baited
one another.

'Come over and give me a match?'

'Your face and my arse.'

'*Fuck you.*'

'Fuck yourself, you're used to it.'

Further back, where the lights didn't reach, those lucky
enough to make a Saturday night connection didn't have to
drink or smoke at all. They wound around each other like
vines gagged by their own embraces. Cars continued to

arrive, headlights following single file up Bowen Hills and through the ballroom's iron-lace gates.

Soon Monica came out to look for me.

'What are you doing?' she asked. With her white hair and green dress she looked like a little girl about to appear in some school play. Except that her cheeks had a slutty flush.

'Go back to Johnny. I don't give a shit.'

Monica came around a column and looked me in the face. 'What?' She pushed my shoulder. 'What?'

But Johnny came out, followed by our beery mates.

'What's going on?' he said with the ease that made him the most well-fucked of our school. 'Everything's cool.'

I turned to Johnny and saw his two dimples.

You know the way Count Yorga attacks his victims in those old scary movies? I rushed at Johnny just the way the Count would, hands outstretched. What a joy it was to bring out my beautiful hating anger at everything and nothing. *Fuckitfuckitfuckitfuckitfuckitfuckit!* I had Johnny right back against a wall and our friends were shouting and Johnny started shoving back at me. My feet slid over sand and gravel. We had each other by our shirts but in my fist I was also scrunching that voodoo-magic tie. And then it ripped away from Johnny's neck and I flung it onto the ground and stamped on it. Johnny looked as if I'd just murdered his grandfather. Everyone danced around us, then poor good-hearted Paulie Chang put his chunky body between us and copped one in the cods for his trouble. He gripped himself, eyes crinkled up, then slowly he sat down on a step.

'Ohhh-ohhh-ohhh-my-nuts . . . ' Paul muttered.

Someone helped him put his head between his knees.

Johnny wasn't in a fighting mood any more. He just picked up his ripped tie and with a mournful gaze at me sat down beside the still-mumbling Paulie Chang.

Monica was gone.

Someone pointed in the direction of the iron gates. Head-lights flashed. I took off after Monica but she had a head start. I jogged down the winding road, more cars passing me, Fords, Holdens, Toyotas, Datsuns, then ahead, reflected in a combination of headlights and moonlight, the silk and rayon of her dress.

'Monica!'

Monica stopped. She turned around. Mascara dripped under her eyes. 'Fuck you!' she cried out. 'Fuck you!'

I walked toward her and I couldn't think of a word to say; all I knew was the sight of her made a thunder in my heart.

She put her head down and breathed heavily. It was as if she was deep in thought. Her hair fell over her eyes. Oh she seemed too young then, too innocent, but wasn't she the one giving me my education? Why did I feel so much older and so much bloodier?

I said, 'Jesus Christ, Monica, let's just get out of here.' The look Monica gave me then will always stay with me, but I didn't let it faze me. I went right up to her. 'Come on, where will we go?'

She kept looking me in the eyes. 'All right. Somewhere fucking peaceful. New Farm fucking Park.'

I said, 'Fine'.

And then Monica grabbed my face and she kissed me as if she was starving to be kissed, she bruised my lips, and for the life of me I never even came close to understanding what made her do that.

A sixteen-year-old's lips and the sour catfish smell of the

river; another perfect Brisbane day and the taste of blood.

'How do you feel?'

Her hair was in a ponytail and her hands were long and white, and there was what felt like a cavernous split in my lip.

'You made a lot of noise during the night, talking and swearing and going on.' Her eyes crinkled at the corners. She was young enough to still have bad skin.

My face and ribs felt as if I'd been hit by a truck. She wiped my forehead with a warm wet washcloth. I liked the way she did that. I liked the way she looked. There wasn't too much incentive to get out of Dr Johnny Armstrong's wanton old four-poster.

'What time is it?'

'About one in the afternoon. You had a lot of sleep, but you had a lot to sleep off. You smelled like a petroleum factory. What hurts worse, your bruises or your hangover?' She brushed the hair away from my eyes, a gesture of so much familiarity it rattled me. 'You still smell like a petroleum factory. Romeo Costanzo, from Sydney's beautiful Bondi Beach. Interesting name, "Romeo". I took a look at some of your things, in case I had to get you to a hospital.'

'Who were—' It hurt most where the jaw meets the skull, a dull ache. 'Who were they?'

'I was hoping you could tell me. They must have been ready to break in when you arrived. TV, video, stereo, Johnny's lost all that stuff before. I was asleep in my vee-dub outside.' She smiled and nodded, 'I'm Mary,' and her eyes watched intently for her name to have some effect on me. Then she said, 'Do you know me?'

I shook my head.

'I should be in Switzerland right now. A little ski village

called Wengen, prettiest place you've ever seen—that's how
our Johnny described it. I was waiting outside for Johnny last
night. Two a.m. He hasn't returned any of my calls. You're
a friend of his?'

'Only from a long time ago.'

'Yes. He didn't speak of you. I was under the impression
the dog was going to a pound and the house was going to
stay empty.' Her eyes were hazel and her voice was even,
penetrating, but even. Nothing like the tremulous voice on
the answer machine. It was difficult to believe this was the
same person. 'You've heard from him?'

'No.'

'Neither have I.'

'He went early,' I said, trying to be careful. 'Yesterday
morning.'

'Yes. I've spent the morning ringing around. I left all the
travel plans to him. It seems he never bought me a ticket,
even though I gave him my money. He never meant to take
me with him. Isn't that nice?'

It was none of my business. I wished she would shut up
about it. What did I care about their relationship? I shifted
uncomfortably in the bed.

She could see what I was thinking. 'Don't worry. It's
not your problem.'

In spite of myself I looked at her and said, 'He left me
a note'. God, she was eighteen or nineteen at most, to Johnny's mid-thirties.

'A note? Have you got it?'

'I threw it away.'

'Jesus. Well, we'd been planning this holiday for a long
time. It was supposed to bring us closer together. I didn't
realise he was too much of a coward to tell me the truth.

I've even deferred my second semester.' Mary fussed with the towel and played with her ponytail. 'Fuck him.' She seemed to get the clasp in her hair right. 'You're lucky, you know. I'm a nurse. Which is how I met Dr Armstrong.' Mary sniffed a little but kept herself together. After a second she went on, 'Just a first year student nurse but I know enough to take care of you. You might have to stay in bed a few days, there's always a chance of concussion. I've already checked my books. Now that I've got nothing better to do. Do you feel nauseous at all?'

Mary touched my face and made me wince.

'For some reason they didn't really get a good poke at you. I've seen worse. You must know how to fight. The most is bruising, especially on your face and torso. I don't think there are any broken bones.'

She pressed my ribs and I took a deep breath, ready to scream with a punctured lung, but nothing hurt badly. Did this kid really know what she was doing?

'I bet your jaw feels good, though.'

I nodded. 'Hurts to talk.'

'Didn't pop that either. You're pretty tough though you look like you've been on a starvation diet. Loose skin,' Mary explained. 'Are you sick?'

'No.'

'You're sure you're not sick?'

'Just not eating.'

'Mmm. That's easy enough to fix. You might get to a dentist in the next few days. Your teeth seem okay, then again, I'm not an expert. You've got so many fillings you ought to be ashamed of yourself. What did you eat when you were a kid?'

'Coco Pops and Froot Loops.' Even smiling seemed to

pull my lip apart. 'Call the police for me, Mary.'

She had wise eyes, this Mary, wise and startling. 'You think you know who did this, don't you?'

I nodded. 'Uh huh.'

'Who?' she asked.

I shrugged and thought about telling her. Then I thought about telling no one. 'Doesn't matter. Don't call the police.'

'Why not?'

I was thinking of Nigel.

Oh what the fuck was the point, he was a kid the same age as Mary, and without a home. What could you do with someone like that? What would the police teach him, and prison, and what would a hundred hours of community service do to change him? All those recent memories of Monica made me remember too well my own witless teenage years. I touched the split in my lip and the tender bruising of my face. I had a headache. No. I'd find my own way to deal with Nigel—and his putrid companion. The man with the half-eaten face.

I looked at Mary's bad skin. 'How old are you?'

The question seemed to surprise her. 'Eighteen. Next birthday. Why?'

And what was so earth-shattering about a thirtysomething doctor with a young nurse? Only that Johnny was in Switzerland and Mary was here. Why had he been so cruel, so cowardly, so utterly duplicitous?

'I think I need a glass of water.'

'Sure.' Mary stood up from the side of the bed and I saw how tall she was. She and the ex-school sporting genius Dr Johnny Armstrong should have made a great couple. 'Don't go anywhere,' she said.

When Mary left the room I felt a little tug in my heart,

but I wouldn't let myself dwell on it. Her manner rattled me a little, the way she cared for me, the way she ran her long white hands over my bruises, but I liked her and I liked the way she was perfectly at home in this house. After all, it was more hers than mine; I was the stranger.

There was a padding sound through the doorway, then Blue jumped aboard and curled himself up at the foot of the bed. I raised myself onto my elbows and pushed him away.

So what would Mary do, buy herself a real ticket and go after Johnny? Something told me that wasn't about to happen. And why hadn't Johnny at the very least contacted her now—surely he must have known he was leaving me to deal with her? Was that the intention? My first instinct was to run screaming from this place—just as I'd run screaming from Sydney. But where could I run away to now, after a life of running?

Oh, fuck the prick.

It was difficult to think of Johnny as *Doctor Armstrong* when my best memories of him were as a seventeen-year-old Lothario. We had kept in contact over the years, but always by telephone or postcard. It struck me that I really didn't know much about him any more. He was a medico in a big Brisbane hospital and had never married and played indoor cricket because he was scared of the hole in the ozone layer. So said Johnny in our last telephone conversation. And that was about it. With too much passing time my oldest friend, my oldest adversary, was just a distant acquaintance.

I eased myself from under the covers and held onto the wooden banners of the bed and put my hand under the heavy mattress.

Mary returned with a pitcher of water. Slices of lemon and cubes of ice floated in it.

'What are you doing?' she said, and she helped me back into the bed. She had no fear of a naked man. Mary gave me two aspirins. I could hardly get a mouthful of water down but she helped me, full of patience.

'Florence Nightingale, I presume?'

'Funny, I have got a "Florence". Mary Florence.'

'Very mellifluous . . . '

'Mmm. Good word. My mother gave me my middle name after the Biograph Girl. Florence Lawrence, ever heard of her? No one remembers her. In the early 1900s she was Hollywood's most popular female performer. She was so famous she initiated the star system in American films. That's the end of my trivia.' She smiled down on me from her position at the side of the bed. 'Mum was a little batty.'

I drank more lemon-tinged water. 'Mary.'

'Yes?'

'Your non-existent air ticket cost you $1,767.'

'That's right.'

Mary's expression changed as I handed over Johnny's white envelope. She held the white envelope and her bottom lip trembled, and that was all. How could she have left such half-crazy messages on the answer machine?

'Where was it?'

'In the doll's house downstairs, along with the front door key.'

'With no message.' Mary closed her eyes. 'You'd think Johnny hated me.' She took a deep breath. 'How long have you arranged to stay here?'

'Until he came back. But, you know——I'll go.'

'Oh, what's the point?' she said with exasperation. Mary pulled the clasp from her ponytail and loosened out her hair. 'I've been paid off. Johnny's buggered off. I've got no right

to be here.' She stood up from the bed. 'Get yourself down
to casualty if you think you need it.'

I looked away, out through the bedroom window at the
blue day, and when I looked back I said, 'Mary, if you want
to, please stay.'

Mary gave me a look I didn't like.

Did I remind her too much of Johnny; did I carry the
weight of my untrustworthy generation and sex? How long
ago had Johnny looked at this young trainee nurse and said,
Mary, please stay.

Now Mary said, 'No'. She seemed to think. Then,
'Maybe. Maybe. I'll hang around a little while. Just to see
how you go.'

I said, 'Okay'.

'I want you to sleep now.' There was a new authority
in Mary's voice. 'I think you'll need to sleep.'

'Just one thing.'

'Yes?'

Blue had jumped back on. 'Can you get that bloody ugly
mutt off the bed?'

Mary folded her arms and looked pissed off and shook
her head. 'No. No, I don't think so, Romeo. And please
don't talk to me like that again. This bed is Blue's place. I
bought him for Johnny's birthday. It broke our hearts when
he lost his eye and his ear. Since then he's been a bit highly
strung. Right there is where he sleeps. He's a fixture in
Johnny's life. If you don't like it, there's a very nice couch.
I use it often.'

I was treated to the spark that could radiate from her
hazel eyes.

'Rest well, Romeo.'

Then Mary left the room.

At the foot of the big four-poster bed Blue made panting noises and lovingly licked his privates. So I had this girl called Mary, and Blue, but if I'd had the strength I would have kicked Blue the fuck out of there, kicked him out of the house, battle scars, Doberman neuroses, big black balls and all.

A weight had been placed on my soul, something I hadn't expected, a sort of moral disgrace at being clubbed like a mongrel dog, and it took a week to go away.

F. Scott Fitzgerald has written that a mark of a good mind is the ability to hold two contrary and opposing ideas at once. I lay in Johnny's bed day in and day out, one side of my mind repulsed by the reality of violence, the other side remorselessly making plans for Nigel and his friend. So, I knew I had a good mind, if not a good heart.

And every day Mary moved more of her things into the house.

The first night of my recuperation Mary came into the bedroom with a dinner tray. On the tray were covered plates and a pink rose from the garden. The rose had aphids but I didn't let on. Mary uncovered the plates and there was the most glorious homemade soup, and—garnished with steamed broccoli, tomatoes, parsley and carrots—a t-bone steak.

Meat.

'You can go back to your starvation diet after you get better, but for now you're going to get lots of protein,' she said, meaning every word. 'And,' she added with greater emphasis, 'I mean lots.'

She was off in the daytime.

Too late to enrol into the second semester of her degree, Mary spent the ensuing days looking for work. Sometimes she visited her mother, which was where she said she had been semi-living while semi-but-not-really living with Johnny, and every night she was back. There was an air of mystery about her and I liked it. There was a touch of intrigue to her smile. There was a sort of assurance in those hazel eyes.

Mary made her bedroom in one of the spare rooms. More appropriately, we should have traded places, but she was happy with the way things were. So was the mutt. Often when I was reading myself to sleep I would hear Mary still throwing the ball for Blue, speaking to him softly, calling for him to come for his evening walk around the hilly neighbourhood.

Oh but we were sharing house, such a city thing to do, me and Mary and Blue, and by providence it was what each of us needed. A hassle-free togetherness, caring without love—the only problem was that being stuffed with so much protein seemed to give me too many protein-rich dreams.

Mary kept her distance.

After a week I'd had enough of dreaming alone.

So one morning, my face a lighter green and a lighter blue of fading bruises, I took myself out of the bedroom and into the shower. My smashed lips ached under that hot water but I stripped sticking plaster off my skin and told myself I was sick no more. I went and sat in the morning sun, in the fresh and fragrant air of coming winter, and read another of my books all the way through. The next day I left my pile of books alone and was bottom-up in black rich soil. Within a few more days I was once again turning that garden into a beautiful place.

And being happy.

So we Costanzos truly are bred for dumb labour. *La*

buona terra lifted the weight from my shoulders and *il bel sole* revitalised my spirit. That night, after a long, long bath, I turned all the house lights on and restlessly waited for the moment when Mary would walk in the front door. It was the night of this century's last total moon eclipse and it was due around 11:00 p.m. It had been advertised like the premiere of a television station's blockbuster movie. During the eclipse, we were told, the moon would give off a brown-red glow. I looked out often but there were too many clouds and the moon couldn't be seen at all.

But the night of the century's final lunar eclipse is an occasion. I wanted to do something special for Mary.

So here is how you make a proper Sicilian sauce.

First you fill your house with music. It has to be music good enough to put you in a mood for cooking. Second, you uncork a bottle of red wine, drink one glass and keep another handy, and then, third, you start cracking a lot of garlic.

Johnny had a CD of that great pop-opera, *Carmen*, and in the fridge Mary had left a bottle of chianti. I got busy cracking garlic and was soon pan-sizzling beef mince in extra virgin oil. Blue kept me company but he whined until I fed him. I knew how he felt for inside me there was a hunger different from any I was used to.

Maybe it was just the aromas of the kitchen.

With more wine, and a soprano singing, I chopped mushrooms, tomatoes, hot peppers. Mary couldn't have read my mind better if she'd tried, almost everything I wanted was there in the kitchen. When I had all the ingredients bubbling in the covered pan I went looking for candles.

The house took on a gossamer glow.

I went onto the verandah to try and see the moon but

it was still obscured by clouds. Blue sat by me and let out a fart. I said to the absent starlight, *Mary come home.* Her ugly green Volkswagen pulled up, engine rattling, and I went back to the kitchen. The sauce simmered that special orange-red of meat and ripe tomatoes.

Mary was covering her ears.

'It sounds like a carnival. Can I turn it down a bit?' Which she did without any prompting. Her face was drawn and her black and white clothes were stained. 'Candles. And you're cooking.'

'There's a lunar eclipse. I thought I'd make something special for the occasion.'

'I think it'll rain.'

'It's still an eclipse, even if you can't see it.'

Mary stood in the kitchen with me. 'I've been working today. Cash in the hand. I'm caring for a grandmother who should be in a nursing home. But her family can't bear the thought of letting her go. She's a little senile and very—' Mary looked down at herself '—incontinent.' She seemed uncomfortable. 'They wanted me to start right away. Grandma Henderson has a weight problem. My back is killing me. And I need a shower.'

I uncovered the pan. 'This'll be waiting for you. And a glass of chianti. Okay?'

'Okay.'

Mary left the kitchen, shaking her head at my new-found zest for life. I stirred in the pan and washed endives for the salad and salted the boiling water, then walked around the house with another glass of chianti. A few days earlier I'd realised there were no photographs anywhere. Plenty of art, but no photos.

'It's extraordinary,' Mary had told me. 'Johnny doesn't

like himself very much. You won't find a photo of him anywhere.' Or of her, it seemed. Well, I wanted her to know
I liked her.

The shower was going, I listened, and then the shower
stopped. *Carmen* finished. Mary would be drying herself with
one of Johnny's thick towels. I went to the corridor and the
blistery glass of the bathroom door was misted over. There
were dribbles of condensation running down the glass, steam
seeped out from the crack under the door, and inside Mary
was pink and naked.

I hurried back to the kitchen.

When Mary appeared she was wearing a daggy-baggy
tracksuit, as if she had dressed to put me off. I gave her a
big glass of wine and saw her cuffs were rolled back many
times—Johnny's clothes.

'God I feel better,' she said. 'What a bloody day.'

There were dark smudges under her eyes and her skin
wasn't good.

I gave a final stir in the pot. The *spirelli* pasta was ready.
With the serving spoon I picked up a little of the sauce.

'Have a taste.'

Mary's hazel eyes gave me a prolonged look before she
leaned toward the spoon, mouth a little open, pink tongue
showing. With a hand she kept the hair away from her face,
droplets of water beaded in her tresses.

'Mmm, it's good.'

We were standing beside the warm stove, Mary's hand
still holding her hair from her face. I put my hand over hers.
Hazel eyes looked into mine. I felt lost in the steam of garlic
and basil and tomatoes, in the rich black dirt of Johnny's
garden.

I kissed Mary.

Mary said, 'Please let go of me, Romeo.'

I held her tightly. I squeezed her tightly and felt the breath exhaling from her mouth. I put my mouth in her hair and her heart pounded against my chest. How could I explain the emotions that made me just want to hold her?

I said, 'Please, Mary, let me—'

Somehow Mary was out of my arms. She was out of my arms and my chest longed to feel that beating of her heart again, and then she was twisting my thumbs in a way that felt like the joints were about to snap. Mary stood in front of me and made me a helpless slab of man-meat.

'This is called a thumb ride, Romeo. You couldn't guess how many times I've had to use it.'

'Ow—fuck! Ah—' was all I could get out. Mary increased the pressure, bending me down to the ground.

'No, that's right, it doesn't feel very good to be helpless, does it, Romeo?'

I went on one knee to relieve the pressure but Mary was relentless.

'Look at all this, candles, music, food, and then you won't let go of me when I ask you to.' With a harder twist I was on both knees.

'Stop it, stop it—' but she wouldn't stop it. 'How can you—hate me so much?'

'Don't be stupid, I don't hate you at all.'

'Mary—stop—'

'It's just that your generation is corrupt and I'm not having a bar of it. It's not your fault you come from a time of instant gratification of needs. Just think about it. Work backwards. You had the greed-is-good cult of the eighties to make easy money. In the seventies when your glands were going berserk you lived off the ongoing hubris of the pill,

you didn't need to develop a moral code, you just went out
and had your fun and life was great. I assume. And in the
sixties you were too young for the social upheaval and the
radicalism brought about by the Vietnam War. So you read
comic books and listened to the Beatles. Isn't that right?'

'Ouch!'

Mary let go and I fell forward onto my hands.

'I've had a hard day and I've been covered in an old
woman's shit, but you have to reach out just because you
feel like reaching out. I don't want to be cruel to you,
Romeo, but you only think this is what you want.'

Stranded on all fours on the kitchen floor, I looked up
at her.

Mary said a little more kindly, 'Oh, come on, get up.'

So I did.

And then she revved up again.

'What are you doing in Brisbane? What was so awful in
Sydney that you had to run away?' Mary contemplated me.
'I told you I went through your things that first night. Lots
of books and lots of photographs of a woman with black hair.
Why didn't you bring her with you?'

I said, 'I was married, but she died. Leave her alone.'

'She looked nice in the wedding photograph.'

'Leave her the fuck alone. *She's dead.*'

How had it failed to strike me just how cold Mary's eyes
were? She said, without pity, 'You married her and made
her life miserable? Or did you try your best to fall in love
with her, all for nothing?'

'Jesus Christ! It wasn't a good marriage. So what? Fuck
off!' Wasn't Dr Kolner so proud of my ability to say that?
Or was he only paid to be proud? Whatever, I couldn't stop.
'Fuck off! Fuck off!' And then something like a block of

concrete weighed in my chest and I had to sit down at the dining table.

'Oh, Romeo. You and Johnny might as well be brothers. You mistake kindness for lust and lust for love. You're like zombies, good and dead inside.'

I couldn't look at her. I hated her. I said, 'Mary, if you think that's what we are, what are you doing here?'

Mary stood in front of my chair. Her presence was electric but I still couldn't look at her. She was breathing fast and I was afraid. No wonder Johnny had run the fuck away, what could you possibly do with a young woman like her?

'Don't you know what I'm doing here?' she said, then she went into the kitchen and heaped a white porcelain dinner plate with my sacred Sicilian pasta. 'Don't you know?' Mary let the serving spoon and the lid of the pot drop to the floor.

With her plate she went down the corridor to her bedroom. The door slammed shut; there was the click of a latch. And then silence.

I got up from the dining table and went and stood on the front verandah. Blue was disturbed from his sleep. His one eye took me in and he seemed as jittery as me. We watched the night sky, where low clouds had parted to reveal just a little of the moon. The moon had begun its move into the shadow of the earth. There was a partial eclipse. I walked up and down the spongy timber of the long verandah then just kept going.

Into a chilly, other-worldly night.

Blue trotted beside me as we followed Raintree Avenue toward the stark outlines of the city of Brisbane. Rounding a corner, I saw the Fourex brewery billow great bales of smoke from its stacks. Blue started to lose interest, his steps faltering. Finally he stopped altogether. He put his grey-flecked snout up to the increasing eclipse and wailed. I didn't let him unnerve me.

After all, what could I be scared of? Mary had said I was a dead man.

The further I walked the greater was the chill in the air. Blue's wailing faded into the distance. The night grew darker. Everything became silent, the streets, the suburbs, the sky. It struck me that I couldn't hear my own footsteps, it struck me that I didn't cast a shadow.

No matter how I searched, no shadow at all.

The moon disappeared.

FOUR

The Devil's Moon

Nigel was hunting along the Underworld's queue for a friend to pay his way in. The Keith Richards-trash, Madonna-slut, Evan Dando-dreamy, Janet Jackson-sexy and Eddie Vader-intensos weren't going for it. A lonely Morrissey lookalike did watch intently but he didn't give any money. Undaunted, Nigel threw the baseball cap he wore onto the ground and improvised a twisting and turning tap dance that was in time with the beat from inside and out of time with the decade. In clothes not quite as good as those he'd worn the first night I met him, Nigel's skinny frame went up and down the queue, through the queue, and the kids laughed.

But no one was about to drop a coin into his cap.

The bouncer let people through while he kept an eye on Nigel's act. Now Nigel was twirling upright, then he was spinning on his backside like a New York breakdancer from 1984. He was perfectly eclectic in his influences, any generation would do. Tap dance, breakdance, moonwalk, boogaloo; I wondered if he could do a rumba. Nigel should have been making a fortune in music videos—if I wasn't so intent on beating his brains in I would have considered becoming his manager.

I dropped the eleven dollars Nigel needed into his cap. He hadn't seen me, the fall of money made no sound, but Nigel stopped in mid-routine as if he had a sixth sense for cash.

'Hey, Romeo!'

Nigel's eyes were freshly smash-jaffa'd. It didn't affect his coordination at all, but if he couldn't afford to get into a nightclub, where did he get money for drugs? He caught his breath and bent down to scoop up his cap. I took his arm and straightened him to me before he could reach it.

'Shit, you going to kiss me or what?'

A satin sheen of perspiration covered his forehead and he quivered a little at the sight of my new face. I could feel the skin and bone of him shaking in my grasp.

'Someone take a sledge-hammer to you, Romeo?' Nigel's long fingers came up and touched the bruising. 'Fucking good job all right. The question is: will the ladies go for this look or will they pass?' He grinned at me. 'Let's go in and find out.' Then Nigel's grin became half a grimace. 'That's an arm you're squeezing, old matey, in case you didn't know. And that sure is a grip you've got, Romeo.'

Nigel still tried to wriggle free.

I let him go. Nigel scooped up his baseball cap, pocketed the money, and rushed to the end of the queue. I'd expected him to try and bolt but there he stood, excited as a colt. So I went and stood with him. Nigel kept chattering, trying to get on my good side. If only he'd known; in Sicily they say that when a man walks under a full lunar eclipse, what they call a 'devil's moon', a man doesn't have a good side at all.

We were into the Underworld's grub and grind.

Nigel said, 'Where are those ladies? You made a big impression, you know that? They're gonna be happy to see you again.' He gave me a curious look. 'Only this time try and make a little conversation, would you? They thought you were a bit disappointing in that area.'

The smoke and mist machines were working overtime as someone danced alone in a gold lamé bra and miniskirt. Then the beat intensified and more dancers took to the floor. I noticed a sign, THE UNDERWORLD PRESENTS THE GOLDEN AGE, and the crystal anniversary disco thump of Sylvester's 'You Make Me Feel Mighty Real' brought the boogie out in everyone. When had AIDS silenced Sylvester's falsetto, 1988, 1989? It didn't matter—in bad nightclubs he and Andy Gibb and Freddie Mercury were forever a holy trinity.

Nigel looked through the non-dancers for his friends. I was already at the bar. People were three-deep trying to get their drinks and the bar attendant was hassled and copping plenty of abuse. Those not pushing toward the bar all seemed to be sniffing amyl nitrate and drinking little bottles of natural spring water.

In the free-for-all I lost sight of Nigel.

His friend wasn't working that night. The burly bar attendant who gave me my vodka and ice wanted six dollars even though the drink was all ice and very little alcohol. My

mood got bloodier. Then, as I stood beside four towering
young men in hot pants, I saw Nigel slip out through a fire
exit. I supposed I'd spoiled the little bastard's night.

The safety bar of the fire exit snapped the door open and
I was out into a black alleyway redolent of rubbish and faeces,
cats' urine and tar. The moon's total eclipse covered the city
with black; there wasn't even that reddish-brown tinge in the
sky the newspapers had promised. If it hadn't been for a
sputtering streetlamp I wouldn't have seen a thing, but there
Nigel was, a stick-spider leaning in the shadow of a high brick
parapet. He must have thought he'd made good his escape;
he acted as if he had all the time in the world. His shadow
made a crooked stroke across the ground.

'Nigel,' I called softly, and he turned with a magnificent
look of surprise on his face.

He was rolling himself a joint. He should have had the
patience to wait until he really had made a good getaway. I
went to him and thumped him in the guts and, while he was
doubled over, I held him up. I remembered him and his
smelly friend kicking at my sides and bashing at my jaw. I
pulled back my fist to really let him have it.

But Nigel went to water too fast.

So I kept holding him upright and it was as if there was
no weight at all. His dancer's legs were loose and a trickle
of spit hung from the corner of his mouth and I realised
Nigel would always have all the fight of a dish-rag. I let go
of him and he did a boneless slide down the brick wall and
he ended up as a puddle at my feet. Oh, what a fool I'd
been.

It was only then I saw that the many bundles of rags and
newspapers in the alley were lonely sleepers. How many? It
was too dark to discern. One bundle shifted; another grunted

in the grunge behind a gaggle of black wheelie bins; from a mass of newspapers and rags there was the sound of grinding teeth.

And footsteps click-clacked down the alleyway.

Nigel's friends were drunk or stoned. The poor light made them ghostly, well, as ghostly as is possible in gold lamé. Only Julie wore something different. Black. Appropriate. The three came down the alleyway and sour-sweet smoke came with them.

One held the fat joint out to me. 'What's happened to Nigel?'

'Too much to smoke,' the other said. 'He should take better care of himself.'

'Oh well,' the first said, then she looked at me. 'You're not much on conversation.'

So Nigel had been right.

We passed the joint around.

They were tired and haggard and stoned, Nigel's three nightflies, as if their big Friday night had started at midday and their exuberance had finally been bled dry. Julie wouldn't say a word but she wouldn't take her eyes off me. She was either the worst or the least plastered of them. When the joint was stubbed out I made to go.

'Wait,' Julie said. 'I want to show you something.'

So I waited.

The high heels of her friends zigzagged away back down the alley, past grumbling bundles of forgotten humanity. Nigel's friends meant to leave him right there amongst the vagrants. Maybe he was used to it. I looked down at how he slept so peacefully and then I looked at the sky. The lunar eclipse was coming to an end and a slice of moon had appeared, as if by magic.

Julie stepped back from me until her shoulders were against the brick parapet. She shook back her hair and carefully spread her feet over Nigel. A sliver of moonlight fell across her features and what she probably used for a smile only looked like a devil's leer. Nigel slept on right there between her feet.

'What's so important?' I said.

In the shadows Julie reached down with her tiny fists and eased her tight little black skirt up to her hips. Her legs were plump and pale and she didn't like underwear.

Nigel mumbled. He was an ancient turtle slowly coming awake; he had that slumbering turtle indolence you see in nature documentaries. Nigel's eyes opened and he looked up at Julie's black bush and then his red, sleepy-sleepy eyes fell shut again.

What a long way it is, I thought, what a long way it is from Cloudland to this stinking fucking alleyway in the back of the Valley. That 727 hadn't crashed me into paradise, no, we'd gone wrong somewhere, for this was hell.

Dear Monica, my lost angel of the past, where are you? Can you hear me, can you see me? Can you still feel me deep inside you?

Monica lives in New Farm with her parents and her older brother. They have a red brick house and a yard with a creaking clothes line dead in the centre of it. They have two cats, a cocky named Cocky, and two budgerigars. Her maternal grandfather used to live with them but he was in his nineties and senile and one day walked off a precipice near the Storey Bridge and wasn't fished out of the Brisbane River for three days.

Monica's father runs a small Italian restaurant called Il Vulcano. The place is named for Sicily's Mt Etna, which is where he was born and where his romantic but melancholy ideals come from. The restaurant is in Petrie Terrace, up in Spring Hill, and Monica's mother is the cook, though not the only one. Monica's mother was seventeen when her first child, Antonio, was born. Now she's in her mid-thirties and is as ravishing a woman as you are ever likely to meet in the flesh. Her name is Gloria and though I call her Mrs Aquila, or Signora Aquila, every time I see her I think that first name suits her just fine.

Mrs Aquila took her time in getting used to me.

Maybe she found my silent ways hard to take, or maybe she was worried what her daughter was doing with a Sicilian donkey for a friend, but whenever I arrived to visit she would give me a hug and a kiss anyway. I liked that very much. I liked it because her breasts were big and warm and smelled of honeysuckle. It made me wonder why Mr Aquila tended to brood; if I was going on fifty and I had a young wife whose big bosom was scented of honeysuckle, I wouldn't be moody at all.

But that's the Sicilian male for you.

Sometimes Monica and her brother Tony have to serve tables in Il Vulcano Ristorante, but now that Monica is in her last year of high school and Tony is in his second year as an apprentice mechanic that doesn't happen too often. Monica's parents work all day and all night six days a week. Tony works all day and all night five days a week. On the weekends he takes his mates either up or down the coast in one of his deconstructed Fiats. He likes to take away as much upholstery and padding as possible so that he is left with pure machine. Tony loves Fiat cars and he says they will make his fortune. He says the word 'Fiat' is an acronym for Fix It Again, Tony, so his first million is written in the stars.

Tony is an idiot and he doesn't like me.

He caught me reading a book in the Aquila backyard and he's been aloof ever since. It was only John D. MacDonald, for fuck's sake. Anyway, he has suspicions about his sister and me. Mrs Aquila has suspicions about her daughter and me. Mr Aquila has no suspicions at all; he just sets that melancholy gaze of his straight into my soul and broods very hard.

It's Saturday.

Bloody hot and I'm on my way to Monica's house, where I will find her, the cats, the cocky, the budgerigars, and no other humans. She'll be studying because we're getting on toward our final exams. After that it's university or work, college or the dole queue. Fraser the Razor has made it more likely to be the dole queue, at least for me, and I don't care. I don't study at all, I just read the books Monica gives me. And there have been piles of them. Graham Greene, Ray Bradbury, George Johnston, F. Scott Fitzgerald, Patrick White, Albert Camus, Joseph Conrad, Thomas Keneally— and sometimes I sneak in something mind-numbing like a John D. MacDonald.

Some of Monica's books bore me stupid, some of them I want to throw across the room, and some of them make the world melt away and the hours nothing but the smell of ageing paperbacks. Monica gave me *Portnoy's Complaint* to read, which I did in a day and a night, and after that I couldn't face her for a week. If she understands that book then she understands my soul just as well as her droopy-faced father does. Then she gave me *The Thief's Journal* and I wanted to keep washing my hands while I read it. But Monica devours them all. It's knowledge and experience that Monica wants; she wants to possess all the rapture and passion and pain that she reads about; she wants to live in a world where all of these things are real and not just made-up stories in water-stained pages.

Maybe that's why she's got me.

I've been in Brisbane three months now.

My mother rang last night. I told her I was studying hard. Lies. She says I ran away from home because I'm full of the fiery blood of youth. She says I'm a living example of that volcano that sets the tone for all our family. She says she and my father have been too tough on me. She's right, and she's no fool either. So we'd struck a deal soon after I arrived in Brisbane. Seeing as how they'd driven me away from home, we agreed I could stay in Brisbane with my cousins Lucia and Pasquale Torino. The deal stands as long as some criteria are met. As long as I go to a good school. As long as I earn my own money. As long as they don't hear any bad reports about me.

It was a bargain. Ma expected me to come running home in a week. She was wrong.

Cousins Lucia and Pasquale never had any kids and they like having me in their guest room, for they are destined to be the last of their family line. Cousin Lucy got me into a good state school, and then I started earning money by stacking shelves in a big Coles supermarket and by sometimes accompanying cousin Pasquale on some of his more back-breaking jobs. He's a bricklayer and he knows he can load me up like a pack mule; bricks, blocks, bags of cement, I never complain. So my parents aren't likely to get any bad reports. Sometimes I hear cousin Lucy on the telephone to my mother, *'Ma lui e piu santo che ragazzo'* meaning, in her kind way, I am more saint than boy.

Well, this boy-saint is about to see his girlfriend and the

thoughts in his mind will never get him into the kingdom of
heaven. My pocket holds one rubber, one franger, one fred,
one whatever you want to call it.

It's a good day for it. But it's only two o'clock in the
afternoon. I'm loafing along Brunswick Street because
Monica asked me to not come over until later. She wants
to get her study done. I couldn't wait until later. Jacaranda
trees are exploding purple, mango trees drop sweet summer
fruit in backyards, and wooden houses on insect-leg stilts
poke up out of the green suburban valleys. How much
more slowly can I walk? My heart aches for the sight of
Monica, but my dick aches too. The dichotomy of human
existence. So I concentrate on my surroundings to get my
mind off all my troubles. An old man in brown crimplene
shorts and with blue-veined bug legs sits out of the sun
and mops his mottled forehead with a handkerchief. An old
woman with great hips and blue hair collapses on the bus
stop bench beside him, her string bags fat with largies of
Fourex, Liptons tea bags, Tip-Top white bread. The two
don't talk, they sit profile next to profile and wait for their
bus, which doesn't come.

Brunswick Street undulates up and down on its way to
the brown Brisbane River. If you were to follow the street
all the way in the opposite direction you would find it
becomes Lutwyche Road and then Gympie Road and then
the Pacific Highway and then the Bruce Highway and then
you're in Cairns and you're sweltering in heat a hundred
times muggier than Brisbane and you haven't needed to take
a single detour to get there.

I'm sweating like a pig as it is. The distances shimmer
with water mirages. The franger in my pocket is probably
melting, but my desire is intact. I can picture Monica's room,

her bed, her sheets, the perspiration sheen across her breasts. And that's it. I've already driven myself half-crazy. I read something once, *when the balls are full the brain is empty*, and of this I'm guilty as hell.

Monica's quiet little street is full of iron-roofed wooden homes and rows of majestic camphor laurel trees. The street is shaded and the trees are ancient and fragrant. Monica is known to sometimes make a bed of fallen leaves and lie with a book and stay in the wood-scent until the ebb of daylight. Sometimes under the camphor laurels she'll make me play a scene from Shakespeare with her, me as Fool and her as an appropriately white-haired Lear: *Blow, winds, and crack your cheeks! rage! blow!*

As I arrive—three hours early—a breeze blows through my shirt. A breeze, not a cataract. It's a blessing and I take a great sigh. And who should be right there waiting for me on the patio, but Monica. She's wearing a skirt and a black halter top; she's barefoot and her hair catches the sun. One of the cats is in her arms, a tawny tom. The cocky is bobbing its head and squawking like a crazy beast. The budgies are singing.

And I'm running under those trees.

Monica puts the tabby down and it scoots for its life.

Cocky screams, 'Pretty-boy-pretty-boy-pretty-boy-pretty-boy-pretty-boy,' on and on, and then, 'Mo-ni-ca-mo-ni-ca-mo-ni-ca,' also on and on.

Everything seems worth it just to touch her and kiss her.

But though she holds me Monica is also not fool enough to miss out on her chances of being dux of her school, which is very likely. So after I've kissed her and held her and wondered aloud how she knew I was arriving then, right then, three hours early, and she says she knew, she just knew,

Monica smiles and gets herself out of my arms and leads me
into the house and down to the rumpus room. All her books
and notepads are spread out on the floor.

We spread out across those books and I kiss every part
of Monica I can reach. Her cheeks grow pink, so does her
neck, her throat, all the way down into her halter top, which
seems now as wonderful and filmy as tissue paper. Monica
wrestles with her conscience but she also wrestles me around
and sits on me, and I look up at her, dazed by the way her
nipples poke through her top.

Somehow I'm able to get the prophylactic out of my
pocket.

Monica gets off me and goes and opens wide all the
curtains and windows of the rumpus room. Why isn't she
closing them? She catches her breath and then she turns to
me, smiling in that crooked way of hers, big eyes alive and
teasing.

'I have to tell you something. I went on the pill, Romeo.'

I say, *'Jesus'*.

But we can't do it then, we have to study, and I realise
that this is part of Monica's *thing*, to anticipate, to savour
the yearning and make it delicious, to relish the ache of
wanting each other so badly.

The seconds drag and the minutes jerk.

Every now and then I harass her but we can only go so
far, and then she wants to get back to her books. Monica
seems to grow more and more excited by all this, even as
she studies Hammurabi's Code, but after two hours of this
so-called sweet anticipation I've sunk into as bitter and black
a melancholy as I've known. We have a break and Monica
makes tea and raisin toast. She brushes a few crumbs from
my shirt and runs her fingers through my hair.

'I hate studying.'

'You're not studying, Romeo.'

'I hate *you* studying.'

Monica gives me a look and says, 'I'm going to make you something special for dinner. And then,' Monica kisses my hand and rubs her soft cheek on my calloused palm, 'we've got all the time in the world.'

I'm almost convinced.

She adds, of course, 'In another hour.'

Donkeys have bad moods, I can't help it if I'm surly. If only I could know what she feels when she looks at me, what she thinks when she thinks of me, maybe then I would be in a better temper. But she's cross-legged on the floor again and questions like those will never come out of my mouth. I watch Monica leaning over her books, one hand holding her hair away from her face. She'll get sevens for her final exams, win the history and the English prizes, be dux of the school, and give her class the shits. And me too.

The tree-lined avenue is luminous with autumnal light by the time Monica decides she's had enough.

Finally!

'I want to do something really special,' she says. She couldn't have read my thoughts more perfectly. Except what Monica means to do is to make me a proper Sicilian pasta dish. Why can't we do what they do in Monica's precious movies? Did anyone ever bother to make James Bond a pasta sauce? Why can't we do what they do in Monica's precious literature? Did any of Jean Genet's grubby protagonists think half a minute before sticking it into the nearest hole? Where does all this *restraint* come from? As if I care about anticipation or foreplay; mood-setting or the sweet ache of desire; temperance and abstinence—give me your body, Monica!

Like a randy mutt I'd be happy enough to mount her shin bone.

Oh but that husky quiet voice of hers, the way she gives the sexiest undertone to the simplest things she says, and it's all for her mother's Sicilian pasta sauce.

Vaffunculo Sicilian pasta sauce!

As I trudge up the stairs toward the kitchen I want to grab her elegant *culo* from behind with both hands, strip her halter top and feast my eyes like the filthy-minded pervert from Sydney I am. It crosses my mind that Monica is a goody two-shoes, a little Italo-Australian princess from a family made royalty by their economic success and I only like her because every now and then she undoes my fly and rubs away with an impetuous rush. All the rest are my idealised projections. What do I know about the ballet and piano lessons she took, the subtext of impenetrable Ingmar Bergman films, the lunatic ravings of Nietzsche, Kierkegaard and Gurdjieff?

I'm just trying to fit an image so she won't send me away. I can make myself an expert on European cinema, world fiction of the thirties, the poetry of electric guitars— for what? I'm selling my soul through my cock; Monica and I are so worlds apart it's not even funny, yet for the touch of a silken palm I'll develop Deep Love for any Fine Art she cares to mention.

'You're very far away,' Monica says all at once.

Ha!

Monica sets little jars and spices out, gets the knives and cutting boards ready. She's always very structured in the way she goes about things. Everything has a beginning, middle and end. She follows these little paths of hers meticulously. She seems to think she holds all life's great recipes, including cooking recipes, in her mind.

'I'm okay.' I just want Monica to get on with it, to get it over with. I can't see the sweetness of what she's doing, the meaning, I only start to think about going home and abandoning the whole thing.

'Sure you're okay?' When I turn around from pouring myself a glass of cold water Monica is looking at me. Her expression makes it seem I have somehow opened the terrain of my evil thoughts to her. She says, 'Can you do me a favour, Romeo? Will you go into the garden and pick some of Mum's Sicilian basil? That's the smaller-leaf one.'

I wonder if maybe along the way I should lock myself in the bathroom and do it myself, pull away with my own impetuous rush, just to get rid of the headache that's developing.

'Yeah, yeah.'

So I go outside and have a good poke around Mrs Aquila's garden for this so-called small-leafed Sicilian *basilico*. I don't know, it's all news to me. Basil, oregano, fennel, what else is there? Parsley sage rosemary and thyme. Don't they all come in jars you buy from Woolworths?

The moon is already hanging low in the early evening sky. Monica comes out to see why I'm taking so long.

'Which one is it?'

'That one there, right in front of you!' she calls from the patio.

Monica returns inside.

I survey the little herb garden. Why am I so stupid— what does basil look like? The wind whistles and whispers in the avenue's dinosaur trees, at the intersection a streetlamp comes on. The herb garden is secluded and quiet. Its scent is astonishing; yet even more astonishing is the fact that there is an overriding perfume of honeysuckle. I don't understand this at all. No one can see me so I undo my trousers and try and urinate into the bushes but Monica has messed me up completely. I'm stiff as a week-old corpse. So I might as well die. When I walk back up the front steps my hands are full of bits of every herb in the garden.

Monica turns from the kitchen sink and she's wearing nothing but a big pink and white apron. Her halter top and skirt are gone. The apron covers her from neck to knees but it's open at the back and her long spine and buttocks are golden. She can't help but give me a shy smile. *This* was her secret, *this* is the life she wants to lead. I can't smile at all. My heart is a slow and heavy pounding.

Monica isn't annoyed that I can't tell one herb from another. She takes all the bits of dirt-plucked herbs from my hands and lays them end to end on a breadboard.

'This is oregano,' she says. 'Here, mint. This is rosemary. *This* is lavender, which isn't a herb. This is normal basil, see, with the big leaves, and this one here is the jackpot. Sicilian *basilico*.' Monica keeps smiling up at me, light catching the few freckles on her cheek. She tweaks basil leaves between her fingers and holds them up to my nose. 'Smell. We just need a little more of it, that's all. I'll come with you this time.'

Monica takes me by the hand and we go outside. She has no fear of the neighbours. The hulking trees and bushes protect us anyway. The moon is full and white. Monica kneels down on the lush green grass like Bernadette before a vision of the Virgin Mary. Her fingertips in the different herb flowers are as gentle as Bernadette's must have been when she washed the Virgin Mary's feet. Monica puts the basil she picks into the apron's pocket. My eyes are fixed on the golden down across the base of her spine, on the bow that ties the apron together. Then Monica stands and wraps her arms around me and keeps smiling her shy smile. That scent of honeysuckle is in the air again. As I hold Monica a bead of sweat runs down the cleft of her back. It's as if her temperature has jumped by whole degrees. She kisses me but holds my hand to stop it wandering.

'Come on,' Monica says, 'you have to help me now. There's someplace I have to go and I don't want to go alone.'

Holding hands, we go into the house, through the rumpus room, through the laundry and garage, and to a door. Monica holds my hand tighter and opens that door to the odours of must and damp.

'Switch on the light,' I say.

'There isn't a light,' Monica replies. 'Dad's superstitious about it.'

'About what?'

'This is where he keeps his wine.'

Still holding onto my hand, Monica fumbles around in the darkness. I can just discern the outlines of wooden crates stacked along the floor. When I touch them I find they are covered with damp hessian. No wonder Monica doesn't like to come in here alone. But the darkness, the smell of damp earth, the hazy lines of crates that resemble covered coffins, is somehow too exciting. Monica is a small mysterious shape in the dark. She doesn't fight because she feels it too. I press to her and this time her body presses back to me. Her hand is rubbing my cock. The apron twists away and her back goes against one of the damp walls and her hard mound pushes into my groin.

Monica's mouth is buried against mine.

And a telephone is ringing from upstairs.

Monica pulls away from me, I'm cheated again, Monica

grabs something from an open crate and then she flees.

'Quick!' she calls back, running ahead, apron flying. 'I know who that is!'

At the internal staircase Monica takes the steps two at a time. The unmistakable shape of a bottle of chianti swings from her hand. Monica makes it to the kitchen-wall telephone and it's Mrs Aquila on the line, just as she had known it would be. Monica's Sicilian dialect sounds as rough and earthy as the atmosphere of that dark little wine room. She straightens her apron and redoes the bow while she speaks; she takes the basil from her pocket and passes it to me.

So I go to the kitchen sink and rinse the leaves over and over.

When Monica hangs up and comes over to me she says, 'Boy. Mum always wants to know how my study is going. Okay.' She gets herself together. 'Now, Romeo, the first thing we have to do is get a good red, something just right to put us in the mood for cooking.' She uncorks the bottle and pours two glasses. Her hand is shaking, but only from the close encounter with her mother. Before I'm allowed to drink, Monica goes to the living room's old record player. It plays 78s, and she chooses Caruso with his sweet-voiced arias. His voice rises over the crackles of a bad needle.

Monica says, 'This is from about 1904. It's Puccini. *E lucevan le stelle.*'

So this is a ritual. I start to smile. I might even start to understand.

'Let's crack some garlic, and that's your first cooking lesson. Once you get the basics right, the rest just falls into place.'

And so it does.

* * *

Our bellies are full when later we lie cuddled in her single bed. We stink of garlic and meat and basil. It's still hot. We perspire over each other. Moonlight fills Monica's room and illuminates her angel's face, and when she cries out nothing is more important to me than the sounds of her tight breathing and voice. The pain in the pit of my stomach finally relents. But the pain in my heart is greater and will never go. It's a pain I want. I know now what Monica thinks of me; she was right to hold off for so long. I wanted copulation but she gave me consummation. For her it's lust versus, well, love. Monica holds me close, her face on my arm. I can hardly breathe I'm so fucking happy.

We have until about midnight. That's when her parents will close up the restaurant and think about their own bed.

'Monica . . .'

'No,' she says straight away, with a smile. 'You could hardly confuse it. I really wasn't.'

'Neither was I,' I say.

'In America they call it your "cherry".'

'I know. Somebody else got yours and somebody else got mine.'

Monica says, 'Oh well. What does it matter?'

I like the way she is so matter of fact, but I say, 'So why wouldn't you let me touch you all this time?'

Monica shuffles around in the narrow bed and stares into my face, full on, amused. 'I don't know about you, Romeo, but I've got school to think of. If we'd started this earlier I wouldn't have been thinking much about school.' She laughs at herself. 'Not much at all. We'd be doing this *constantly*. I *want* to do this all the time. Just think what we've got to look forward to.'

We grin at each other and hold each other more tightly.

All that time, those stabbing looks from Monica, those kisses, all those simple things that said she was imbued with electricity—all of it was real.

'You know what, I've been planning a surprise for when school finishes.'

'Wha-at?' Monica asks slowly.

I like the excitement in her face; I hold off saying it for as long as I can, like announcing the grand prize on a game show. 'Two weeks at Stradbroke Island. In Johnny's parents' cabin. What do you think about that?'

Monica goes dead silent.

It takes me a half hour to get her to say anything.

Finally, two notches in front of midnight, the moonlight in her hair, Monica says, 'Well, there's something I want you to know.' There is nothing capricious in her steady gaze. She brushes a wisp of hair from my forehead, then she tugs my hair forcefully. 'Henry Miller asked why it is that lovely faces haunt us so. He asked, *do extraordinary flowers have evil roots?*'

'Yeah?' I say. 'Ahm Monica—what the fuck are you talking about?'

With a jerk Monica lets go of my hair.

She says, 'It's Johnny.'

'What do you mean "It's Johnny"?'

Monica can't answer me. She seems scared. Something in my face is truly frightening her.

Maybe I don't have to bolt like a thief in the night, maybe a few more minutes will make everything all right inside me and inside Monica, but that's just what I do, I don't talk any more and I don't listen any more because she's not going to say anything. It's so nice and clear anyway. I just get up out of that bed. Donkeys have bad tempers, it's their way. It's

my way. *Fuck it. Johnny? She wants both of us?* I'm not going
to weep or wail. Monica has succeeded in finding that stony
core of me I always feared was there anyway. There's no
need to be afraid again. As the song says, *I won't get fooled
again*. This is liberation. For I am a stone, inside and out.
Monica wants Johnny *as well* as me? Good. If you ask me,
Monica's read one weird book too many; seen one Ingmar
Bergman film too many; listened to one too many soppy
arias. Who gives a fuck? I'm gone.

But why was I given the name of 'Romeo', the romantic
lover? It should be Pietro, the rock on which I will build my
church of lovelessness. The world is as hard as nails and I
will *never* be crucified by it.

The vast ugly house is all quiet and dark around me. I
pull on my shirt as I look down at Monica wrapped in her
white sheet, her cheeks and her eyes shining. The prophylactic drops from the pocket of my trousers. I pick it up and
look at it and throw it in Monica's face.

Then the moonlight shines through the trees and from
the avenue the red brick house, mantle of success that it is,
looks no better. There are no lights from anywhere in the
rooms, not even an outside light to welcome the Aquilas
home from their labours. Monica is awake and alone in her
bed, the cages of the cocky and budgies have been covered
and those three brainless birds sleep their brainless sleep.
Monica's cats, bitch on heat and male stalking like a gun-
slinger, are out on their midnight prowl.

So, midnight and moonlight.

From the river there comes the smell of catfish, for this
night has used up every bit of honeysuckle. There's a wind
in the high heavy branches. I get the fuck away from there,
walking fast down to Merthyr Road where it's not so dark.

I wipe my face furiously to get rid of Monica's kisses. My shoulders start to shudder and my teeth start to shake, and this premonition comes over me, this really shitful Sicilian sort of premonition, it's a sense that somehow, in the name of love, Monica just hasn't done sticking her knife in my heart.

Nigel rocked in the back seat with me. The driver glanced at us through the rear-vision mirror. He gave the impression of having seen all this and more most Friday midnights—but he was still on the nervy side.

'Fight?' he asked.

'My mate can't take his drink.'

The driver's eyes kept glancing into the mirror. I kept forgetting that my face resembled a not-very-good prize fighter's.

'I don't know about moon eclipses exactly,' the driver said, 'but very uncivilised events always follow the full moon around, you know that?'

'Yes, it's a popular myth.'

'No, no, it's real. Fatal traffic accidents, for one, matey. It's proven. And suicide too, or suicide attempts. The moon affects suicidal activity in women more than men.'

'Uh huh.'

'You bet. Research again. In spite of popular belief women's menstrual cycles don't average 29 days, but are usually 29.5 days, exactly the length of the interval between two successive moon phases. The average length of pregnancy is 266 days—exactly nine lunar months. So maybe the moon has a reason to affect women's depression more than it does for men. Then again, research also shows admissions to psychiatric hospitals on days of the full moon rises for both sexes, and you know what, sometimes it's as much as the combined admissions of the ten days before or after.'

'Are you for real?'

The driver stopped talking at a red traffic light. The green made him continue. Maybe he'd been a cabbie too long. Too long a cabbie with a science or psychology or *Readers Digest* degree.

'Offences with the highest correlation to the full moon are homicides and anything to do with family and children. Now this is the part where people should start thinking. Wife bashing, child bashing, the really ugly stuff. Car thefts have the lowest correlation. Of course. They're not crimes of passion.' The driver sniffed significantly and his eyes met mine in the rear-vision mirror. 'So what did you do, smack him one?'

'Oh well—'

'Deserved it, huh?'

'The wrong fellow.'

'Still deserved it.' The driver might have had a science degree but he'd failed race relations and peace studies. 'Can't stand them black dogs,' he said.

We pulled up, I paid him, and I dragged Nigel out of the back seat. The taxi tyre-screeched away. As I half-carried Nigel across the footpath his legs found a little volition.

Nigel murmured awake and said, 'Do you mind if I throw up?' and I got him over the garden and held his woolly hair away as he heaved. I concentrated on the camellias. When he finished he wiped his eyes and mouth, and looked at me sadly. 'What came over you, Romeo?'

'I thought you were somebody else.'

He didn't understand and he wasn't in the mood for conversation. Who could blame him? His skinny frame trembled as he gawked at the house and dark surroundings.

'What are we doing here, Romeo?'

The house was quiet. Though the eclipse was over, clouds obscured most of the moonlight. There was a strong wind that would get rid of those clouds soon enough. The trees and shrubs rustled alive.

'This is where I live.'

Nigel looked around. Like the trees and shrubs, he was trembling in the wind. 'Please don't hurt me. I'll do anything you want me to, Romeo.'

'I just want you to have a place to sleep. I'm sorry for what I did.'

His eyes were big and round and he didn't believe a word. 'I don't need a place to sleep. Thank you. Really. Thank you.'

'No, I'm sorry. I really am. Let me make it up to you.'

Nigel moaned, on the verge of tears, 'Oh, Romeo, I wouldn't have picked you for a moof.'

I said, 'But I'm not.'

Then he threw up again, all over the camellia sasanqua bushes, and his legs wobbled under him. I picked him up and carried him inside and wrapped him in a doona. On the lounge-room's fold-out bed Nigel watched me, gift-wrapped and unhappy.

'Do you want some dinner, Nigel?'

'No.' He stared at me. 'What have you got?'

The microwave reheated my pasta and Nigel sat in the bed and ate slowly and deliberately. He had three servings before he gave a terminal burp. I sat with him for ages, until his troubled eyes just had to shut. Nigel started to snore. I wondered how I could have been so utterly blind.

The night had turned very cold. The wind shaking the house didn't help. I wanted my bed but instead I went to

the corridor and tried Mary's door. It was bolted shut. In
the black I burst the door wide with my shoulder.

'Who's there?' Mary said, sitting upright. She was sleep-
shaken but something that looked like a baseball bat was
already in her hands. At the foot of her bed Blue growled
and moaned a little but he knew it was me. I saw the outline
of Mary's baseball bat, and it was shaking.

'It's Romeo, Mary.'

'Get out of my room.'

From the futon Mary's head and shoulders were silhouetted against an uncovered window. Out in the night I could
see the swaying of the backyard's impossibly tall palm trees.
Mary was wearing a nightdress with a bow tied under her
chin. I could hear her breathing. I could hear Blue breathing.
In the lounge room Nigel snored and snuffled.

Mary didn't move from her bed but she kept the baseball
bat up.

'So who were the two men, Mary?'

'What two men?'

'Come on.'

'What two men? What are you talking about? Get out
of my room before you're sorry.'

Blue shuffled around and farted before resettling himself
over the blankets.

'You had them waiting that night. Only they were
waiting for Johnny. Johnny was going to be taught a lesson
for treating you so badly, right? It was dark and your friends
mistook me for him. You didn't know Johnny was gone.
When you realised I wasn't him you came to the rescue.'

Blue's ear pricked up, like a bat's. In the window behind
Mary and Blue the crazy mop-tops of the palm trees swayed
in front of a luminous moon.

'How far would you have let them go if it had been Johnny?'

The wind eased a moment and the palm trees rested. The house stopped creaking.

'Far enough.'

'Who were they?'

'I like to call them my brothers.'

'One of them must have an interesting face now.'

'He needed six stitches.'

I moved away from the doorway. 'I'm not leaving this house, Mary, but I think you should. Tomorrow morning will do. And mind the lounge room, we've got a guest staying over.'

'You fucking bastard, Romeo.'

I let her be.

I sat a few minutes on the side of my bed and stared at the wall, then I undressed and slid under the covers and stared at the black ceiling. Winter was coming and I shivered before settling down. I looked at the moonlight past my bedroom window. Poor Nigel. And in a way, poor Mary. Now she really did make sense to me. She was bitter and she wouldn't be walked on and she would go that extra bit to make sure she wasn't.

Through the open curtains I focused on those two tall palm trees swaying in front of the face of the moon. The westerlies had cleared the clouds away. The old house shivered and groaned, and the floorboards creaked loudly as Mary moved around her room.

Good. Good. Let her pack and leave now.

And let her take the mutt with her.

Bitch and hound.

Footsteps, creaking floorboards, then the metal scrape of a doorknob.

Mary came into my bedroom. She was out of her night-dress and her back was straight as she walked around the four-poster. She climbed into the other side of the bed, shuffled under the starchy covers, and gripped me between her thighs. Her legs were warm. Her breath was tinged with garlic and basil.

'No one has to leave this house,' Mary said, but I grabbed her hair and pulled her face away from mine. She was a puzzle, absolutely so.

Blue came padding after her. If he was another to jump into the bed with me I'd break his skull open.

Mary didn't grimace. Instead her long white hand stroked a line down from my eye to the corner of my mouth. 'I'm sorry about your face, Romeo. And I'm very sorry about your dinner.'

I let go of Mary's hair and she rubbed her head into the hollow of my shoulder. The tops of the palm trees covered the moon, revealed the moon, covered it again. I closed my eyes. What do I see when I close my eyes? The moonlit leer of a dirty alley cat; a silhouette of Mary; and Monica wrapped in a white sheet, reaching out to me.

'Romeo?' Mary quietly said into my shoulder. 'I've got some condoms.'

Mary went back to her room for them and then she shushed the grizzling Blue out into the corridor. She lay down with her hair spread over the pillow. What had Monica tried to tell me so long ago about extraordinary flowers?

FIVE

Il Vulcano

Sicilian premonitions, don't make me laugh.
Love, don't make me vomit.

I haven't seen Monica in weeks and I like it that way. I see clearly Monica was like a god with good thighs who wanted to make me in her own image. Music, books, dancing; Sicilian pasta sauce, Sicilian chianti and Sicilian basil. Give me a break. This is Australia. Our families left the old country far behind, long ago, and forever. Why should kids like Monica and me perpetuate old-world myths, old-world romance? Old-world bullshit.

Exams are over.

I heard on the grapevine Monica missed out on

becoming dux of her school but she's in Queensland's top
five per cent for academic achievement anyway. Now the
little bitch queen can choose whatever future she wants. I
failed every subject bar English. My parents are hysterical
and they've gone back to their old ways. They're demanding
I get on the next train to Sydney. Or else my father is
on the way up, leather belt in hand. Let the old fart come.
He'll be hard-pressed to find me because summer's here
and the time is right for fucking on the beach. Christmas
is around the corner. Can't my parents *imagine* what these
Queensland beaches are like right now? Probably they can,
only too well. So I failed, so what, it was all probably
written in the stars the day I was born, like Tony Aquila's
attachment to Fiats.

Johnny and I never worry about Monica.

He can do whatever he wants but he can't be doing too
much with Monica because I'm always with him. I don't hate
Johnny, I'm happy to be with him. He says he put Monica
away a couple of times after their dance at Cloudland, and
then she got all clingy and started talking about love and
going crazy about not knowing how to choose between him
and me. All it does is make me realise how gullible I can be.
So am I going to ruin the only real friendship I've got because
of that little slut-bitch-whore? I look at Johnny's profile
sometimes while we sit on the beach. I imagine him putting
his cock in Monica and I imagine her telling him that she
loves him like the stars above and will love him until the day
she dies. And I imagine what went on in Johnny's thoughts,
the silent laughter at her stupidity, the blind and obdurate
need to just *fuck* her.

Monica hurt me and Johnny hurt Monica. She deserved
it and I deserved it for being so blind.

So we head off to the beaches as often as we can, Johnny and me, off to where all the girls are on holiday. They're out there lying in the sun, bikinis and cheap magazines and sun hats everywhere. We spend our days in the surf, lying in the hot sun, chatting up girls until they let us rub sun cream onto their shoulders. It's weird. Now that I'm free of Monica I don't seem to have any problem getting what I want. Maybe girls see the emancipation in my face. Maybe it's more alluring to be cruel. Maybe the colours of my aura have changed.

Things are good.

My two jobs give me plenty of money and I don't have to study any more. I don't have to read stupid books and listen to stupid records. I turned seventeen. To celebrate there was a big illegal beach fire at Mooloolaba, and we drank too many cheap flagons of moselle. Now that I'm seventeen I can buy a car and I won't have to wait for Johnny to drive me to the beaches, the nightclubs, the lovely dark parking spots in Mt Coot-tha where it's almost as if you're the only people on the planet. Johnny and his date are always in the front seat, me and mine are always in the back. A happy, quarrelsome foursome. The things we hear from each other's cramped quarters are enough to turn your hair white, but it's all part of getting rid of a fear of the future we never allow ourselves to talk about. Or am I the only one with the fear of the future? The girls we end up rooting are always going into the public service or saving to travel overseas or already buying bridal magazines. And Johnny got into medicine at university, just. Wouldn't it be a fucking joke if it turns out I'm the only one cast adrift?

Ah, forget it.

So it's nearly Christmas and of course it's around now

in the progress of my fun new poisonous life that Mrs Gloria
Aquila decides to call the house.

I wasn't answering the telephone any more and my
cousins Lucia and Pasquale have been well-trained to ensure
that any caller isn't Monica. Whom they met only once. The
sight of Monica's hair was enough to scandalise them. What
kind of good Italian girl dyes her hair like that, this is what
they wanted to know. A little henna, a little black, a little
brown, nature sometimes needs a little help—but white? To
them Monica is a five foot harpy and so they were only too
happy to ensure her calls never got through to me.

But this is different. This is *la Signora Aquila*, whom
everyone venerates.

It's a mid-week evening and my hands are blistered and
aching. If it's not the big concrete blocks I have to cart
around for cousin Pasquale, then it's the freezing vats of
mince in the Coles meat section that I have to pack into
handy take-home trays. Anyway, my cousin Lucia is pointing
that heavy black telephone receiver in my direction and
there's nothing I can do to avoid it.

My guts start to squirm.

'Hello, Romeo, how you are?' Mrs Aquila says it as if it
isn't over a month since she's seen hide nor hair of me. She
acts like it was only last Sunday she cooked me a good dinner.
'How you holidays, darly?'

I'm sweating too. 'Good,' I say.

'You family?'

'Good.'

'You cousins?'

'Good.'

'You results?'

'Good.' I listen to the pause, it's obvious Mrs Aquila

doesn't believe this. 'Well, not so good,' I say, and with the first break into honesty I know I am lost. And Mrs Aquila knows it too.

'No worry, young man,' she says, going on in that nice way of hers. '*Basta*. You must be wonder why I call you.'

I say, 'No' but now that Mrs Aquila is on to me every lie is like throwing a piece of shit into her face.

She says, 'Ah, so you use to the women they calling you on the telephone. *Oh Romeo, oh Romeo*.' She laughs, it's the only Shakespeare she knows. 'You too young to be lady killer, no?' Mrs Aquila waits for me to say something but I just let her go on. 'My husband Michele and myself, we were wonder if you can help out. We got the little problem. Romeo. You can help my husband and myself?'

She's a sly one, that Mrs Aquila.

I'm lost.

A few days later I'm back in the red brick mausoleum and Mrs Aquila is sizing me up for an Al Martino/Las Vegas entertainer outfit from her husband's closet. Except of course that I'm not going to sing, I'm going to serve—at tables. Il Vulcano Ristorante's tables. This has to be a set up. Mrs Gloria Aquila is as romantic as they come, it's easy to see she's the quintessential Sicilian mamma. Warm and loyal and romantic. Three handmade lace hankies in her purse when she goes to the cinema. *Gone With the Wind* nearly ruptured her spleen and *Casablanca* almost put her in hospital. Knowing this about her personality even I, meathead that I am, can't be uncouth enough to try and wriggle out of what she's got planned. But at least Monica's away today, Mrs Aquila was kind enough to tell me that straight out.

We're alone in the house and I look at Mrs Aquila's face as she does up the black buttons of another ridiculous pink shirt. I keep wondering if Monica has put her up to this because, you know, mothers and their daughters, they're the unknown world. Mrs Aquila tells me I'm to be serving at tables in the restaurant during some big Italian wedding, and of course, 'Is Christmas Romeo we no can find anyone half as hard-work like you to help out and of course the pay she be okay and you get good *mangiare* and maybe later in the night you can have dance and maybe a couple glass of the bride and groom champagne but definitely yes a couple glass of my husband his best *vino rosso*.'

The family paying for the wedding party have more money than good sense. The florist's bill alone would send an ordinary family broke and the courses chosen to be served are classic Mediterranean too-mucho. So naturally everyone has to be dressed right, even waiters and waitresses, and that's why I'm being sized up for one of Signore Michele Aquila's poofy pink shirts. The other staff are going to be wearing the same type of outfit—it's a little consolation, but not much. It makes me wonder what monstrosities of fashion await us from the wedding party and guests. Maybe at least there'll be a good laugh to be had.

Mr Aquila and I are about the same height but that's where the similarity ends. I can't fit into his trousers. Already at seventeen my thighs are like tree trunks, but his shirts fit me okay, more's the pity. He must have the same donkey stock as me.

Mrs Aquila says, 'You look *simpatico*.'

As if.

'I order you a nice pair black trousers, with the stripy down the leg. What size you waist? Lemme measure. And Monica, she will look nearly the same, just with the long black skirt.' Then Mrs Aquila just gets busy with her tape measure.

'Monica is going to be working?'

'Of course.'

'Signora Aquila, you know, I can't—'

'Romeo. Is very big wedding. And Monica she on holiday. She have to work. Antonio too.'

Mrs Aquila is on her knees. She's got some pins stuck in her mouth. Without much hesitation she measures my inside leg. I see again Monica kneeling at the little herb garden, showing me what's basil and what's not basil, showing me her little *culo* and bare legs through the open apron. Mrs Aquila looks up at me but she doesn't say anything, and then slowly she gets to her feet. She takes the pins from her mouth and I can feel a flush coming to my face.

What does Mrs Aquila know and what doesn't she know?

We're in the bedroom she shares with her husband, we're standing by an ornate clothes cupboard, in front of a full-length mirror. It's not dark but it's not all that light either because the afternoon has slowly faded. I know Mr Aquila is at the restaurant, but where's Monica today?

Mrs Aquila's face is like an angel's.

Monica got that from her all right. There are lines, the lines of comfort and understanding. Her hair isn't the wiry black of we Negroes of the Italian south, no, it's what people call honey-brown. Shoulder length and shining. Her dress just accentuates how womanly she is. Like Gina Lollobrigida in her heyday, Mrs Aquila is any sane man's dream. To imagine her as both lover and mother seems the only right thing to do. I can see the person Monica will be right there in the compassionate lines of Mrs Aquila's face.

Her lips are parted in just the way Monica's would be

before she kissed me. Mrs Aquila looks at me and if I'm not careful I'll break into a thousand pieces. Somehow Mrs Aquila knows this because she reaches out and holds me the way I've always wanted to be held. I can't help myself, in my pants I'm as stiff as a pole, but Mrs Aquila doesn't move away at all.

She just takes her time and lets me settle down.

And then she says, '*Romeo, I don't understand why you want to be bad boy when you're such a good boy. Why are you wasting your life when you could do better? Why do you act the fool when you've got a good mind? Your parents might be tough and cruel but that's no reason to turn your own future into shit. Do you want to be bitter like them? Do you want to be lonely like them?*'

Mrs Aquila's chosen to speak in Sicilian, the language I have faith in. It's dirty and clear, no elaboration, no airs and graces, no bullshit. You speak it with honest shit on your shoes. The proper tongue for anger and for love, for berating beasts of burden and for lulling children to sleep.

Mrs Aquila holds me and caresses my hair. Her breasts don't smell of honeysuckle but I feel her steady and soothing heartbeat. Her hands are in my thick hair and she kisses my face and I imagine Monica in her womb, nursed by that steady heartbeat. Mrs Aquila takes up my hands, calluses, blisters and all.

'*Look at what you've done to your poor hands. My God, look at what you've done. Romeo. Tell me, go on and tell me. If you love my daughter, you should tell me.*'

The light is fading and her hand still follows the thick waves of my hair and I can't say a thing.

'*You ran away from home because you were sad, and now you're here and you're sadder still. If you've got a broken heart it's because you love my daughter. So why do you stay away?*'

I see our reflection in the mirror. We look like a noble-
woman and brute, loving each other.

Mrs Aquila says, *'Romeo, how did you ever let Monica break
your heart?'* and I begin to weep because it's too hard a question, because I haven't a clue. But then something happens.
Every piece of shit seems to lift from my shoulders. I put
my face on her breasts and I know Mrs Aquila has done this,
somehow, with her absurd and romantic heart she has made
me see what needs to be seen.

That I love them both, child and mother.

In the morning Mary hummed a Gershwin tune and found
the time to break open another of her nonoxynol-9 smeared
condoms. Then from shower to towels to thick dark stockings and a white and black outfit, Mary hummed the same
piece of Gershwin over and over, not looking at all like
someone preparing to deal with an old woman's
incontinence.

Halfway between corridor and living room Mary called,
'Your guest didn't wait for breakfast.'

Saturday morning and I was a rich man lying in bed with
newspapers and coffee.

'The fold-out's empty.' Mary came into the bedroom to
look at me, her hair pulled back in a bun. 'And the front
door's wide open. Something must have scared him off.' She
slipped flat shoes on and looked in the mirror and saw me
watching her. 'Maybe we made too much noise. Have
another coffee?'

Mary zipped the back of her black skirt. She was sexy
and young, wise and untrusting. When she returned with
another big mug of coffee for me I put down the newspaper.
I took her by the arm and made her sit on the bed, held her

and searched her face for tenderness. Maybe there wouldn't
be a sign of it in my face either. Something in my heart
shuddered. Like a dreamy kid I wished a night together could
change people completely and give them fairytale hearts.

Mary went into the bathroom and ran the taps and
when she came again to the bedside she kissed me lovingly,
as if she'd read my thoughts. She said, 'I've left some
lipstick,' and wiped the corner of my mouth. Mary's head
went onto my shoulder. Her long white hands ran along
the scratches she'd put in my back. Brisbane was constantly
mutilating me.

And then Mary whispered, 'Romeo, I'm not what you
think I am.'

A little later the front verandah door slammed shut. I
read the Saturday papers and did my best not to think another
thing about her.

In the late morning I took the flat-wheeled wheelbarrow
and two sacks of horse shit into the garden. The shop assistant
had wanted to deliver the sacks in his van but I preferred to
put each over a shoulder and grunt along the weedy footpaths
of Auchenflower. Mary's food and succour had just about
turned me back into what I'd been. And this time I liked it.
I was myself again, solid donkey, not a vegetarian of love but
a true carnivore. It was hopeless to try and be anything else.
A good night with Mary mightn't have left me with a fairytale
heart, but it helped me accept I wanted flesh and the devil
as much as I ever had. And if I was a kind of werewolf then
maybe Mary was a kind of vampire.

No. I didn't want to think of her.

I had a plan for the garden, but most of all I had a plan
to atone for my sins against Nigel. I knew that without
remorse and a good dose of penance I was no better than a

good piece of rump or t-bone or eye fillet for the predators
of this city.

The birds were singing.

Blue kept me company as I cleared the garden beds and
spread the good turdy manure around. The sky was a clear
pale blue and the garden was alive with colour and light and
living things. Grasshoppers and wasps prospered. Eventually
both would have to go; the grasshoppers would be easy
enough and one day I'd get around to burning the wasps
from their nests. For now though I liked their helicopter-
whir and busy company; the grasshoppers were somnolent
but the wasps seemed to have as clear a plan as I did.

The hot dirty work reminded me of a song my mother
used to sing when I was a kid, when I used to get down on
my bare knees with her in our family vegetable garden. With
her apron full of flat broad beans and her hands tending the
tomato patch my mother would sing,

> *Oh, campagnola bella*
> *Tu sai la reginella*
> *Negli occhi tuoi c'è sole, c'è colore*
> *C'è la valle tutte in fior.*

and I always understood that once upon a time my mother
had been that beautiful country girl with all the sun and
colour of the flowering fields in her eyes.

At the end of the long hot day I gave in to Blue and his
soggy tennis ball.

I led him around the big old house and down to the flat
back part of the property. From in between the stocky trunks
of the palm trees I tossed the ball for him, endlessly watching
him scamper away into the lantana and undergrowth.

Somewhere in tree-hidden back streets another excited dog
was barking, and children were laughing, all of us playing the
same Saturday afternoon game in the same failing light and
wondering what the evening would bring.

Johnny's house was precariously high on its fifteen-metre
stilts, somehow too far away, like a distant house on a hill.
From it came the sound of the telephone ringing, as it had
done all day. I concentrated on the soft insect-buzz of the
late afternoon, broken by Blue crashing through the thick
vegetation, and by a radio somewhere playing grungy guitar
pop tunes. I remembered the messages left on Johnny's
answer machine, Mary's voice coming off the tape again and
again and again, pleading and lost. I threw the ball and wondered what had been going on with Johnny and Mary, why
nothing seemed to add up, why it was as if little pieces of a
complicated mosaic had been thrown away.

The sound of the telephone went away and I stood in
the quiet of Johnny's rainforest paradise. Light faded and a
breeze drifted through the thick canopy of branches. Two
orange blossom trees gave off their perfume, and Blue spied
a goanna poking its great head out from between two rocks.
The soggy tennis ball dropped out of Blue's mouth, his head
went down, and he shot forward like an arrow.

'Blue!'

Blue crouched away with his living trophy, a growling
coming from deep in his throat. The goanna—long as a
forearm and nuggetty as a piece of shale—thrashed in his
mouth. My heart was pounding and Blue wouldn't come and
I saw Mary again, long and naked and pale, and with her
teeth on my throat.

The droning of insects stopped while Blue dragged the
goanna away up the garden terraces. He was half-grinding his

yellow teeth, playing, drawing the crunching and the killing
out. The goanna had its own sharp teeth and claws. If it
could get at Blue there would be a real battle of blood and
backbone. I caught up with Johnny's mutt and grabbed him
by the collar. He twisted and turned. After I punched his
skull he gave the goanna up with a resentful cough. Blue
didn't try to bite me; with an affronted eye he watched the
reptile limp and scurry back to its world of moss and rocks.

'Get into the house! Pieceashit!' and I gave him a kick
to get him mobile.

Blue trudged up the terraces, his eye downcast, his tatty
ear flat against his skull. I threw the soggy tennis ball to
buggery and followed him and stuck him in the room with
the futon. Like Nigel wondering why all this had happened
to him, Blue was too frightened to even whimper.

Though there had been all those telephone calls during
the day the machine had no messages. I was sure it was Mary.
The evening approached and I knew I didn't have a word to
say to her. My heart chugged with dread. I'd come crashing
out of the sky to fall into the belly of a beast, and the beast
was Mary. And now I could see Mary and me in a domestic
scene, cooking together, drinking wine, ripping away clothes,
and when I displeased her, her two 'brothers' would come
to make a Romeo-bone-stew of me.

I had a shower and dressed and got away from that house
before I heard the throaty rattling of Mary's ugly green
Volkswagen.

It was a fresh night. Crowds already gathered in the Fortitude Valley mall, and even in the sea of unfamiliar faces my
mind would not stop racing. Bars were busy, nightclubs were
quiet. The Underworld too, padlocked, empty, windows
dark like an amusement park ghost-house. It was just too

early in the evening. In a few hours all would find a way
back to that lively hell.

I had to pull myself together.

The Empire Hotel's public bar teemed with beer-barrel-
belly drinkers, no Nigel. He wasn't bludging a meal off
anyone at any of the restaurants. I walked around and
around and Nigel's skin and bone profile was nowhere to
be found. Wherever I walked there were loving couples.
Would it have been such a sin to swallow my misgivings
and wait at home for Mary, to promise her a night on the
town, to consecrate our communion with cheap champagne
and bad music?

There was enough bad music in the mall, and street kids
fighting. Two officers, and then four, and then six with a
paddy-wagon broke them up. The kids went scampering away
and none of the police went after them.

So might Nigel be one of those kids? Did he live in the
street or in a St Vincent de Paul collection bin; did he have
a mattress busy with fleas, stolen nightclub clothes lovingly
arranged on wire hangers, a picture of Fred Astaire or
Michael Jackson tacked to a wall above him?

Yet again I was around the Underworld.

The alleyways behind the club were loaded with cats and
that familiar stench of rubbish and faeces. It was just possible
that sometimes Nigel made this place his home. Over there
was the parapet where Julie had leaned. I preferred the alley's
maze to the bon vivant gaiety of the mall cafés. I undid my
fly and urinated against a pile of empty crates. Curiosity made
me follow the alleyways further, deeper into the hidden guts
of Fortitude Valley and to a nest of vagrants trying to keep
warm under cardboard boxes and newspapers.

I would have asked these rotting and forgotten souls if

they knew anything of a kid called Nigel, but I was too close
to losing my nerve. There were the glowing paper embers
of a fire that hadn't taken. Pieces of wood, cardboard and
rubbish were constructed into a boy scout's camp fire.
Someone had lost interest. The air was cold and so were the
embers. Dusty human bodies shivered under their cardboard
coverings and evil permeated the deep alley.

Matches were scattered on the ground. Maybe some poor
vagrant's hands had been shaking with too much palsy to
strike enough of them. I picked up a handful and struck them
all together and lit the old newspapers, fanning the flames
with the flap of a cardboard box. The fire went up and I felt
the heat on my face. A bundle of old clothes, held together
with a flashy leather belt, held out a claw, palm upraised.

'Please . . . please . . . '

There were a few lamps at the crumbling back sections
of old buildings, over the rickety legs of fire stairs, at the
end of the alley. The weak light showed the bright intelligent
eyes that looked out from a wicked Rip Van Winkle face.
By the licking flames of the fire the long hair and long beard
were grey and white. But those eyes held me, and somehow
they were filled with knowing and wonder.

The claw became a pointing finger, stabbing at the stinking air, indicating me, me, me. Movement then amongst the
half-hidden bodies as they gathered closer to the warming
fire. *Jesus Christ*. I lost my nerve and took off for the merry
lights of Saturday night. When I looked over my shoulder
that same long-haired ghoul was coming after me, finger still
extended. He might have been a ghoul but it was like he'd
seen a ghost. I hurried. There was no way he could catch up
with me. It was like out-stripping passengers on the way to
the safety of the airport's marshlands. The ghoul fell behind

and I was out into a sweet safe night of coffee beans and coriander.

Coffee bars and Thai restaurants, they'd never been so comforting. If Nigel lived in those alleys he could stay there. So much for my plans. I rushed up to the mall and found an Italian café that advertised beer and wine as well as fettuccine and focaccia.

The night was cold and, after that alley, I couldn't get warm. I felt like getting good and drunk again. The nearest waiter took his time in coming to me. There were better tables for him, the tables with young women sitting in threes and fours. The waiter's eyes ate up the low-cut blouses and soft necks before he sashayed over to me. 'Sir?'

I asked for a double whisky.

'Sir.'

He bowed curtly, to mock me, to point his tight tush in the direction of the largest table of females. I heard their reaction and so did he. It was his night. Such self-confidence would never be in danger of failing.

While I waited I looked around and tried to gather my wits. Slowly, two people at the table nearest me turned in my direction. They stared, others too, then the big table of young women did the same. The waiter was returning with his tray held over his head. People kept looking at me, then I realised, past me. I jerked around in my chair.

The ghoul had found me.

He pointed at me, gnarled finger shaking in my face. No wonder everyone was so transfixed. I was transfixed. The ghoul's bright blue eyes were anchored to me as if I was some strange and wonderful thing. His seaweed-straggly hair reached his shoulders and his beard grew to his chest. His mouth was open, all gums, except for a grey front tooth protruding like a gravestone from a weed bed.

His lips twisted. It was the best smile he could manage. A croaky voice said, 'Oh, *lupo mannaro*.' Again, with affection, '*Lupo mannaro*.'

God help me but I understood him.

The waiter arrived. With a wink of his eye and a flounce of his bottom toward the big table of young women, as if there was nothing strange at all he set a whisky between my two dead-cold hands.

A week later Il Vulcano Ristorante is full of Italians who look like movie extras, and me, who looks like a *finocchio*. Sicilians, Neapolitans, Calabrese, all kinds of regionals with all kinds of dialects, they're all there. The young woman getting married is the daughter of the Italian club's president; the young man getting married is the son of the local consul. So for one night and one night only the Aquila restaurant is a melting pot for communities who wouldn't normally spit at each other.

Tony Aquila introduces me to Robert, George, Mario and Gus, all waiters wearing the same outfits. We look like a carnival conga line but at least there's strength in numbers. Tony of course somehow avoided the pink frills. He's dressed in black, like a gunfighter. As well as we young Italian boys there's one waitress, and she's not Monica. She's a Calabrian porker by the name of Luisa and she keeps finding time to admire the black trousers Mrs Aquila had made for me. They've got a black satiny sheen and a stripe down the sides, and in the first half hour of serving the multitude I've ruined these trousers by tossing a great bowl of ravioli over myself. Tony is coming one way, I'm going the other way, the swinging doors are swinging, and—WOOMPAH!—ravioli and sauce everywhere.

The night is young.

Well, Tony is more resourceful than I thought. Without anyone in the kitchen noticing, without his mother or father noticing, and especially no one of the wedding party noticing, he scoops the ravioli right off the floor and back into the ceramic serving urn. He gets me to sprinkle some parsley and parmesan over the top and everything's magic again. Robert, George, Mario and Gus are pissing themselves. There's something about the excess of this wedding party that none of them like. At least the floor looked clean enough to eat off. I get onto my knees and wipe that floor until it is sparkling again, then I go and serve the ravioli while the band play 'Delilah'.

In the kitchen the two chefs, identical twins I can't tell apart, are already screaming the same mezzo soprano. They want one of us layabouts to come collect a serving that's been ready a millisecond. So I hurry in and get it. On my way out I pass Tony again, and he's grinning, so I say, 'Hey, Tony, when does your sister start? She's a little late,' and Tony looks at me and his big grin is gone for good.

'What's it to you, fuckface? Get the fuck out of here and serve the fucken customers.' He grabs another waiter, George, by his frilly pink shirt and shoves him toward the twins—who are now invisible behind the hissing steam of their pots and pans. 'Go get the fucken gnocchi—what the fuck's the matter with you?'

George scrambles, as do we all, because Tony's vocabulary makes him the boss. I don't even want to be here and I'm copping this abuse. It's going to be a long night.

There are 376 guests, not including the wedding party. The wedding party consists of two sets of beaming parents,

one bride, one groom, five bridesmaids, five groomsmen,
three flower girls with flowers in their hair, and three page
boys in ducky white suits. The priest who performed the
marriage is up there at the bridal table and he's tippling away
because the wine we're serving is a class above any altar wine
he's used to. In fact the church is well represented because
we've got a few nuns, three Christian Brothers, a bishop,
and to show a liberal attitude, a Protestant minister with a
drop-dead gorgeous wife. I wonder if any of these Catholics
wonder why God so smiled on a Protestant?

Anyway, it feels like I've got to cater to about 300 of
these guests. I'm pouring wine like a sonofabitch, bringing
out carafes of red and white, bottles of lemonade and orange
juice, Coke, Fanta, mineral water, serving the starter of anti-
pasto, the next course of ravioli and gnocchi, the next course
of veal, the next course of a chicken dish fragrant with rosemary, out come more buns and hot rolls and dollops of
creamy butter, salads with black olives and oily artichoke
hearts; we've forgotten to bring out the vinaigrette of *pipi*
and oregano and extra virgin olive oil. Some crabby old jerk
is ordering anisette and another more ancient but just as
crabby old jerk wants Galliano. I tell these scrofulous old
farts to go to the bar where they will find two bar attendants
whom they will know as bar attendants because of poofy pink
shirts just like mine. The two old pricks won't get up to go
to the bar because they want *me* to go to the bar for them,
then I notice their walking frames so I *do* go to the bar for
them, setting a precedent none of the waiters are crazy about.
Everyone is then asking for more of the vegetables and just
a little more salad, as if they haven't been fed enough as it
is. The twin chefs have taken to abusing each other instead
of us waiters. Finally we bring out the *pipi* with oregano and

extra virgin olive oil and no one seems to notice the bad timing because it all gets eaten up in a second anyway. That porker Luisa actually pinches my bottom as I pass her and I give her a filthy look and she smiles as if I've tweaked her tit. With that reasonable voice of hers Mrs Aquila does her best to calm down the chefs, then a great grandmother without any teeth and in a Gloria Swanson–Norma Desmond evening gown advises me loudly to soak my trousers in salt water and lemon juice to get the very large sauce stain out. Mrs Aquila's reasonable voice has got her nowhere with the temperamental chefs so now she starts screaming at them, really screaming, and Mr Michele Aquila is nowhere to be found though we all have our suspicions. The previously foul-mouthed Tony Aquila has turned sweet as a pussycat because one of the bridesmaids has been whispering to him with every course of the dinner he has personally served her. In his black outfit he looks like, and has adopted, the demeanour of a character from *The Good, the Bad and the Ugly*. We, the abused, agitated, aggrieved waiters in unrewarding pink know exactly what she's been whispering because it's written in the increasing flush of Tony Aquila's idiot face. And then just as we've finished serving the food and clearing away the crockery and the silver cutlery and setting out the champagne glasses for the toasts, and the master of ceremonies is about to get up and start with the speeches, some tuxedoed dick-head who is pissed as a fart, with perfectly white, perfectly swept-back hair, stands on a table and bellows a wildly inappropriate *Nessun Dorma* at the unsuspecting bridal party, much to their horror and much to the greater outrage of the intolerable six-piece band who believe they possess a monopoly on all Italian wedding music because they're booked twelve months ahead for all weddings of this nature all over Brisbane and are always written up and lauded by their journalist relatives in the ethnic newspaper, *La Fiamma*.

And *then* we get the speeches.

Out the back, flanked by our sulking chefs, we waiters shake champagne bottles up and pop innumerable corks as loudly as is possible. George aims at me, I aim at Robert, Robert aims at Mario, Mario aims at Gus, and somehow The Man With No Name lets off two simultaneous corks in the direction of the twins. Tony's got the gunfighter image down pat.

'Eh *vaffunculo!*' the twins yell, both wielding sharpened meat cleavers.

'Stick it up your arses!' Tony yells back.

So we're laughing, but in all this I'm still looking around and waiting. No Monica.

Mrs Aquila is standing over at the kitchen's back doorway. She catches my eye and signals me to join her. I put down the extra case of champagne I've hefted up from the cellar, and leave the others to their games. I see there's colour in Mrs Aquila's cheeks, probably from yelling at the chefs. She looks more ravishing, more exquisite than ever. Beside Mrs Aquila the bride is a hag, and the bride, we have been told, is a photographic model. Luisa and Tony and George and Robert and Mario and Gus troop out with trays loaded with bottles of champagne. It's just me and Mrs Aquila and the twins left in the kitchen. The chefs grumble and drink beer and pick at leftover pieces of garlicky chicken.

Mrs Aquila doesn't say anything. She leads me out onto a fire-stair landing, then she shuts the back door behind us. Below is a paved courtyard bounded by fern trees and palms. It's quiet and warm. The stars are out.

The amplified wedding speeches are like the distant bee-hum of traffic. On faraway roofs there's a cat fight. I appreciate this chance to get away from it all, the waitering life is definitely not for me, then of course, thick-head that I am, I see Mrs Aquila's pink cheeks have nothing at all to do with the chefs. I watch her profile. If I was twice my age I'd run away with her into the hills and make her love me. I'd spend eternity with her. Mrs Aquila would just have to name a place, Tuscany, Provence, Biloela, anywhere, I'd be there.

'*Romeo*,' she says softly. '*Will you do something for me?*'

'*Si, signora*,' I say respectfully.

She leads me down the fire stairs to the courtyard. It's dark. Under the stars it's as romantic as life gets. I wonder what's going on. This has to involve Monica. I expect to find her down in this courtyard waiting for me. Mrs Aquila, faithful angel that she is, is bringing us together at last—but no, it's not Monica I find, and neither is it an expression of some hidden desire in Mrs Aquila.

Signore Michele Aquila is sitting on a garden bench right at the back of the courtyard, under the fanning branches of a big pineapple palm. He is singing a little song, watching the stars, wearing a black tuxedo. With his mournful eyes and dark good looks and cowlick of hair carelessly dropping over his forehead, he is a sad-faced gigolo, a southern Italian James Bond. Marcello Mastroianni in *La Dolce Vita*. His legs are crossed and he languishes under the stars and quarter moon with a glass in his hand and a bottle of champagne by his side.

'*Drive him home, Romeo. Here are the keys.*' Mrs Aquila talks to me but she is looking down on her husband. '*I could ask Antonio but I don't want him to see his father like this.*' She hands me the keys. '*Please drive him in his car. This is the front door key to the house. I trust you to do this for me, Romeo.*'

Mr Aquila keeps singing up at the stars. I have the impression our presence means very little to him. He seems happy, adrift, quiet, totally within himself. Then he looks at me.

'*Look at the stars, young man,*' he says, speaking in Sicilian. He looks at them himself and goes back to his song.

I say to Mrs Aquila, '*But where's Monica?*'

'*When Monica found out you were working tonight she wouldn't come. She's got her own mind.*'

'I understand,' I say in English, hoping it will put Mrs Aquila off. I've heard enough. The disappointment I feel is overwhelming.

'*She was very upset with me, Romeo. I thought it would do you both good to get together here. I'm sorry.*'

'It was a good idea, signora.'

'*You should talk to her, Romeo.*'

'All right.'

'*You should talk to her,*' she emphasises. '*Don't just look at each other and say* "Oh, my heart, how she is-a beating!" *Tell the girl how you feel.*' She sighs, the gorgeous Mrs Aquila, wanting to do good but failing to find the means. '*Look at him,*' she says, but it's her only slip and she catches herself quickly. '*Take my husband around the side here so no one can see. Then you can go home too. Thank you for your help tonight, Romeo. I'll send you your wage.*'

'*Will Monica be*——?'

Mrs Aquila shakes her head. '*She went out with her friends, just in case. You understand. My daughter won't be home.*'

I understand. I understand that I could not have spoiled things more completely.

Mrs Aquila smiles at me and I ease Mr Aquila into a standing position, then half-carry, half-drag him toward the family Valiant. He goes into the passenger seat easily, then we're backing down the driveway and no one has seen a thing. I'm not used to automatics so I drive slowly as we leave Mrs Aquila and the wedding reception fairy lights behind.

Mr Aquila isn't singing any more, he just stares out the windscreen at the passing night.

'*Guardi,*' he finally says.

So I look.

Up at the peak of Bowen Hills the Cloudland ballroom is bright with colour, the big arch lighting the sky. The quarter moon is white and the stars twinkle. It's such a pretty sight I want to throw up, mainly because Monica is probably dancing there with her friends.

'*When was the last time you were in Sicilia?*' Mr Aquila asks, his accent a lot thicker than his wife's. A lot thicker and a lot darker. I've never been to Sicily or any other place so I tell him so. '*You've never been to your country,*' he says as a statement. '*But you speak the language. It's not your country. I think you're a pretender.*' He stops a moment as if he has lost his way. '*Is it your country or not?*'

'Nuh. I'm an Aussie.'

Mr Aquila is slumped, his shirt now a little out and crumpled over his cummerbund, his hand loosening his wing collar and bow tie. He doesn't look too much like James Bond any more, but his voice is even, if a little quiet. 'Where you parents they are from?'

'*Provincia di Catania.*'

'*Siciliano to the bone. Where in Catania?*'

'*A little town called Piedimonte.*'

'*The feet of the volcano.*'

'*That's right. That's what the name means.*'

'*Etna.*' Then he's silent for a long time and I think he's nodded off to sleep. He says, violently, '*Why do you think my restaurant is called Il Vulcano?*'

I shrug to put him off, but he won't be put off.

'*We come from the same town!*'

'I don't think so.'

'*Why do you speak English to me?*' he shouts, lively for a second, but I just concentrate on the driving. Then he's nodding to himself, the name of my parents' town is a revelation to him. I'm cautious because if we go too far we might find we're related. Monica and me, distant cousins. It just doesn't bear thinking about.

I concentrate harder on my driving.

He mutters some unintelligible things, then, '*At night, you know what you see from the streets of my town?*'

I shrug again.

'*Guardi.*' I follow his pointing finger toward Cloudland at the top of the hill. '*Etna,*' he says, '*Etna with a fire that never goes out. It's the only thing you can see, day and night, the volcano always there above you. Always on fire in the belly, always with fire coming out of its mouth. We came here and we saw Cloudland and we felt like we were home again. So we wrote to our friends and our relatives and they came and they stayed too.*' He smirks at me. 'You tink you can understand dis, Mr Aussie?'

'Sure.'

He seems satisfied by this. '*In Piedimonte, when the volcano erupts, the townspeople have a competition. A very good competition. Good for men. It goes back too many generations to remember when or why it started. The men take the front doors from their homes and go up the foothills. As far as they can, up toward the volcano, and they hold the doors over their heads for protection from the falling lava. They go to see what it looks like, their volcano exploding, they go to see how close they can get to the molten rivers.'* Mr Aquila is looking at me. *'It's a true story.'*

I say, 'Yeah, bullshit,' because he's a drunk and moody old fart who doesn't appreciate his wife or his daughter or anything his new country has given him. If I have to hear any more about Mt-fucking-Etna I'll go crazy.

'My father always won,' he goes on. *'They're mad in that town, always working, always fighting, always fucking, you understand? The Greeks used to say a monster named Typhon lived under Etna, and Etna held up the sky. When Typhon twisted and turned in his sleep, then the sky rained fire. So who can blame us for being a little crazy? We're always rumbling too, eh? You and me. Always ready to explode, no warning, no nothing.*

Yeah, sure, I think to myself. I glance at him. Mr Aquila's eyes are glassy and he has slumped more deeply in the vinyl-covered front seat. He's rambling and he makes no sense.

'If you're a real Piedimontese you've got that blood. There's nothing you can do about it. I've got that blood. My wife hasn't got that blood. Antonio has got that blood but Monica, you know my little girl Monica, she hasn't got that blood at all.'

Enough of this romantic fucking bullshit! How far to New Farm?

But Mr Aquila's voice is softer now, a kind of dreamy sing-song, and I think I'll be spared any more. We continue on in a silence interrupted only by sporadic lines from some old Italian folk song. I drive carefully and keep wondering where the clutch is; every now and then I get a glimpse of the Cloudland Ballroom and I think of a monster named Typhon restlessly sleeping beneath it. The old guy's made me nuts too.

The traffic is quieter in New Farm. Mr Aquila sits up

straight. Maybe he's just had a quick bad dream. He says, *'You love my little girl Monica?'*

I say with as much insult as I can, 'Nuh.'

He says, *'That's good. I don't like you.'*

And we're in the red brick mausoleum's driveway.

I get out to open the garage door. The house is dark. If Monica's there, she's asleep. I get back into the car, park it, then find that Mr Aquila's not as helpful as he was earlier. His feet slide across the lawn as I drag him to the house. Behind us, in the moonlight, we leave tramlines in the grass. For some reason Mr Aquila has gone so rubbery I can't put him over my shoulder. He is silly putty, always slipping out of my hands.

'Put me down before I kill you,' he says as we go, tramlines lengthening. *'I'll cut your fucking throat.'* I'm getting him up the front steps. *'You should be a policeman when you grow up,'* he says. *'You don't listen to anybody.'*

I fit the key into the front door lock and drag the man of the house to his bed, where I let him tumble. Mr Aquila lies in a human shambles and he's singing again. I take off his shoes for him but that's as far as I'll go.

Out of the blue, like the snap of a light going on in black, Mr Aquila says pleasantly and loudly, *'Romeo, get me a drink. You'll find the bottle in the cupboard above the refrigerator.'*

He is definitely the undrunkest drunk I have ever come across. So I go to the cupboard above the refrigerator and find a bottle of Famous Grouse. I'm about to pour a glass for Mr Aquila but then I wonder at the sense of this. Instead, I take a long pull from the mouth of the bottle and despite what might be expected the whisky goes down straight and easy. So I take another pull.

The front door is open. I tell myself to stop farting

around and to stop hoping and to go home. It's too late for
a bus, it'll have to be a taxi. Ah, but why do I lie to myself,
why do I *always* lie? I shut that front door and go to Monica's
bedroom, and still in my pink poofy shirt and black stained
trousers I lie right down on her single bed. Fuck Mr Aquila.
Fuck them all. I put my hands behind my head and wait. I
wonder who will arrive first, Mrs Aquila and Tony, or
Monica. It's dangerous business waiting there but I don't give
a shit. What's the worst that will happen? Monica will scream
at me? Mrs Aquila will scream at me? Mr Aquila will tell me
again he doesn't like me? Tony, the man in black, will beat
my brains out?'

Monica's perfume is in the sheets and it's as if she's
already with me, just quiet. My silent companion, my beautiful friend. I don't care that she wants Johnny. I'll take
anything of her I can get. So I lay my face on the sheet and
drink Monica in, forever, forever, into my heart and soul. I
drift, I think, I sleep, I dream. It doesn't matter what, the
whole time I'm with my Monica.

A car pulls up however many number of hours later.

It can't be Mrs Aquila or Tony, not with the car parking
on the street. Monica's bedroom is dark and it's dark out in
the tree-lined avenue. I kneel on the mattress and lean against
the window sill. My forehead's against the window pane.
There's not much to see, just Johnny Armstrong's car. Oh,
what a fuckwit I am. Something about all this doesn't even
surprise me. All our girl-chasing, all the drinking and the
surfing and the partying we've been doing together, and he's
still onto Monica like a blowfly onto a ripe piece of fruit.
What can you do with a man like that?

Fuck you, Johnny, fuck you, you lying fucking cunt. Fuck you
and may you eat shit and may you fucking die.

Time passes and Monica doesn't get out of the car. My eyes have lots of time to adjust to the dark. I watch and wait and wait, and then I see movement, in the front seat. They're cuddling and kissing, and it looks a lot like Monica's legs are open and my mate Johnny's hand is up between them. I bite down on whatever it is that makes me want to sick up. I should go down there and tear them both limb from limb.

I get up to go down, but I end up sitting on Monica's bed cracking my knuckles one by one. Then I hang my head and wait. Everything seems taken out of me. What does Mr Aquila know about volcanic emotions and crazy Sicilians? I know I should commit murder yet all I can do is weep. I don't want to hurt anyone. And I don't want that crazy blood Mr Aquila says is in my veins, he thinks it's so romantic, but it's all just homey Sicilian bullshit. My heart just aches.

And still Monica doesn't come inside.

There's the sound of a car door creaking open. I know that sound so well, it's the sound of Johnny's front passenger door. My legs won't hold me up but I force myself to go back to the window and see what's going on.

Monica is standing at the front of the car. The headlights are off. She's staring hard at the windscreen, at where Johnny must be sitting. Then Johnny gets out of the car and slowly, as if he is frightened, goes around to her. Monica pushes him away. Even from up here I can see that bitch-fire in her face. Johnny tries again and from Monica's expression I wouldn't advise him to try any more, unless he wants a kick in the cods. Monica walks toward the house and Johnny leans on the green bonnet of his Holden. He folds his arms and he is looking down at the ground, and for an instant maybe, just maybe, I see that side of him that only some girls see. Jeans and a t-shirt, a strong profile and lots of Elvis Presley, but he leans there looking quiet and full of sorrow.

It's just the moonlight, for sure.

And then Johnny cries out, 'Fuck!' loud enough to wake the dead, and he grabs all his Elvis Presley hair in both hands, and then he gets in the car and he's gone to buggery.

I hear Monica coming through the quiet, darkened house, and in a second she comes to her door. I sit down on her bed again, and crack all my knuckles again.

Monica snaps on the switch and in the flood of light I see her recoil. Her hair is jet black. It's as if she's a new person. The black hair makes her look a little pale. I get up from the bed and touch her black hair and put my arms around her.

Monica says, stiff as a corpse, 'You should stop crying, Romeo.' Then she pulls away from me and shoves me with both fists in my chest. 'You bastard,' she says. 'What are you doing here? What are you doing here after so long?'

I say, 'Monica, Monica,' and the breath dies in my chest. It's like something is suffocating me. I might as well be the monster Typhon with the weight of a whole fucking volcano on my chest, because that's just the way it is. Mrs Aquila told me to tell the girl how I feel, but I don't know how I feel and I can't find the words anyway.

Monica stares at me, her look killing me.

Then it comes to me. It does no good to be weak. Donkeys are stubborn and they do just what they want to do. So I say quick and sharp and tough, 'I had a holiday planned for us over Christmas and I think we should take it. I think we should just go and straighten ourselves out. You owe me that. This is bullshit. I think going away is the only right thing.'

'What!' Monica spits and snarls, ugly and angry. 'What!
Who do you think you are coming here? Who do you think
you are?'

She shoves me again and then she whacks me. Once,
twice, three times, and I stand there and take it the way
donkeys have to take their beatings. I tough it out and hope
she'll hit me until she can't hit me any more. The blood in
my face is burning. Monica stops before time. She's run out
of strength and she's crying. Her raven-black hair suits her.
This is the real Monica at last, a black angel with volcano
blood—I want to laugh that Mr Aquila doesn't know his own
daughter.

Monica wipes her eyes. Her mouth is twisted. She stares
at me some more and just like that she says, 'All right'.

So I say, 'All right' too.

The deal is done. Monica comes closer. She grabs the
front of my pink shirt and twists it in a funny way. She says,
'This doesn't suit you, Romeo.'

I kiss her everywhere. Monica holds me so tightly I know
she won't let go.

But Mr Aquila, old rubberlegs that he is, sways into the
bedroom doorway. He's got the bottle of Famous Grouse.
From over Monica's shoulder I see him take a swig.

'You no get me drink,' he says very quietly, having forgotten the Sicilian dialect. He studies us with a sense of great
world-weariness, and takes in the fact that his daughter and
I have been eating each other alive.

Monica says tersely, 'Papà, go to bed!'

Mr Aquila gives a slow smile, a rare event.

He says, looking at me, 'Huh. What I tell you? Is in you
blood. You like the *lupo*. The *lupo mannaro*,' he accuses me.
'When you got the wolf in you house you must cut his troat.'

Mr Aquila leans forward and gives an evil grin. 'Hey, Romeo. I tink I must cut you fucking troat.'

And then Mr Aquila lurches backward into the shadows and thumps unseen to the corridor floor.

SIX

The Question Mark Man

So I was bringing another stray home. Another stray, but this time with a clear intention.

Beside the racing taxi the Brisbane River wound its way to its source. I wondered if I was doing the same. Somehow I stopped myself from shaking the answer out of that poor befuddled piece of shit beside me. My old nemesis, the always mournful Aquila, hummed an old folk tune. He'd lost his ear, his melody was off-key and he didn't know the words. As if I cared about *him*.

'Where's your daughter Monica?'

'Oh, Monica. Mon-i-ca.'

In the mall it was about the first thing I asked him. I knew she had gone overseas years ago, but was she still there? One Christmas I rang Mrs Aquila and she told me Aquila the Alcoholic was kicked out and Monica was studying in Bratislava. A Christmas later Aquila the Alcoholic was still kicked out, Mrs Aquila had remarried, and Monica was living in Montreux. I sent Mrs Aquila a wedding congratulations card. The last time I called Monica had some low-paying job in the Prado. The locations grew more exotic and less likely with every call. She was also getting married. To a nuclear physicist. I got the hint. Nuclear physicists exist in Alfred Hitchcock motion pictures and nowhere else. Mrs Aquila was just making sure to keep Monica at arm's length from me. Maybe *la signora* heard the term 'nuclear physicist' in a daytime soap opera. Her romantic attitude toward me had gone missing. My last contact was one more wedding congratulations card, this time to Monica, and no reply came and that was fine and that was that.

Mrs Aquila might have known best, anyway. What good would it have done either Monica or me to look at each other as the woman and man we'd become, to hear the new music we listened to, to read the books we now read—how could it have helped?

Things change.

The taxi turned off Coronation Drive into Park Road, sped past the Savoir Faire complex with its counterfeit Eiffel Tower, and rocked Aquila beside me. His voice was croaky and wasted, just right for an atonal old Italian love song. If I closed my eyes I could just believe this was the man I'd once known. Wherever Monica was in the world, Aquila would help me find her. He was a gift from heaven. As if he sensed my thoughts Aquila cuddled into me.

'Eh Romeo,' Aquila said, cackling, holding me close, 'I tink I cut you fucking troat, eh?'

He stank like an old shoe. Still, if I could grow to love virgin garden manure I could love *this* smelly jewel. I put my arm around Aquila's shoulders and held him and wondered what vermin beat a path from his body to mine.

'What was the number again?' the driver asked in a resentful tone. He probably foresaw he would have to hose his taxi out.

'Twenty. Please hurry.'

'I am, mate.'

Aquila took my chin and waggled it. 'The Romeo is still the good look boy. You marry? You got the children?'

'No.'

'No? Some thing she no change, eh? Then you still live like the *lupo mannaro*,' and he laughed. It was Monica who all those years ago had explained this stupid Sicilian slang to me.

It means werewolf, Romeo. You know how quixotic he is. He's got this thing about the moon and the volcano, and blood. Dad means you can never be satisfied. He means you'll always be hungry because you'll never understand what you're hungry for. Of course he's talking about himself. This is his sole insight into his own life. Maybe it's a compliment that he sees you as a twin. Actually, I think he likes you.

Monica's voice was so clear it was as if she whispered in my ear. I shivered right down to my bones. Aquila's ruined face glared at me. 'No, Mr Aquila, I don't think you can say that. I think you're wrong. It's not like that.'

'Oh no?' Aquila jumped up and down in the seat. 'No? Ha! Ha ha! Ha ha!'

At least Aquila's humour had changed over the years. For all his ruination he was less melancholy than he'd ever been.

Many things amused him, and most of them seemed to do with me. Aquila cackled in my face and slapped my shoulder and bounced in his seat, and he let me know he knew better than a dumb donkey like me ever could.

The cab driver checked us out in the rear-vision mirror, miserable at having picked us up.

Mary was waiting on the front verandah. Mary and Blue. Mary's arms were folded and a glass of wine was balanced on the rail in front of her. Blue was on his haunches, tongue out. With a screech of tyres the taxi disappeared. I tried to help Aquila down the steps from the front gate but he saw Mary and would have none of it. He slapped my hands away and his feet sort of shuffled along.

'Romeo, what you got to eat?'

'Well, I think there's—'

'I tink it better be good, huh? I no use to rubbish.' He took in the verandah and the garden. 'I very hungry.'

I couldn't meet Mary's eyes. 'Hi,' I said.

'Who this is?' Aquila said. 'You wife? You the Missus Romeo? Where the chidren?'

Mary stared at the ghoul I'd dragged home. Blue's nostrils flared. Mary said, 'Romeo, where have you been? Who is this?' She couldn't stop staring. She cleared her throat. 'Is this your friend from last night?'

'No. This is Mr Aquila.'

'Mr *who*?'

Aquila toyed with the hobo cuffs of his shirt and edged toward Mary. Mary didn't wilt. Aquila gave her the best effect of his piercing blue eyes. Neither hair nor beard, neither beggar stench nor question mark shape could obscure the intelligence and craziness in those eyes. He did his best to straighten his back and push out his chest.

Aquila said, 'You the very beautiful woman, Missus Romeo. How you are?'

Mary said, 'No. No. I'm definitely not Mrs Romeo.'

'Mmm, the bad luck.' Aquila said to me. Then to Mary, 'I am Michele Aquila.'

'Aqui—?'

'A-qui-la.'

Mary gave a bit of a smile. 'Beautiful name,' and while she watched him and took him in something came into her face, something that looked a lot like heartbreak. I read it as clearly as I've read anything in my life. It jolted me, this humanity of Mary's at a soul's misfortune. Aquila wasn't blind to it either. I wondered if he was already making schemes for how he could milk us two saps. Then, perfectly on cue, his legs went and I caught him.

I liked his timing.

'I okay,' he said, hanging in my grasp like silly putty. 'Is nice to meet you, Missus Romeo.'

Mary took his claw. 'Mary,' she repeated. His fingernails could have punctured her. 'Hello,' she said.

Enough was enough. I wouldn't let Mary be sucked in by Aquila. As soon as I discovered where Monica lived he would be back to his alley. So I dragged Aquila into the house, his feet dead and skidding over the living-room's carpet, and dropped him into a couch. He bounced once.

'No, don't leave him there,' Mary said. 'Bring him into the bathroom.'

I said, 'No, here's good enough.'

'No, the bathroom.'

Mary and I stared at each other, and she won.

'He's been living in the street, hasn't he?'

'That's where I found him.'

'I'll get him cleaned up. Would you like that?' she asked Aquila as if talking to a baby.

Aquila's eyes were alight. He'd walked out of his hell into the gates of Mary's heaven. 'Oh, I tink so. Yes.' He smiled his one-toothed smile. 'Mary.'

I said, 'Mary, you can't be serious.'

She turned on me and the bitterness that was there all along was clear. She said, 'Why else did you bring him here? Don't you want to help him?'

'Yeah, but he's just an old family friend, on hard times.'

Mary came closer, looking into my face. She said, 'What are you up to, Romeo?'

I said, 'Where do you want him?'

So Mary had another patient.

I said to Aquila, 'Come on.'

He sighed heavily. 'Oh, is hard.'

I said, 'Oh. Is hard,' and held my breath while I picked him up again.

'I'll give you a good bath,' Mary said. 'And that hair. It's got to go.'

Aquila tensed and it was harder to carry him. 'No. Nothing is cut.'

'We'll see.'

'No!'

I lifted Aquila into the bathroom and sat him down on the lid of the toilet. Mary ran water for a bath then she switched on the bathroom's electric heater.

I said, 'Was your day all right?'

Mary said, 'Oh God, don't try, Romeo,' and kept herself busy, finding fresh towels from the bathroom's deep linen drawer. She smoothed the towels with her hands then looked at me. 'You know what? I was expecting a better night than

sitting around here waiting for you to come home. I watched
TV and read a bit of one of your novels. I had the feeling
you'd run away. There's a lot of it going around.'

'Has Johnny called?'

'Johnny? You think I expect him to call from Switzerland? I don't want you to mention his name again.' Mary
turned to Aquila. 'So who is he?'

Aquila was watching us. Blue was watching us. Aquila's
gamy smell made the bathroom unpleasant; I still couldn't
help but think of fresh horse shit.

'I used to be a friend of his family's. I lived in Brisbane
when I was a kid. I came across him in the Valley while I
was looking for Nigel.'

Mary said without a trace of humour, 'And who the fuck
might Nigel be?'

'He's just this kid.'

'Yeah? I think you've got a problem, Romeo.' Mary
rolled back the sleeves of her sweater as if preparing to give
a colonic inspection. 'I also think we need some disinfectant.'

'I hungry,' Aquila reminded us.

'And make yourself useful in the kitchen, the poor man
can't remember what a decent meal is.'

Aquila's shoulder had slumped against the wall. With a
blue-veined claw he scratched at Blue's ear. Blue sat quietly
by the toilet pedestal, his all-seeing eye growing languid. I
guess it was love. Aquila breathed heavily and I thought it
would be just my luck for him to die right there.

'Do you think we should get him to a doctor?'

'What's a doctor going to do?' Mary said with vehe-
mence. Even Blue's head jerked sharply toward her. 'What
would a prick like Dr Armstrong do with a patient like this?
Stick a needle in him and toss him back to where he came

from. They've got stuff to make him throw up if he takes a drink. You think that would help?'

'He could be sick.'

'Of course he's sick. He's an alcoholic. Now get the disinfectant and go and get busy in the kitchen.'

Aquila croaked, 'No *alcoolizzato*.'

Mary said, 'Oh yes, good for you. Please get out of those things.' Aquila's blue eyes stared at her and she said, 'Hurry up, I don't want any nonsense.' Somehow in Mary's brief career she had skipped being a trainee nurse and had gone straight to matron—some traits are innate, after all.

Aquila fumbled with the buttons of his shirt. Mary pushed me out of the bathroom and slammed the door, pissed off *in extremis*. I stood in the draughty corridor and listened to water gush into the bath. Through the door's dimpled glass there were the reddening bars of the electric heater; then I saw the spectral outlines of Mary undressing the old man.

I went for a bottle of eucalyptus disinfectant. When I returned I found the old man languishing in Johnny's semi-circular love bath, his wrinkled skin turning lobster pink. Aquila wasn't as emaciated as I would have expected. He was wiry, with protruding knees and shoulders, but naked he seemed a fairly hardy old man with a heavy torpedo-shaped *pene* straight from the pages of a pornographic magazine. His long beard and hair dragged in the bath water like seaweed.

Mary poured a good half-bottle of eucalyptus disinfectant into the bath. And then the rest. It didn't seem all that scientific but I didn't say a word. Aquila would come out smelling of the fresh outback. Mary pulled on a pair of purple washing-up gloves then got down on her knees beside the bath. She started to shampoo and scrub Aquila's head and beard. His great big cock lurched and listed with her vigorous action but his eyes, the clearest sharpest blue, never left her face. Blue lay on the bath mat, tongue lolling.

Mary said, 'You don't have any scabs on your scalp.'

Aquila nodded with dignity. 'I no *alcoolizzato*.'

'Didn't I ask you to get some dinner ready?' Mary said, barely looking over her shoulder.

So my place was the kitchen and to my place I went.

Thoughtful, uninspired, I made tea, toast, fried bacon, grilled tomatoes and poached eggs, and wondered why nothing made sense. Why did Mary have to take such a nursing interest in Aquila, and why did Aquila seem a most unlikely derelict anyway?

Soon Mary was walking through the house. Aquila's derelict clothes were wrapped in newspaper and she held it all away from her body. She went to the living room and pushed the clothes into the combustion stove. Then she stripped off the washing-up gloves and threw them in as well.

'Burn those,' she said.

Mary's hair was in a ponytail. Her jeans and sweater made her look too young for a night like this. In the bedroom—my bedroom, our bedroom—a paperback lay open on a pillow. As Mary had said, she spent some of the evening with the novel I was reading. Waiting and waiting.

'How is he?'

'He's all right. I've got him soaking in Radox. I drained the bath water twice. That water's so hot his balls must be poaching but at least they'll be relaxed. After this I'll get him to rinse under the shower. He'll be fresh as a daisy.'

Aquila had become less a man and more a particularly stubborn decontamination exercise. Mary spoke softly, restraining herself. I could see she wanted to forgive me for not being there when she got home, for leaving Blue locked up in the spare room, for not showing more affection. Her eyes betrayed everything. Mary was still too young to have learned how to hide, a problem I didn't have any more.

'He doesn't have any body vermin at all. Fleas, lice, not even crabs. No bruises or discolouration, which they usually have from the type of life they lead, though he has lost his teeth. Some might have gone in fights. He won't say, he gets vague. I've seen worse. But he's definitely got the biggest thing I've ever come across.'

'Uh huh.'

Mary pursed her lips at me. 'Your friend can be very charming. I had to stop him touching my hair while I bathed him. He asked me if I knew any songs. It wasn't enough that I should give him a bath, he expected me to sing to him too. So he sang some love song for me. You know that expression "a voice like sand and glue"?'

'I've heard him sing.'

'Right. He's been drinking a long, long time.'

'He was well-off once. His wife kicked him out and remarried.'

Mary considered me for a while. 'What do you know about his family?'

'Nothing. Not any more.'

'Well your friend's not dead just yet. So far he's mainly interested in me washing his thing. This is a good sign. And he wanted me to condition his hair and beard. He asked me if it was a good conditioner. I made him do it. Once he had his arms moving he was okay and he got an erection. That made him happy. How long are you letting him stay?'

'Tonight.'

'Just tonight? Well why did you bother?'

'I don't know.'

'Bullshit.' Mary's usually expressive face became impassive. 'You might as well have left him where you found him.' Then she softened. 'He doesn't want his hair or beard cut but he let me trim his nails. He could have disembowelled someone. That thing of his is amazing. A cold spoon wouldn't do much good. He's so big you'd need a soup ladle.'

'Will you stop talking about it?'

Mary came closer to me. Then she covered her face and said, 'Romeo, don't you understand anything at all?' She was too tired. She had come from her Mrs Henderson only to encounter Aquila. Mary wiped tears from her eyes and it struck me that maybe I'd made all the wrong connections about her. I tried to pull her to me but Mary said, 'I'll have to scrub. There could be other things.'

'Like what?'

'Have you got any idea how many different species of worms there are?'

So I let her go.

In the stove, the flames licked over Aquila's clothes. Maybe it was a sign that his destitute life was over. The blow drier was going in the bathroom as Mary dried his hair. Aquila had struck pay-dirt all right. I wondered what a blow-dried ghoul would look like. Like mad Lear, that's what, and of course it would be appropriate because I remembered only too well Monica playing Lear under New Farm's great phalanx of camphor laurel trees. Not for her the parts of Goneril, Regan or Cordelia, no, in Monica's world all main roles were hers. With my hard body and thick head she always left me the supports, Gloucester, Kent, Fool.

Blow, winds, and crack your cheeks! rage! blow!
You cataracts and hurricanoes, spout

Till you have drench'd our steeples, drowned the cocks!
You sulph'rous and thought-executing fires,
Vaunt-couriers of oak-cleaving thunderbolts,
Singe my white head!

Aquila came to the kitchen doorway and he *was* Lear's ghost, and a badly dressed ghost at that. He was in some of Johnny's clothes. An old pair of jeans mended at the knee and held up by a leather belt, an out-of-date western shirt with silver stud buttons. He smelled of eucalyptus and shampoo. Mary had combed his beard out. His hair was a fright wig. An urge to laugh came over me but the seriousness of Aquila's eyes stopped me.

'Smell good,' he said. 'You got good bread? You should get the Sicilian bread. The Australian bread is no like bread should be.'

'I'll bring you a cup of tea.'

'The Australian bread is dead! You know that? I like cup of tea. No use the bag, eh?'

Mary pulled a chair out for him. Aquila's movement was easier. He seemed content. Having one erection and two Radox-relaxed balls is a fine thing for a man.

'You house, Romeo?'

'No.'

'What you do here?'

Mary moved behind Aquila and started to plait his hair. I brought in Aquila's dinner and didn't answer his question. He sipped his cup of tea, added two spoons of sugar, sipped again, then very slowly went about the business of eating. His hands didn't shake and he sat as straight as he could. I poured myself a cup of tea from the pot, then one for Mary. Her hands were busy and she plaited expertly. None of us had anything to say. I buttered Aquila's toast and set it beside his plate, and though it was dead Australian bread he ate every crumb.

Then Aquila said, 'I eat no more,' and with a shaking hand he put the plate down at his feet. Blue thoroughly and noisily finished the eggs and bacon off, then gave a silent fart of contentment. That dog must have had something wrong with its digestive system. Aquila turned his tea cup this way and that way. The veins of his hands were knotted green and blue but his nails were neatly pared. Arthritis had left his fingers the claws of children's nightmares.

'Romeo.'

'Yes?'

'Romeo.'

'Yes.'

'Romeo.'

'*Yes.*'

Aquila wheezed a little then started again. 'You know I lose everyting.'

'Uh huh.'

'Because I go crazy from the drink. But I no *alcoolizzato*. Once upon a time but no now. I was but I finish. I go down to bottom. Then I see bottom and I come up.' Aquila made the hopeful gestures with his hands, going down, coming up, evening out. 'Long time pass. Many year. But is no good because my family they gone and they no return. Eh. My restaurant she is gone and she no return.' He put up a gnarled finger. 'Huh. That what they tink, Romeo. That what they tink. They tink I finish. But you know what? My wife she is stolen from me, and my business it is stolen from me. Stolen. This is what happen. But I make promise long time ago. You want to hear my promise?'

Mary and I exchanged a glance.

'My promise is I bring everyting back to me. My wife, my business and my family. What is stolen must be return. Until then I no cut my hair or my beard. No cut. Until then.' His blue eyes had gained much and lost much since I'd known him in 1976. 'What you tink, Romeo?'

I shrugged. 'Ahm. Okay.'

'Romeo! Where is you blood?' Aquila quickly slapped the side of my face. '*Okay*,' he mimicked. 'You help with me. Eh? You help with me.'

I wouldn't let myself rub my burning face. I said after a minute, 'Do you know where your daughter is?' and Mary stared right at me.

Aquila's eyes widened a little. 'Ah,' he said. 'Ah,' and he sipped his tea. He added another two teaspoons of sugar then he slowly stretched out his hand and with tenderness touched Mary's cheek. Her skin seemed too soft next to that arthritic claw. Mary drew away. Aquila asked, 'How you call this place?'

Mary said, 'This house?'

'No.'

'This suburb?' she said. 'Auchenflower.'

He nodded. 'Now, Romeo, like all the time you got the wrong tings in you mind. You help with me and maybe I help with you.' Aquila said to Mary, 'I tired.'

'We've got a spare bed.'

Aquila stood but he was crooked, a question mark man. Distress seemed to cross his face and he touched his stomach. He said to me, 'Tomorrow make you happy?'

I stared at him. *He would take me.* My God, Monica was that close. I hadn't even considered the possibility.

'Yes.'

Aquila touched his stomach again. He said, 'Why after so many year you no learn you got the wrong tings in you mind? Why you so tick?' More distress crossed his face. 'Oh, *merda*,' he said, and took quick shuffling steps toward the verandah.

Aquila did his best to hurry.

Out in the cool of Johnny's dark garden Aquila kneeled down as if to pray but instead he leaned forward onto his hands and brought up his dinner. He stayed on all fours like a dog. After a few minutes I helped him back inside. He was shaking.

I looked up to Mary, who waited for us. She didn't say anything but she watched Aquila and me with an expression I found hard to like. She had made up the bed. I got Aquila out of his clothes and into the bed and sat with him until he stopped shaking. Blue jumped right onto the foot of the fold-out; Aquila weakly called Blue to come closer to him. In the time it took me to brush my teeth, man and dog were cuddled together. They were in the glow of the combustion heater still burning derelict clothes to ash.

Soon Aquila snored. Blue's eye followed me while I turned out the lights, but he should have trusted me. For once I wasn't going to throw him out.

I found Mary sitting in all her clothes by the side of Johnny's big double bed.

She said, 'Well, you seem very interested in that man's daughter.'

'She's a girl I went out with when I was seventeen.'

'Wasn't that half your life ago? What's her name again?'

I opened the curtains and the moonlight came into the room, the most absurdly beautiful moonlight. 'Monica.' The sky was clear and the stars were out.

Mary said, 'Your plan is to find this Monica after all this time?'

'Yes.'

'Don't do it,' she said.

The room was too light. Mary watched me undress. I felt her eyes on the scratches she'd given me. I got under the covers and it crossed my mind I was foolish to lie back, to leave myself so vulnerable. The tip of Mary's tongue showed between slightly parted teeth. With her survival skills she could probably have struck like a cobra.

Mary said very slowly, 'Okay, I see where I stand.' Then I saw the pale light washing through her hair as she loosened her ponytail. Mary seemed tired, resigned, as if being angry was too much of an effort. She said, 'Oh, fuck it,' and restlessly shook out her hair.

The bedroom was cold and out past the window Johnny's palm trees swayed. Soon it would be another winter in Brisbane. Mary never seemed to feel the cold. She slipped off her sweater. Her breasts were taut and her nipples were hard and unloved. For a moment I thought I saw more than just a rocky world in her eyes, but when she moved that startling moonlight made her cheek glisten.

I said, 'What is it? What's the matter with you?'

Mary said, 'Oh Jesus, just forget it.'

I said, 'But what is it you want?'

She said, 'Oh, for God's sake, why don't you read your own books? Is it all just bullshit with you?'

I didn't have a clue what she was talking about.

Mary lay down on her stomach with her face turned away from me. I rubbed the knotted muscles of her back and thought of her cleaning Mrs Henderson's incontinence, lifting Mrs Henderson into a chair and lifting Mrs Henderson into a bed. I thought of Mary kneeling at Johnny's semi-circular love bath and scrubbing Aquila's armpits and groin; Mary preparing for a Swiss holiday with Johnny and being left behind; Mary coming to my bed, naked and straight-backed.

She murmured. I massaged her strong back for so long I lost track of time and space. I felt her relaxing; she was just a young girl after all. When I put my face down to hers she was falling asleep. I put my cheek on hers and closed my eyes.

We slept like that until dawn, when the first rays of sunlight came crawling in. I was still holding Mary. My mind was clear. My chest felt like granite and my heart felt like iron.

Mary's long hair was away from her face. She had long eyelashes too, such fine long lashes. I lifted her hair, savouring its texture, its lightness, its magic. I studied her cheek and the line of her white neck. It was as if I saw Mary for the first time. It was stupid to feel such antipathy toward her. The bed covers were crumpled down to the small of her back. She would be cold. I pulled the covers to Mary's shoulders but her skin wasn't cold at all, it was blood warm. She sighed; I passed my hand over the small of her back. She sighed again.

There was a rustling in the backyard.

Shivering naked to the window, I looked down at Johnny's rainforest. In the misty morning light Blue crashed through flowering brush and scrub. Aquila came into view, his hair still in its curiously appropriate plait, his back crooked and his feet shuffling over the lawn's heavy dew, leaving tracks.

Aquila went carefully through the garden as he inspected each of the bushy terraces. He looked at the orange blossom trees and the white daisies and the closely placed baby's breath flowers. He looked at the wandering Jew ground cover and he found himself a stout branch for a cane. Aquila's face turned up to the broad breaking dawn and neither the misty air nor his flowing beard could hide his exhilaration. Blue leapt out of the lantana. He went to Aquila and endlessly circled the old man's legs. Slowly-slowly, and slowly-slowly some more, Aquila bent down to Blue. Down, down, down, creaking down. Finally Aquila leaned all his weight on the branch-cane as he rubbed Blue's face. All that effort just to rub the face of a dog; a few minutes later Aquila was smiling at the sky again, a happy fool.

I wanted to go to them but they didn't need me at all.

On the floor by the bed lay the novel I was reading. I remembered it open on the pillow when I came home with Aquila, I remembered Mary saying, *Oh, for God's sake, why don't you read your own books? Is it all just bullshit with you?* So I picked the book up. Mary had creased the title page, where there was a quote from Francis Bacon's *Essays*.

> But little do men perceive what solitude is, and how far it extendeth. For a crowd is not company, and faces are like a gallery of pictures, and talk like a tinkling cymbal, where there is no love.

I read it again, and then I lay down with Mary and watched her sleep. I touched her. *Where there is no love.* That was Mary. How far did her sense of solitude extend? I thought it was very far indeed. The dog was yapping. Of all of us, maybe only Blue knew love and loyalty. Mary rolled onto her back and looked up at me and didn't say anything.

I took her hands and held them.

We listened to Blue careering through the underbrush. We listened to Aquila call out and whistle, the shrill sound of a Sicilian shepherd calling a flock. We listened to a crow crowing and birds singing.

Mary sat up. Her breasts were white and her abdomen showed the definition of muscle.

'Oh, listen to that,' she said. 'Doesn't it sound like heaven?' She put her long fingers through my hair. 'What is it? Why do you look at me like that?'

I kissed both Mary's long hands.

Now, because I understood her, because I really under-stood her, I could hold her and I could say, 'Mary, I'm sorry,' and she could touch my hair again and kiss me, with her breasts crushing to my chest and her silky hair hiding both our faces, and I could feel no fear.

Aquila came in. Blue as well. Blue jumped onto the bed as if it wasn't me who always kicked him to the ground. So I kicked him to the ground to remind him of the facts of this world. Aquila had a breakfast tray in his hands. The room was heavy with sex but old Aquila didn't seem to mind. Or maybe he couldn't pick it any more. His breakfast offering was black percolated coffee.

Mary slipped on a white floppy t-shirt as Aquila made his creeping way to the bed. He slid the tray over the covers.

'I once good *cuoco*. You remember?'

I remembered Mrs Aquila's cooking, Monica's, the res-taurant's twin chefs', but that was all. Mainly I remembered Aquila drinking and smoking and looking into the middle distance. So I leaned my shoulder against Mary's shoulder and didn't answer. The coffee smelled good and so did Mary. Aquila's eyes were fixed on her.

He said, 'I tink I like stay here for some time.'

Mary took up her heavy mug and occupied herself with it. She didn't look at me. 'Why not?' she said. 'There's plenty of room.'

Aquila's tooth protruded like a yellow fang. That was his smile. I couldn't believe Mary's answer but I held my tongue. It only took a minute before I worked out this was good for me. Mary could look after Aquila and I could chase Monica. Aquila's gaze turned to me. He knew what he was after and he probably knew what I was thinking.

He said, 'Romeo. Today you come where I live. I have some tings to bring here. And maybe there some tings to teach you, eh?'

'That's a good idea,' Mary said.

Aquila's eyes bored into me. 'Very true. I can no go see my daughter dress like this.'

Trials and tribulations hadn't dented Aquila's capacity for manipulation. I wondered how many years Mrs Aquila had wanted to say *Basta!* to him. Not only was he going to stay with us, but he was going to move his *tings* in.

'So where do you live?'

'Where I live? No where you find me. Nice little boarding house in New Farm.' He went to the door and called Blue to follow him out. 'We go soon, okay?' Aquila pulled the door shut behind him.

'He's off the planet,' I said. 'I'm surprised you want to let him stay.'

'You think you've got the right to bring someone into this house and get what you want and then throw him back?'

'He's just a nut.'

'But he *can* tell you where to find Monica.'

I pushed the tray over to Mary's side and got out of the

bed. 'Don't you think it's a bit childish to be jealous of someone I haven't seen in nearly twenty years?' I went to the window and looked down at the garden. 'He expects me to help him get his business and his family back. All I can say is it's cruel to encourage him, Mary. You can see just as well as I can he's crazy.'

Aquila immediately hollered thorugh the door: *'Pazzo?'* He was miracle-cured of his croaky voice. 'I no *pazzo!*'

I snatched open the bedroom door. Aquila was there, where he had been listening. He was bent and shadowed and standing in the corridor with good buddy Blue by his side. Aquila leaned on his branch from the garden, shaking. His silhouette was like the one you'd expect the devil to make if he chose to pay a visit.

'I no crazy, you bloody *finocchio,*' Aquila said.

Now he was calling me a homosexual. Me, to whom he had just served coffee while I lay in bed with a girl half my age. Me, who had crazy-fucked his own daughter.

'I know what I want and you no know at all,' Aquila said. 'Nothing she changes.' He rattled off toward the kitchen, stopped, looked back at me. 'Eh, Romeo. What you call that baby worm? Oh, poor little worm. You put you pants on!'

Mary was laughing.

I slammed into the bathroom and took a hot shower but it was for too long because before I knew it Mary was bashing on the door and calling out to me and then dragging me from under the water. Aquila was watching and so was Blue and I dried myself and cursed loudly.

Mary just went on with what she had to do to get herself ready for another day of playing Florence Nightingale. To top it off Aquila was tapping his foot with his branch-cane and still smirking at me as he said, 'Stop the play around, eh little worm, is time we go.'

Blue was ready too. And Aquila wanted to go off on foot.

Fucking hell.

An eighteen-wheeler belting along Raintree Avenue gave an ignominious fart. The Milton Fourex brewery belched grey clouds of hops and hangovers and future fist fights. Blue jumped fences and had barking battles with the dogs of the yards, always to come back and cock his leg against the telephone pole or gutter or car parked out front. Aquila walked with his attention on his slow steps, his head bent as if fossicking for coins. Even when the odd house dweller yelled for us to get our dog out of their Sunday-quiet yard, Aquila didn't waver.

After a half hour of this creeping-walking Aquila grinned as if he had made a great achievement. Maybe he had. 'You know what I sometime tink I want more than anyting?'

'What?'

'More than my home?'

'What?'

'More than my money and my business?'

'What?'

'More than my wife?'

'*What!*'

'The new teeth.' Aquila put his fingers in his mouth and wobbled his gravestone. 'I tell this to Mary when I take my bath. Is hard to be the man without the teeth. When I got my money back I get the false teeth. First ting, Romeo. What you tink?'

I was looking at the street. It was a hot day. 'I think we should take a taxi.'

'Taxi? Eh Romeo. You be a good boy and shut the fuck up.' Aquila's English had a way of improving when he was motivated, and it always motivated him to be rude to me. He said, 'You no understand. For now—we have to walk.'

Aquila was slow-slow and we still had such a long, long way to go. A snail could have lapped us, then again, I found the further we went the more the years seemed to fall away from Aquila. His arms started to swing and his steps were just that wider apart. An hour, an hour and a half, and from somewhere even more strength was arriving. Maybe this was what Aquila wanted me to see, that he still had grit and determination in his old bones.

That look of exhilaration was back in his face.

Maybe Aquila saw more than this Sunday's sunshine. Maybe he saw a day when he was again the owner of a successful restaurant, when he was again his wife's husband, again the proud owner of a full mouth of teeth. Then he could cut his hair and shave his beard and wear fine clothes. If this was his dream it wasn't too different to my dream about Monica. So is it a sin to grow old and in the process learn how to dream again? The alternative is worse, isn't it, to lie dreamless and lifeless in some Fortitude Valley alley-way, some New Farm flophouse, some hospital ward for the permanently dazed and confused.

I put my hand gently on Aquila's elbow. He made a sour face and shook it away.

The sun climbed to its highest point. We passed all the Park Road restaurants and outdoor cafés, with their groups of well-dressed boys calling out like idiots to any passing being with tits and legs. Blue was up ahead crapping over a manhole grate.

Aquila said, 'Soon will be enough, Romeo.'

'Good. There's a taxi rank.' Aquila wagged his finger and gave me a knowing look. Then I said in a rush, 'You mean Monica?'

Aquila finally took my arm and held on to me. 'Get the Monica out of you head for now, eh? For five minutes you forget about her!'

'Well, what then?'

'Eh.'

One day somebody would shake the life out of Aquila for a straight answer. It might be me. We had to keep going before I could find out what his mystery was about, all the way down to the Brisbane River and a bicycle path that shadowed the silty water and went on forever in both directions. The path was busy with Sunday riders in stack hats and t-shirts and colourful trousers.

A gecko ran across our way. A multitude of these crazy-crawly things sunned themselves around the undergrowth. Aquila held Blue by the collar to stop him chasing them. Three skiffs crowded with oarsmen competed in the river. No one was winning, all three skiffs were neck and neck. Maybe that was the idea. Sailboats with bright logos dipped in the sunlight. Aquila went to a green bench. He sat down and wiped his face with his crooked hands. Blue curled up at Aquila's feet but kept his eye on the darting geckos.

Aquila grinned at me. 'Soon we take ferry, Romeo. Is very nice on the ferry. Is very easy to get to New Farm.' He shoved my shoulder. 'And no complain, you sound like little girl.'

The midday breeze was perfumed with dead catfish. Little ferries crossed the river from shore to shore and bigger charter ferries churned the silty water. Across the river the Pioneer cement works was closed for the weekend. Families

on Italian or French mountain bicycles whizzed by us, then
I noticed it, this thing that was so big I'd taken no notice of
it at all. Aquila watched for my reaction. It was built right
on to the Brisbane River, all white sails and black glass and
outdoor timber decking. A very discreet sign read,

Il Vulcano Ristorante
by the river

and there was a surrealistic impression of a volcano making
a red lava flow of the river, and it steamed straight into the
city centre.

'So look what they do with my business, Romeo. They
burn down the old restaurant and they build a monster. They
say the prime minister he like to come here when he come
to town.'

Couples and families strolled into the place for their
Sunday lunch. There was an air of activity. Waiting staff
showed people to their tables. Through smoky glass I saw a
crowded circular bar. The outside decks were busy with
alfresco diners.

Aquila carefully curled his gnarled hands into his lap as
if he knew those hands were like relics from a prehistoric
age. I tried not to look at him. To have a dream is one
thing—but this. The size and opulence of the place diminished Aquila's dream into what it was, a hopeless, hopeless,
hopeless concern. How could a rowdy little restaurant in
Petrie Terrace have turned into this—*thing*?

Aquila ran a hand along the length of his beard and then
he tugged at it gently. He didn't bother to look at me, he
knew what I wanted to know. 'Many year ago the *lupo
mannaro* understood good when I talk.'

I said that, yes, I still would.

'Ah,' he said. 'Then I tink I tell you a story.'

So in his favourite dialect, my favourite dialect, as the sails skittered along the river and the bicycles whizzed by and the geckos sunned themselves, as cold chablis and chardonnay and champagne was served on the floating restaurant's polished decks, I listened to the story Aquila had to tell me.

Romeo, my father had one lesson to teach me in life, and no more. It came when I was six years of age and the lesson was about a filthy whore of heaven who could seduce all men. My father liked to call her the angel of forgetfulness.

In the vineyards neighbouring our town of Piedimonte, men and women picked black and white grapes and took cold water from the centuries-old well, and cursed the holy trinity for giving them a dynasty of padrones with so many vineyards and this hot day to labour in. I worked there, and so did my young brother, and so did my young sister, and so did my mother. When night fell and the stars came out and the women and the men from the fields prepared their meals, my father sat away from everyone and ate green olives and drank rough mountain wine. When he had his fill of his own silence he crooked his finger at me to join him. He pulled up his right trouser leg and, by the light of a wood fire, pushed it at me. You see, Romeo, his right foot had been blown off by a World War One land mine. This night he made me hold the stump of his ankle in my hands. He slapped my face until my hands stopped trembling. He slapped my face until I stopped crying. His mood was bloody. That morning the town doctor had told him that on top of everything else, my father had diabetes. Soon my father's stump would have to start higher, at the knee, and after that, higher still.

The women worked over their pots and tore chunks of their corn bread and soaked those pieces in virgin oil and oregano. The women didn't sing. They knew this hard day was only the first of what promised to be a miserable and hot season of vendemmia, the grape harvest. The men and the mules were unsettled and grumbling for their dinner. The men gathered around open camp fires. The mules were kept at the back of our mud brick and stone huts, high in the hills overlooking the vineyards. Only the stars rejoiced. A relative who was crazy enough to know about such matters had taught me the names of the constellations. The sky was so clear I could see them, Sagittario, Capricorno, many others.

So, Romeo, my father pulled my face away from where I tried to escape into those stars. Wine ran down his chin and into his shirt. He held me close and he made me touch the scars and the stitches of his dead stump. To impress them into my memory. Then he told me the story of how our family had been touched by the angel of forgetfulness and how, unless I spat in her face every day, our children and our children's children would repeat the same mistake until the end of the world.

And that mistake is of course to grow confused and forget what is important in life.

By then I was more interested than scared. I asked my father how it could be that forgetfulness could take away a man's foot. He squeezed my face in his hands as if it was a custard apple and he had to crush it. My father told me that while he had been in the fascist army and his company had been crawling its way through the mud on the outskirts of the Veneto, for a moment he became possessed by the idea of rolling himself the most perfect cigarette to smoke this world has ever known. He went onto his back like a turtle and lay in the mud and with a wet muddy face and wet muddy hands he carefully rolled that perfect cigarette. And then, smoking it, hanging it from the corner of his mouth as all army men did, he forgot to follow along the path the advance party had mapped as being free from land mines.

Why he was so crazy to smoke such a perfect cigarette at such a bad time can only be explained by the presence of the angel. My father, who declared he knew at every moment just where all the jigsaw puzzle pieces of his life lay, pushed himself out of the mud and rose to his feet. He inhaled deeply and exhaled into the rain and cried out words unintelligible to either himself or his companions. The men begged him to get back onto his belly but my father unsnapped his pack and smoked his cigarette and took it upon himself to wander away into the rain. He stepped badly it's true— and when the mine exploded the enemy came screaming from their wet muddy trenches and used bullets and bayonets and rifle stocks to slaughter the company to a man.

Except for him of course, because bloody and in a few pieces, they took him for already dead. So as with all things in this divine comedy we call life, in 1968, the fiftieth anniversary of that slaughter, the president of the Republic gave my father the posthumous title of 'Cavaliere' and a bronze medal and a gold medal for his heroism. But Romeo, eh, that's another story about the blind stupidities of this world.

That night in the vineyard hills my father drank and cursed and by midnight was howling like a wolf at the moon. He slapped me and shook me and kept saying I would have to carry the angel's curse and keep watching for her touch. I was the first born. My father's bad luck would be my bad luck. That is what he cried, but I sensed my father's despair was because he knew that in the end nothing could help me.

At six years of age my knees trembled at the horrors that awaited me. At ten, the same. At twelve and fifteen and seventeen and twenty-one and thirty—the same. I could never forget my father's howling. I could never forget that stump at his ankle that became a stump at his knee, and then because the doctor's fears were true and my father's diabetes was worse, more and more of him was cut away until in the end there wasn't much left of a man to bury at all. But it was my life that had been taken away. I kept myself

*apart from all that could harm me and lived and worked dutifully
in those vineyards. There I made my life and there I grew up to
believe I was safe. The worst that could happen was the bite of a
brown snake or the night-time visit of Beelzebub.*

*But at the age of thirty-three the angel found me and visited
me. She touched me with her wings the moment I met a child of
fifteen, a child whose name was Gloria.*

'Wait a minute, wait a minute,' I said, and Aquila gave me
his best dirty look.

Children rang their bicycle bells and parents called for
those who strayed too close to the river's edge. On the
restaurant's decks big umbrellas were unfurled and awnings
loosened to protect diners from the sun. In the river the skiff
race had been won. Together with the catfish perfume there
was now a scent of sunflowers and coconut oil sunscreen.
Aquila, Blue and I were in our shady spot on the bench.
Sunday life passed by and for some reason I was listening to
a fable about peasant supersitition, vineyards, and the hills of
Sicily.

Aquila said, 'Eh Romeo, you like better to be up there
with the cold wine and the women?'

We watched tables being served. Even from our distance
the beads of sweat running down the sides of champagne
glasses were clear.

I said, 'Oh yeah, I think so.'

Aquila gave me a shove in the ribs. 'Why you make me
stop?'

'What does this story have to do with anything?'

Aquila's tooth showed in a grin. 'You listen, Romeo.'

'Why don't you tell me while we have a nice ferry ride?'

'No be smart!' He shoved me again. 'We stay here!'

'*All right.*' I resigned myself to playing it Aquila's way. 'Okay, okay. So your wife was only fifteen years of age when you met her?'

'Eh, tick-head, I tell you to listen!'

She was swimming in the stream outside the town. It was unusual for me to be there because I lived in the foothills of Mt Etna; most of the townspeople and even my family were as good as strangers to me. But that day I was overcome with too much heat and, for once, more than that stinking heat, too much loneliness. Mt Etna was smoking. The night before I had seen the fire in its mouth burning brighter than ever before, as if somehow it had become the place where hell and magic and pain all meet as one.

And the stream, cool and clear and seductive, it was the same place—except I didn't yet know it.

The rules of the stream were that the boys should stay where it was deepest and the girls in the shallows, where they were always hidden by weeping willows and rock pools. But this stranger and I didn't have to follow rules for we were excluded from both groups. I for being so much older, she for being a gypsy, an outsider. Without speaking we swam closer and closer, and discovered a game to play. We dived between each other's legs and always tried to close our legs just in time to catch one another like twisting silver fish. I let her catch me again and again, and every time she did I ran my hands up and down her slim and slippery thighs. If my father had seen he would have killed me. Any adult of the town would have killed me.

The sun sank behind the red glowing mouth of our volcano and the day turned to that familiar bite of country evenings. We stayed and lay over the smooth flat rocks beside the stream. She had a strange accent. Her name was Gloria, so named, she said, because when she was born she could bawl the glory of God louder than any baby. That evening at the stream Gloria had a way of looking at me. And just like that she came out and said she believed she could see the glory of the countryside in my eyes and in my mouth.

As days and weeks passed Gloria would come all the way up to the vineyards and wait for me until I and the other field labourers had finished our work for the day. With camp fires burning and the women singing and the men clapping their hands she would show me her dance step, and I would learn them well, just for the chance to be close to this, God's most beautiful creation. In front of the flames her hands danced and her bare feet pounded the dust. On her wrists she wore leather straps shiny with pearls, on her ankles she wore silver and bells. I understood sheep and goats and the seasons of grapes, but even I could see Gloria didn't fit the world of those hills or of any towns nearby. She was a traveller, a girl of the gypsies who sometimes lived by the stream, sometimes disappeared, sometimes reappeared a month or a year later.

All townspeople hated the gypsies.

Gloria might never have known her parents or her brothers or her sisters, but she did know how to dance and she did know how to cook and she even knew how to read, which she proved by reading aloud to me from a book of Russian fairytales. When the other workers were away we stayed like brother and sister in my mudstone cabin, far away from people and troubles. By candlelight Gloria would read another strange story to me. She liked the names of the countries and peoples in the stories; she said her family might have been from Yugoslavia or Latvia, places whose names meant nothing to me.

One night Gloria had that way of looking at me again. The candlelight made crazy shadows across my walls. She reached for the clay pot of red wine and drank deeply, and when the wine ran out of her mouth and over her chin she unlaced her white bodice and let the wine flow over her white breasts and black nipples, over her stomach and into the pleated waist of her skirt, and she invited me to drink.

Who wanted me to marry a gypsy girl with no parents? Nobody. My parents learned of Gloria. My father cursed and raged and there were times you would have sworn the angel of forgetfulness lived in the walls of his home or in the donkey shit of the streets for he spoke to her as directly as if she stood before his eyes. And then my father decided the flesh and blood of his filthy angel was Gloria herself.

Who cared what a diabetic crazy-man with stumps for legs and arms thought?

In the big Sicilian city of Catania I found work cleaning the floors of a café while Gloria sat in a rented room, pregnant with our first baby girl. When she was born dead I saw there might have been truth in what my father screamed. I was young. I believed I could fight whatever black clouds were meant to suffocate us. The solution was to run further than Catania, further away than even the angel of forgetfulness's hands could stretch.

Vaffanculo Sicilia, I thought.

By the time we arrived in our new country Gloria was close to breaking her water. In the Wacol migrant camp a boy arrived, an ugly littly gypsy with devil's lungs. I didn't see the glory of any god I knew in that red bawling face or in those clenched and straining fists. In the next year a girl arrived. Her temper made the boy seem a lamb. Monica would scream for days and nights and nothing would placate her. Her whole little body would shake as if she had to pass the greatest shit the world has ever seen. There were midnights when I would stare down into her evil screaming face and consider taking her by the heels and smashing her into silence against the nearest brick wall.

Still, they were kicking and alive, this boy and this girl, and for all their screaming they were ours.

So in a country of bakeries and Chinese takeaways we had truly escaped the angel, heavenly bitch that she is. Gloria and I built the safe walls of our lives. We took any jobs in restaurants and cafés. We were cleaners and kitchen hands, a waiter and a waitress, cooks, anything, and when we had money and courage enough we made our own place, a place the friends Gloria made came to eat pasta and meet Italian and Sicilian migrants just like themselves.

Eh. The truth is people came for Gloria.

She was growing up in no different a way than our children. She wasn't twenty but already a queen; the queen of our restaurant. Monica was the princess and Antonio was a scallywag prince who you always found between your feet or squeezing your testicles or trying to steal purses and wallets for the treasures inside. Gloria brought music and dancing to the restaurant, she kept track of all the new songs from Italy, and she had records and magazines imported every month. Word about Il Vulcano Ristorante spread so much that soon people we saw on the television were coming to leave their autographed photographs on our walls.

Gloria charmed them all, no matter that they were good actors and bad, beautiful singers and awful, dancers with stringy legs or models with padded bosoms. Political opponents came there to meet and they always left us their photos, and they always came again.

But it was happening to me.

Somehow my father's angel found me. None of my father's warnings could help me, just as no warning could have helped that baby in Gloria's belly from coming out dead. I heard the beating of wild wings days in advance and sometimes I believed it was Monica's screams that gave me away. Sometimes I believed Monica was actually a spy, a collaborator who sent fools like me to that place of hell and magic and pain.

So the angel arrived like all thieves and whores, in the night, and when her wings touched my soul I was lost. I would wake in the mornings with nothing but confusion. As the days and the weeks and the months passed I no longer understood the reasons for living. Why was I the father of two tiny, screaming children? Why was I in a strange country with a strange gypsy who was making a queen of herself? Why did I waltz like a trained dog in front of simple folk who had my spaghetti sauce dried like blood around their mouths?

I remembered my father's misery when he was drunk and howling like a wolf at the midnight moon. God help me but I was now the very same man as he.

So all the restaurant's responsibilities were Gloria's and I was there like a fixture. I kept my eye on everything that went on but if something went wrong I could not imagine what to do about it. Only two things were clear to me: how to waltz with my wife for the delight of our patrons, and how to sit in a corner, that slut of an angel in my lap as she squeezed my cock and poured strong drink down my throat. Those who were once my family and once my friends began to avoid meeting my eyes. I began to avoid theirs, and then I took my leave completely.

As I had done so long ago in the hills of Sicily I now repeated— in my heart.

It could have stayed this way forever. Until one night when I saw the angel had taken flesh. She was with a young man in a good suit and horn-rimmed glasses. This young man's name was Mister Jimmy Blake and he had a popular show on the television. On the television he never wore glasses. In his show people came and talked to him and a big crowd of invisible people would laugh, and sometimes these people who talked to him sang a song and he would sometimes join in and a band would play in such a way that you could never stop your foot from tapping in time. So there he was, this Jimmy Blake who was a television star from Mt Coot-tha and who liked Italian cuisine, and he was still dancing in my restaurant to a Dean Martin record long after everyone had gone, the staff and the cooks too, and long after I had fallen asleep in the back courtyard under a fern tree. It had started to rain. If there hadn't been rain I would have slept on in my beautiful ignorance.

Rubbing my sleepy face, I came into the restaurant and looked at Mister Jimmy Blake dancing with my wife Gloria. I remembered that for dinner he had asked for our specialty, Gloria's own Pollo al Diavolo, with a green salad, peppers in extra virgin olive oil, and some of our cook's home-baked rolls. Jimmy Blake must have liked his dinner very much for now as he danced to Dean Martin's swing orchestra he let my wife Gloria pull his head down to her neck. His mouth closed on her skin. My wife Gloria entwined his fingers in hers and put his hand here, on her breast, and there, between her legs, and a look came into her face, and it was something the likes of which I had never seen before.

Oh, but there was no wife Gloria. There had never been an innocent gypsy girl who was interested in dances and flowing streams and an ignorant country boy. No, there had only been my father's angel, and those wings of hers which destroyed the lives of men.

The young man in his good suit and his horn-rimmed glasses looked up and he saw me. He went to the record player and turned the music off. Gloria saw me and she went and stood in a corner with her shoulders turned away from me.

'You see we're in love, Mr Aquila,' Jimmy Blake said quietly. 'You see, we want to be together and we think that it would be best if we could just get everything done that needs to be done. Do you follow me? We can tell that you don't have any interest in the restaurant any more and that you would welcome being free of it, so you see I've had my lawyers draw up a bill of sale and the terms are very generous, very very generous even though you have no interest any longer. We realise there are many other things that need to be discussed. We're both very practical in these matters, and

of course you have to protect your interests, but then so does Mrs
Aquila. Mrs Aquila cannot be responsible for you any more, Mr
Aquila, and you should do your best to find help because you do
need help. Do you follow me? The restaurant is completely in your
name, Mr Aquila, and it would make everything easier if you could
see your way to study the bill of sale and the very generous terms
I offer you.'

Young Mister Jimmy Blake came right up close to me and his
glasses reflected my restaurant's lights. This made it seem he was a
serious and a kind young man and that he had something important
to say, but he only went on with the same filth.

'Mr Aquila, I want you to know that we've tried to be apart
and we've tried to tell each other we're not really in love, and I've
even thought of going away but none of it works, so you see we
must be honest with you now, Mr Aquila.'

All this the man Jimmy Blake said with that kind and serious
look in his face, and he was standing closer and closer to me while
that thing that was never my wife Gloria stood in a corner with
her white shoulders turned away from me.

'Get out,' I told him before he could get close enough to eat
my soul. 'Get out of here! Get out! Get out of here! What
are you waiting for? What are you waiting for?'

But Jimmy Blake could not understand because in my rage I
said this in a language that wasn't his.

'What's that you're saying?' he said.

'You go! You go to the buggery! You go to the bloody devil!
You take the bloody prostitute with you and I never see you bloody
face one more time!'

'Please think about this, Mr Aquila,' he said. 'And I'll be by
tomorrow with the paperwork and hopefully we can put these things
behind us. You see,' he said again, 'we do love each other so much.'

And then they left together.

Eh.

I found a bottle.

So the next night he did come by again, this brave or stupid Mister Jimmy Blake. The very next night he came to Il Vulcano Ristorante even though the lights were out and there was no food for anyone and even though he would have been safe to expect I would take this opportunity to cut open his chest and take out his heart. I could smell Gloria on him. I could smell her spit on his skin. I could smell her blood in his blood. I should have killed him and he should have known this. But of course what he did know was that angel's wings now watched over him.

When this brave or stupid young man arrived he found me smashing the photographs that hung on the walls and overturning the tables and the chairs. But there Jimmy Blake waited in the doorway, standing with documents in his hands while I tried to destroy all these things Gloria had made.

'This won't help,' he said. 'Oh, Mr Aquila, this won't help at all.'

I sat down with my face in my hands and took another drink. Wine, whisky, beer—who knew what it was?

Jimmy Blake picked up a chair and set it at the table and sat down facing me. He was very neat and he had another good suit on. He put his papers down in front of himself and he watched me. He took off his glasses and handled them and put them back on again. When I finished the bottle I drank from he found another bottle for me and opened it and when I needed it he poured my drink. He lit himself a cigarette and handled his glasses once more. He smoked and handled his glasses and I drank. We didn't talk. It went on this way.

In the morning I was lying on the floor. I didn't know where I was or what I was doing. The place looked as if all the devils of hell had been dancing in there. I fell here and I fell there and then

I saw Jimmy Blake's chair was the only one left upright. It was at the only table that hadn't been overturned. On the table were his papers. Copies of his papers. On the last page I found my signature and Jimmy Blake's signature and a date and the signatures of witnesses.

I didn't remember any witnesses.

I didn't remember signing, but the papers told me I had signed. In the weeks and months that followed I consulted accountants and solicitors and even police, and I was told time and time again my restaurant was legally sold and would remain sold.

Eh.

I found a bottle.

So I decided again that in this world there are many ways to disappear, and I simply found my own true way to do that— I tell you this honestly, my old friend, Romeo—I found my own true way to disappear, and bide my time, until my time came again.

Aquila was hypnotised by the currents in the river.

'What happened?'

'What can happen after that, Romeo?' he said, shaking his head, shaking his plait. 'They live happy and prosper. One day lawyers they find me and they have papers to say I have no wife no more. Gloria and Jimmy Blake they get marry. I lose my money in taxes and in the pub and in many other ways I no like to say.'

'Come on, how could you have lost all your money?'

'I already tell you I no like to say.'

'But how did they turn your old place into this?'

Aquila looked toward the flashy restaurant. 'Oh, one day they find they have to build new place. Old place burn to the ground.'

'You mean you—?'

'Me? Or them! Jimmy Blake a nice man, everybody like. He on television and he smart. He smart enough to be very nice. And is very nice to have fire—but sometimes more things they burn than people expect.' Aquila's blue eyes slowly turned on me. They were the most frightening eyes I'd ever seen. His time would *never* come again.

I said nothing.

For I also realised I could be rid of him. Just like that. Aquila didn't have to be my peace of mind. Mrs Aquila— now Mrs Gloria Blake—was in that restaurant over there and all I had to do was walk in. We'd hug and have a drink and she would introduce me to her new husband, we'd catch up with the news and I would be charming and funny, and sooner or later Mrs Aquila would see I was no threat at all. So many years had passed. She would tell me everything about Monica.

As for Aquila, there was nothing you could do for him. Put him into his bed and shut the door and get away as quickly as possible. Right now I'd take him right back to wherever his New Farm hovel was, and I'd forget him there. Aquila would sink into his boozy nether world and that would be that. He'd never find his way back to Johnny Armstrong's house and his ghost wouldn't haunt me for a minute.

Aquila was grinning at me.

'What?' I said. 'What is it?'

'No, no, is no so easy, my friend. Eh. You tink is so easy? What you tinking, Romeo?' Aquila lay the tail of his plait over one bony shoulder and like a coquette stroked it. 'You tink is easy, but you no understand. You sit here and you listen for so long and you very blind.' He cackled in an unlikeable manner. 'Use the eyes, Romeo.'

'What?'

'Is much we no being told, Romeo. Is mystery, you no tink?'

'What *the fuck* are you talking about?'

Aquila tugged at his beard and played with his plait. He was amused and agitated all at the same time. His amusement went away. He was looking toward the restaurant.

Two bicycles and a tandem whizzed by, then a waddling family in matching beach baggies and bad t-shirts.

So I followed Aquila's gaze.

On the decks around the restaurant a waiter with a balancing problem served a great platter of seafood to three people at a table, the diners all wearing black sunglasses and deeply in conversation. Champagne was being poured into tall glasses. The waiter arranged the platter in the centre of their table. As he finished he bumped the elbow of the waitress pouring the champagne. The faces behind the sunglasses communicated their displeasure. The waiter mopped at the table linen with a tea-towel. The waitress continued pouring into a flute glass. Cool and aloof, she gave the impression nothing on this earth could possibly vex her.

She was wearing a white shirt that might have been silk and an ankle-length black skirt, and her hair was pulled back into a ponytail. I saw what Aquila had seen, that it was Mary. I stared and stared. Then I wanted to call out to her so that everyone dining there and all the happy families going up and down the lovely green bicycle path would hear me and be shaken out of their Sunday pleasures. *You liar! You liar!* But what did it matter that Mary was a liar and I was still a clown you could lead around by the cock?

Aquila took pity on me; he took my arm.

We left the bicycle path and together we went down to

the jetty. One of the river ferries was mooring. Aquila and
I didn't speak at all. We joined a short queue then went to
the open back of the ferry where there was a hard bench to
sit on. No one seemed to mind we had a dog with us. Blue
snapped at the sprays of whisking river water as if snatching
at blowflies. All three of us waited for the departure, bottoms
and balls uncomfortably vibrating to the engine's heavy idling.

The sun burned my forehead and cheeks. By the ferry's
back rail a couple snapped one another's photo. Then the
engine moaned and clamoured and the ferry's propellers
churned the muddy Brisbane River beneath us.

I kept looking back.

Mary was still serving beer and cocktails and champagne
on the decks surrounding the restaurant's black steel and
smoky glass. Those timber decks, I saw from the river, went
right out over the silty currents. There were pretty warning
lights to ward away straying vessels. At night you might stand
with a drink on those decks. You might watch the lights of
the river traffic and you might hold the sweet small hand of
the one you loved while all along you continued to think
your craven thoughts.

Mary's ponytail bobbed behind her. As she moved from
table to table she was full of grace, beautiful. The further
away the little ferry sailed the more Mary looked black and
gold against the sun and currents. I concentrated too hard.
The river and its reaches blurred. *Liar! Liar!* I wanted to
shout, but it was as if I saw Mary floating over the river,
moving with grace, effortlessly walking on muddy water.

That was the new Mary.

SEVEN

Under the Waves and Under the Sky

'Monica, wake up.' I'm kneeling on the bed beside her. 'Come on, Monica, you should see what it's like outside. It's just unreal.' She won't move so I run my hand through her new raven-black hair and clear the wispy bits away from her cheek. 'Mo-ni-ca,' I sing as gently as I can, 'Mo-ni-ca wa-ke u-p.'

She makes a little noise but won't open her eyes. Is she dreaming of Johnny crying out and tearing his hair in the shadows of a lonely old night? No. It's just too much of the chianti we sneaked out of her father's spooky cellar and brought on the rusty car ferry across to the island with us.

'Turn the radio off . . . just another ten minutes . . .'

I turn the volume of the radio up a little louder. The tide is high and I've already been for my first swim and surf and there was a school of dolphins playing out past the crests of the breakers.

'Mon-ica,' I insist.

'It's too early . . . it's too hot . . .'

Now my face is on hers and Skyhooks are on the radio. My hair is wet and salty and so are my lips. I lick Monica's cheek as if there is salt on it but she just buries her face into the pillow. My dick is an albatross in my boardshorts. No matter how much Monica and I have already done this warm-hearted pal wants more, more, more of her. Like a hungry mutt I lick at Monica's cheek and at the corner of her mouth. It doesn't even tickle her.

She's going to have a hangover today.

I leave her alone and lean against the bedhead and though I'm looking at all the broken bits of the little wooden beach cabin, what I see are those dolphins calling out from behind the breakers, daring you to come far away from the safety of the shoreline and swim with them. And then they're all gliding through the rearing waves, twisting and turning above the white water, like vagabond voyagers they're tempting you to follow their lead toward another beach of absolute purity and grace.

Old Aquila led me to a dumpy old boarding house on Brunswick Street.

We entered to the smell of beer and socks. Armpits and tinned food. Bad breath and damp. In the hallways and poor light men of all ages sat in their singlets. Some were outside by the front fence as if waiting for someone or something to arrive. Aquila heaved himself up the narrow steps and I followed. Blue's ear was flat against his skull and he seemed extremely sheepish. Aquila puffed and blew and his hips seemed to give him trouble.

Then we were going down a corridor with black burnt-out bulbs showing in the fixtures. Aquila stopped in front of a door. It wasn't locked and when we went inside I could see why. There was nothing to steal, unless someone wanted tobacco, old photographs, or a bundle of old clothes.

'Home the sweet home,' Aquila said. He went straight to his bed, sat down, found his tobacco pouch and started to roll a cigarette. The wall beside him was knocking. Aquila bashed back. 'You shut up! *Finocchio*! Animals!' He looked at me and his claw scuttled over the covers of his single bed, looking for matches. 'No women they come here,' he said sourly. 'Not even the *puttana* from the street.'

The knocking against the wall intensified.

Blue lay down flat on the floor and didn't move.

Aquila struck his match and drew deeply on his foul-smelling cigarette. He didn't make a move until he had smoked it all the way down to the deep yellow of his fingers. I looked at the photographs that peeled from the walls. Others were in frames on an old dresser. The photographs traversed generations and continents. Smiling faces, stern faces, the crumbling town of Piedimonte in the shadow of Mt Etna. Aquila's restaurant on Petrie Terrace and the person he used to be looking like James Bond or some Italian film star in a black suit, standing out in front of it.

Soon Aquila came and stood behind my right shoulder. We were looking at a photograph in which Gloria, Monica, and Tony held each other. Gloria was showing a lot of cleavage, Monica's hair was black, and Tony was scowling.

'Only Monica she come to see me here,' Aquila said. 'No Gloria, no Tony. But Monica—eh, you remember what

Monica she like. She have her own head. She come here one night with the bottle of wine and a pizza in a box. She make it for me you know, and she make it the way I like, plenty anchovy and the black olive. We no talk very much. I sit there and she sit here. We argue and then we can say nothing. So we eat and have glass of wine and then she go.'

'Did she come again?'

Aquila's head was bowed and his back was bent. The enthusiasm of the morning's walk had fizzled out of him.

'She sit here, Romeo.' Aquila indicated an imaginary chair by the cheap dresser. Blue watched Aquila, and moaned. 'When she go I see that her hand it leave the marks here on top of the dresser.' He touched the place where his daughter's pizza-greasy fingers had once upon a time left their marks. 'I get on my knees, Romeo, and I have to kiss it.'

'Let's get your things together, Mr Aquila.'

Aquila packed a beaten case. He hardly took anything. When he tied an old leather belt around the suitcase he looked up at me.

'You not gonna help me, eh Romeo?' but he didn't mean the suitcase.

I said, 'I'll help you.'

'*Mi promessa, Romeo?*'

'I promise.'

Aquila nodded and contemplated the threadbare floor covering. 'I tink is time.'

He stood in the middle of the room and stripped Johnny Armstrong's clothes off his brittle old bones. With great dignity he dressed in a moth-eaten brown suit that hung in his musty cupboard. He found a grey tie and his gnarled hands hadn't forgotten the peculiar rhythm of tying a windsor knot. The heels of his only pair of good black shoes had split.

I did up his laces for him. His case was light and I brushed cobwebs off the shoulder of his suit coat as he passed me. I stopped Aquila and straightened his plait and tightened the elastic band holding the end together. Then we all went out. If it's possible for a dog to look relieved, Blue looked relieved.

A man of about twenty was perched on the front fence. He was drinking beer and wore army camouflage trousers. Shirtless, white skin, and his head was shaved. It had a grey stubble. The young man cast a jaundiced eye over the brown suit, the windsor knot, then returned to his contemplation of a homely prostitute in a leather skirt and bra walking along Brunswick Street. Then the young man looked back, spat a fat gob at Aquila's feet, and said,

'*Quelle coiffure*. Fucken crazy cunt.'

His French might have been okay but his eyes were good and dead. Further up the street the prostitute leaned with a hand against a tree and two men spoke to her. I wanted to howl but Aquila just shuffled on with his head down. Why couldn't a young man see that between the walls of this dirty place a man's soul had collapsed? So I shoved the prick with his stupid army trousers right off the fence and watched him go over in a flurry of white arms and legs.

'What'd you do that for?' he cried. 'What'd you do that for?'

Fuck that place forever. Seeing it and seeing Mary at the restaurant had opened my eyes, finally.

Aquila and I went and stood in the street, hailing three taxis in a row before one would carry Blue. We sat in the back seat with Blue dividing us. I wouldn't look at Aquila. His suit had thin legs and a patched elbow and a torn breast pocket showing an off-colour lining. It signified something,

something that terrified me. When we were driving up Raintree Avenue and were almost at Johnny's big old house,
Aquila said, 'You make the man keep go, Romeo.'

Oh but I was shaking now. I wasn't ready. I would never
be ready. I already knew the truth about Mary and about
Monica, and I wanted a drink and a one-way ticket the fuck
back to Sydney. Aquila turned away from me. Blue panted
with his great pink tongue out.

'Are you sure, Mr Aquila?'

He said, '*Si*, Romeo.'

I said, 'Keep going, driver.'

The road turned past the southern end of the Toowong
cemetery. In only a moment we were driving through the
cemetery's main gates and were deposited in front of the
sexton's office. A tour bus was parked there and a large
group of people dressed for the beach emerged from the
cemetery's historical museum. Cameras were slung around
pink necks. I wanted to chase them away, shouting.

The tall spire of the Governor Blackall monument was
in the distance, at the far peak of the immense, hilly grounds.
On a midnight in 1976 Johnny and I sat under that monument. We had talked about rooting a girl on a grave and had
worked our way through bottles of beer and packets of potato
chips and had been nauseous for a day afterwards. Boneyard,
necropolis, city of the dead; what did we have to fear from
it?

I walked with Aquila along narrow pathways and down
overgrown avenues. Knife grass was too dry and too long
and black burrs caught in our socks. Many of the grave plots
were crumbling and gone to weed but many more were as
neat as a family's living room. Aquila stopped. Blue stopped
and cocked his leg, but I gave him a shove with my foot.

There was a broken column, universal symbol of a life cut short, and a bunch of greying flowers over a slab.

'I wish I tink to bring the fresh flowers,' Aquila said.

He stood in the sun, grey as those old flowers, and he kept his gnarled hands clasped in front of him. His old brown suit was appropriate for a cemetery on a day such as this. Aquila wouldn't have visited without a proper suit and a tie done in a proper windsor knot. One day when he had recaptured everything he had let slip through his fingers, he would have a new suit and the heels of his good black shoes would be mended. He would have new teeth too. But for now Aquila was just a grey old man and I was a beaten young fool and Mt Coot-tha seemed too green and too beautiful and too near. The sky was blue. I couldn't bring myself to look at Monica's heart-shaped face adorning her gravestone. I couldn't read the inscribed words or dates. Instead, all I could hear was Monica's voice declaiming:

> '*Howl, howl, howl! O, you are men of stones!*
> *Had I your tongues and eyes I'd use them so*
> *That heaven's vault should crack! She's gone forever.*
> *I know when one is dead, and when one lives;*
> *She's dead as earth. Lend me a looking glass;*
> *If that her breath will mist or stain the stone,*
> *Why then she lives!*'

No.

Aquila was talking and Blue was scratching at a flea. I wished I no longer heard Monica's voice.

'Was suppose to be for me,' Aquila was saying. 'All the space they got sold out by 1975. Very popular this place. Still only half-full so a lot of people they must be taking their

time to die. But if you no own you space already you can
only get in if they make you into ashes. So I give my little
girl my space and one day I come here in a little vase.'

Blue was done with the fleas and was cocking his leg
again. I kicked him away but my knees were trembling and
I hardly hurt him at all. In the photograph Monica was
smiling. A wisp of her black hair was curled around her
cheek. Her eyes looked right at me. I had to sit on the slab
to put my arms around the headstone and kiss her. I hung
on until Aquila took me away. As we went Blue trotted ahead
of us, leading, once again more than happy to escape the
baffling places of humans.

Monica is covered in perspiration, a satiny sheen over her
skin as she lies nude and comatose. I go to the bedside and
blow a stream of breath all the way along her body; from
heel to neck, shoulder to shoulder, the hollow of her armpit
down to the dark of her groin. None of this has an effect.
All it does is make me dizzy.

'Hey, Monica, look what I've done.'

It's my first ever attempt at a cooked breakfast, for which
I should be ashamed seeing that I'm already seventeen, but
that's Sicilian family life for you. The menfolk slave like
donkeys in the sun but when it comes to the home the wom-
enfolk have to treat them like royalty. Well, that's the theory
anyway.

I wipe my face with a tea-towel. It's stinking hot.
Outside, the sand is burning but the ocean is a soothing balm.
In the early morning, after an hour in the surf, the ocean left
me fresh and clean and breathless. At least until now. The
cabin is poky and hot and not really the place for the daylight
hours. The sheets Monica lies on are damp. A couple of angry

red lumps mark the backs of her arms. We have bed bugs and sand flies. Mosquitoes and lizards. But an ocean and a blue sky too. I want to get into that clear water again, and this time I want Monica with me.

White gulls with red beaks squawk past the broken little cabin's only window. The window is the shape of a porthole and it doesn't let much air in. I keep the door wide; once upon a time the little window was really a porthole, the framing taken from a wrecked sloop by Johnny's bargain-hunting but still hippy-minded father. The cabin's front door came from a caravan towing accident on the Bruce Highway, and the rickety furniture from some acrimonious divorce sale. Cutlery and kitchen fittings from a Chinese restaurant gone bust and towels and linen salvaged from a loony asylum burned down by inmates back in the fifties. The sheets and the towels still have Saint Michael's Hospital written on them in indelible ink so it's appropriate that Monica and I let ourselves go completely fucking crazy between those sheets.

A breeze edges in through the open doorway but it's not much to talk about. My chest is bare and I kick off my boardshorts. Our cabin is secluded enough that it's okay to be naked and leave everything open. We still need more air; an evening thunderstorm would be an absolute gift from God.

So I have a glass of water from the small fridge, take a pewter plate, and sit down at the rickety wooden table. Through the porthole I can see a patch of dense scrub, a strip of sand, and Cylinder Beach. A kookaburra lets out a throaty aria. To me he doesn't sound so different from that randy fat man, Caruso. Monica'd roll her eyes to heaven if I told her that. I start to eat with my fingers. The sausages crunch and sweat drips from my eyebrows and armpits.

We came across on the Stradbroke Island car ferry yesterday afternoon, even though we don't have a car. It's cheaper that way. Then we hitched from the landing point at Dunwich to the cabin on Cylinder Beach. I like this. Here I am in Johnny's parents' place and it's Johnny who has lost Monica and it's me who is getting her back. Johnny'd always promised I could use this cabin, and he could never go back on his word, and so here I am with Monica. Ha, ha.

I like this turn of events a lot.

There's a bit of scrub and a line of sand dunes between the cabin and the water, but we're still close enough that you hear the lapping of the waves at low tide and the popping of bubbles in soldier crab sand tunnels. Cicadas crackle away in the scrub from dawn till dusk. We listened to all this nature during the afternoon and night and didn't go anywhere near the surf. We stayed in this broken-down cabin with our stolen chianti and a picnic of bread and green salad and bean salad and pasta salad, and made love without a worry in the world. Without any sort of inhibitions—just as Monica told me Caruso's old flame once said of him.

It's never been like this with Monica. It's as if now, together again, we're ten years older. Ten years more desperate and furious in our lovemaking because we know we can lose each other. And Johnny—his influence is with us too. Those images of him won't leave me. In the car with his hand up Monica's skirt; in the night, tearing his hair. And Monica, so fucking wild at him. When will she tell me what's been going on?

'What are you eating?'

In a little while the tide will recede and Monica and I will lie in the shallows and talk about everything and nothing. From the cabin there's not a surfer or swimmer to be seen on Cylinder Beach. No children with pails and plastic shovels, no adults with umbrellas and transistor radios.

'I've been trying to tell you I made breakfast.'

'It smells like it's burnt.' In the bed Monica stretches this way and that. I watch the way her knees bend and her back arches and her white hips push toward the ceiling. Monica says, 'I was watching you.'

'You were asleep.'

'Just now I was watching you. Sitting there. You were a million miles away.' She smiles. 'Crunching a very black sausage.'

'But I was thinking about you.'

'Were you?'

'Oh yeah.'

'I dreamt about you, Romeo. You were swimming.'

'This morning I was. There were dolphins but you missed them.'

'It's not the right time for whales but the dolphins are always around. What were you thinking about just now?'

'Just nothing.'

'Mmm?'

'About what it's been like without you.'

'And?'

I look out the window at this perfect day and say, 'Oh, I guess it was all right.'

'Come here,' Monica says. She lifts her legs and I can see the cream of her thighs. They are covered in down the colour of the sun. 'Come on. Come over here. I'm tired. I just want to lie here and I want you to get on top of me and fuck me, Romeo.'

I look at Monica's glassy eyes. Her hair is messy and her skin is damp and her teeth are dead white. She's spacey with her hangover. I don't get up. So Monica keeps staring at me as she moves a small hand over one breast and touches her own pink nipple. She licks her fingers and slowly-slowly brushes her nipple until it is hard and raised. My legs are like butter and I believe in heaven and hell and all the wonders of this earth.

'Come on,' Monica says in her husky tone.

The old insane asylum sheets hold salt and damp and the shrieks of long-dead loonies. The air is humid. The ocean rumbles and the cicadas are thrumming. Monica is so small and so perfect I have to take care not to annihilate her. The soft sound she makes brings me deep inside her. It's as if with a breath she can engulf me. There is light and colour in Monica's eyes and that's where I lose myself.

We drive each other mad for what seems like hours. Hours and hours, and then somehow we've found the strength to go running down the dunes to the sandy beach, to jump into the sea and tumble in the flotsam and jetsam this earthly paradise sends us.

A family descends from the scrubby tracts behind the sand dunes and comes onto the beach. They carry with them an esky and the biggest beach umbrella I have ever seen. As the family arrives, so too do a school of dolphins. The family stay away from where Monica and I laze in the sand. They set up their umbrella and it sticks out on our virgin strip like that arrogant flag in the Sea of Tranquillity.

There's a bony mother in a bikini, a long-legged father in Speedos, and two toddlers with frilly sun hats. There isn't a breath of wind. The mother opens a heavy book, a kid cradled between her legs. The father takes the other kid to frolic in the wavelets. The father's Speedos are small and show a lot of corpse-white skin.

Of course Monica wants to get a closer look at the dolphins.

'We don't have any swimmers on, Monica.'

'It's a deserted beach in the middle of the week.' She finds the puppy fat in my waist and pinches it. 'I'm sure they've seen it all before.'

'No, no, I don't think we should be flaunting ourselves in front of a family.' I look at the long-legged father trying to take his child a little further than the wavelets and getting a bawling battling brattling for his troubles. 'We'll go inside and put some things on.'

Monica's up and walking toward the waves as if showing her body is the most natural thing in the world. Maybe it is. She looks good. Her hair flicks in the only bit of sea breeze to rise all day. Monica's shoulders have reddened and her lower back is pink. Her small feet leave a trail in the sand.

I don't know why I am so taciturn about this family on our beach. I don't like eyes upon us. I feel as if the family are a bad omen, others must be on the way to look at Monica and me. The waves rumble to shore. Past the breakers the dolphin fins cut to and fro. Monica watches them with a smile on her face, then she's picking at sea shells.

'Look at this one,' Monica says, and she holds it up. The shell has waves in its carapace, colour and light, motes, just like Monica's eyes. I turn to see if the father is watching. He isn't. The sea cliffs and distant rocks have got his undivided attention. Maybe he's a fucking geologist.

There are lots of shells. Monica picks the most exquisite while I keep looking backward. The family man is now flat out at the water's edge, letting the waves run up those long,

long legs, over his chest, and right to his soft little chin.

I say, 'Monica, I think we've been out in the sun too long.'

She says, 'It's too hot in the cabin. Let's get under a tree or something. We can get the radio.'

I don't like that idea either. Under a tree we'd still have eyes upon us. I look sadly at what was our lovely private beach, then I take the shells Monica has collected and make a neat pile of them away from the waterline.

Monica says, 'Romeo?' as I gather her up in my arms and run with her into the swells. It's the only way to hide her. She screams. We've been made so hot by the sun that the water seems ice, as refreshing and stinging as it was the first time we tumbled in.

Monica keeps her arms around me. She's kissing me and her wet hair whips at my face like seaweed. Her mouth is as fresh as the ocean. Monica wrestles with me and I flip her. She likes this so I flip her again. Boy does she look great. Then she tries to do the same to me and the salty buoyancy of the sea makes it easy. She flips me round and round and I think I might have to throw up because in reality I was the one who drank most of the chianti last night. Monica swims away from me and executes a sort of Esther Williams back flip, so graceful in the water but a bit more revealing than Esther ever meant for it to be. The dolphins are forgotten and so for the moment is the family man. I swim after Monica and she wraps her legs around me, but a bigger wave is coming and we have to dive beneath it. When we come up we get a great view of the school of dolphins. Monica tries to get her legs around me again. The dolphins cut this way and that because now a set of humungous breakers is threatening and this electrifies all of us.

Monica lets go and I duck down, the dolphins disappear and reappear, then the mother of all waves gathers and rears right behind and above us. There are heaps of dolphins in it. Monica screams and I take off to catch the wave, yet as I do Monica throws herself onto my shoulders and I end up being her boogie board. We roar along, pushed by all the power of the ocean. The foaming wave rushes us right up to the shore, where we tumble around in a messy tangle of arms and legs.

'You nearly drowned me!' but Monica just drags me from the foam back to deep water.

'Come back out! The dolphins are still there!'

And so they are, for they've been busy catching waves too.

Monica and I swim out as far as our nerve will take us. The breakers have calmed and the sea is flat. This makes the fins of the dolphins seem what they are, not close at all but very distant. I'm tired and sated anyway. My face feels like it's frying. A little away from me Monica dives. I see her underwater, coming toward me. There is no seaweed, no flotsam and jetsam. Monica's white legs kick as she approaches, the round mounds of her bottom move rhythmically, her arms are by her sides, then she is climbing me the way she would climb a tree, her hands and then her breasts going slowly-slowly-slowly up from my ankles and to my calves and to my thighs and to my waist and to my chest and to my shoulders and to my neck, where she traps me, her forehead against mine.

Monica kisses me and her mouth is as fresh as the sea. Her legs wrap me and with two magical sighs she draws me deep inside. All her muscles tense and she kisses me with such yearning, such ruthless longing. I'm lost, utterly lost,

and then I see the family man swimming too close by, his
head just above water, his fair hair all wet and awry, his
smile cordial and sympathetic and encouraging.

Monica murmurs something, eyes tightly shut, but the
family man is a sign. I feel a bad-bad Sicilian premonition. I
try to lose myself in Monica but with eyes upon me it's
impossible. Far behind, dolphin fins etch their way toward
an open olive-green sea.

The gift from God comes. A hailstorm breaks the heat when
the sun is down on the horizon.

With not too much warning lightning skeleton fingers
the sky and the orange tracings of sunset disappear. Fat rain
drops, followed by sheets of nuggetty hailstones. We grab
our towels and books and run for cover. In the cabin we get
all the pots and pans out for it becomes plain Johnny's hippy
father has never bothered to fix a single leak in the roof. The
biggest leak is over the bed and disaster seems to be knocking, but Monica finds a wok salvaged from the Chinese restaurant gone bust and she sets that over the insane asylum
sheets. The raindrops ping like nursery bells.

Rain and hail rattle the cabin. Thunder reverberates
beneath our dirty feet and we crouch at the porthole. All
has been lost, the sea, the surf, the very air around us.
Monica is dressed in a kind of Balinese sarong that she isn't
too sure how to tie. It keeps slipping off a shoulder, keeps
opening to reveal a hip or a thigh or the small of her back.
As we watch the storm Monica's got both hands in my
singlet. The wok fills with rain and I empty it, then the
rain and hail reach a head-numbing crescendo and that's it,
it's all over.

Monica tells me to bring my wallet. Hailstones blanket

the scrub and the beach. The horizon is dark and the evening is fresh. At the end of our beach there is a rocky peninsula so we start climbing even though we're barefoot and it's difficult to see. We're not the only ones with this idea for ghostly shapes wander across the beaches and the rocks. The wind is from the south-west and it shakes the trees above the promontories. There is the vital perfume of life. We look out to the inky sea and watch unnameable constellations emerge.

I've never been on the island before. It's a quiet place. A few little communities that revolve around sand mining and fishing, there are rundown wooden shacks and houses, and you have to hand-pump petrol from most of the bowsers. Even the names have a sense of peace; Dunwich, Amity, Point Lookout. Along with the beaches and the lakes one of the island's attractions is a crumbling graveyard. There the gravestones remember a terrible shipping accident and the era when Stradbroke Island was a community of lepers and their carers.

'Nearly there,' Monica says, catching her breath.

'Where?'

We follow a path to the top of this peninsula, bristly couch grass sticking to my soles. Then there's a new beach below. I hear the waves crashing. Monica leads me down from the rocks. The wet sand is soothing and soldier crabs scurry importantly along, translucent in starlight.

Monica says, 'Look, Romeo,' and she's pointing out to the red dots of remote fishing trawlers. Then she turns and says, 'I think you were absolutely right about coming here.'

Not once have we referred to anything bad that has passed between us. Now I can't think of what to say. Monica seems transfixed by the distant trawlers. Those red lights look like burning stars about to fizzle in the sea. She takes my arm and she smiles at me. She kisses me lightly and the wind blows her hair.

Monica says, 'We've got such a lot of time, Romeo. Let's not worry too much. We can stay here as long as we like.'

'What about Christmas?'

'I'm not expected home.'

'Why not?'

'Because I'm here with you. And because—well, things aren't that wonderful between Mum and Dad. Of course my mother knows where I am, but if Dad suspected, he'd kill both of us. It's a bit of a blessing he doesn't bother trying to work things out any more. He thinks I've gone up the coast with Jane and her family. Maybe it's cruel to exploit his trust.' Monica puts her hand up to my cheek. 'So who's perfect?' She smiles. 'The Straddie is up this way.'

'What's "the Straddie?" '

We traverse the sands of this luminous beach and hold hands. Fishermen stand with their lines out but we're not there long enough to see if anybody is catching anything. We get to the end of the sands and climb another promontory. Monica is puffing. Her hangover has caught up with her. Then we're below the fluorescent lights and lazy hubbub of what looks a very doleful place, the Straddie, the local pub and beer garden.

'Wait a minute,' I say to Monica, and turn her toward me. I tie her sarong in a more decent manner. In a flash she looks trussed like a Christmas turkey. Monica undoes my tight knots and takes the thing off completely. We're in dark scrub. Monica starts again. Before she can get too far I put my arms around her waist and bring her close to me. Monica takes my hand and gently eases my fingers between her legs.

The trees and bushes rustle. We kiss for a long, long time. Monica bites my lower lip and pushes hard against me, but then she moves away.

So we climb the last part of a pathway and head for the pub. I have my doubts about getting a beer. We're under age. We hear crappy music and boozy laughter. Ruddy faces stare out into the night and big bellies precariously balance on stools. Before a dartboard half a dozen men argue. There are just a few women. We enter the public bar and nobody gives us a second glance.

Behind the bar a portly greaser is pouring a jug of Fourex from a beer tap. His belly hangs over a black studded belt with a big Harley buckle. He is in total black and his face is pock-marked. Monica and I stand at the bar in front of him, lay our hands flat on the wet counter mat, and I say, 'Couple of pots thanks, matey.'

The greaser doesn't look up. His hair is carefully arranged with a perfect ducktail at the back. He passes the frothy jug along and starts pouring our pots. His lethargic eyes look us over and linger on Monica. 'Suppose you're both fuckin' eighteen?'

'Oh yeah.'

He nods, 'Oh yeah,' and takes another order. His air of abject weariness says that he has seen all the tribulations of life and has been impressed by none of it. His thick biceps say that he would have clobbered most of it anyway. I pay for the beer and that's it. We find a secluded corner that overlooks some palm trees and the ocean. The tall bar stools are rickety and there is a lot of smoke in the air.

'We used to come over here for day trips,' Monica says. 'The eldest girls used to buy our beer. We used to take it down to the beach and get ripped.'

'When?'

'Oh, a few years ago. I was about fourteen maybe. One time when we came over we were staying in a house up on the hill back there. The whole time we were here it rained and then there was a cyclone.' Monica smiles and drinks more of her beer. 'No beach. We had to stay locked up indoors. It was very depressing.'

'Uh huh. And who were you here with?'

Monica gives me a look. 'Well, my first real boyfriend.'

'Anyone else?'

'Not really, no.'

'Your parents thought you were with Jane again?'

'Well, they like her a lot.'

I don't have anything else to say about it.

'Anyway, he was a musician. Now he's a public servant. It was so depressing in that house with the cyclone. It was the cricket season too, nothing but cricket on the TV. He might have been a musician but he would have preferred playing in his whites for Australia. We wrote a few songs together to relieve the boredom. He was in a band and later they used to play one song we wrote. I did the lyrics and hummed him the melody. He wasn't very good on guitar but he basically got it. They recorded it and made 400 copies and went broke. He used to give them away. That was the high point of the band's career.'

I still don't say anything. My heart aches at this thought of her at fourteen. It should stir the romantic in me, after all, I am *Romeo*. Juliet Capulet was supposed to be fourteen. I'm a lousy Romeo after all. There are dark smudges under Monica's eyes and her glassy look is back. A hard pimple is coming up on her cheek. She's not the greatest Juliet either, I guess.

Monica finishes her beer while I've barely touched mine. She leans closer. 'This was the chorus. Don't you dare laugh.' Her breath is in my ear. Softly and slowly, as in that old black and white news film you sometimes see of Marilyn Monroe singing 'Happy Birthday' to JFK, Monica sings:

'When it's in my heart
To swim out to the breakers
And die
Under the waves and under the sky
To become a part of the breakers
Tonight.'

I look at Monica and she isn't smiling any more.

There are footsteps and before you know it the long-legged family man is standing there with three pots of beer held out in his hands like an offering. Boy, is he tall.

'So you've got a good voice too?' he says. We look up at him and he is beaming. I see that he is in fact extremely tall. 'I thought you might like another drink?' he says. 'Would you mind if I sat with you?'

There are no bones about it. He is very, very, very tall. His neck is very long, as if his head has been stretched from his shoulders. So he pulls up a bar stool and then it's the three of us sitting in this corner and neither Monica nor I have said a word. Sitting, he is as tall as me standing. His head moves this way and that on the stretched stalk of his neck, the most wondrous thing.

'I wouldn't normally just intrude,' he says, 'but my wife and I have got the cabin nearby to yours and we sort of know Wally and Maggie Armstrong. You must be friends of theirs.' He pushes the pots of beer toward us. 'Go ahead. Drink up,'

he says, 'it's on me.' I see that his smile is a little nervy and
a little sweaty and all of a sudden I feel sorry for him because
there's something desperate and lost about him.

'How long have you known the Armstrongs?' Monica
asks, and takes the fresh pot of beer. She's friendly toward
this geek and of course she sees exactly what I see and that
makes her more friendly because she is a gentle soul and that
is why I love her.

'Oh, not long. Just the cabins, you know.' He gives
Monica this creamy smile of his and she smiles back at him.
'And you're friends of their son Johnny?'

'Johnny. Yes,' Monica replies, 'we both are.'

'I like Johnny. He visits a lot whenever he comes over.
I'm Bill Shoemaker. And you're, let me think, starts with an
''M'', right?'

'You've got a good memory. It's Monica.'

I say very softly, 'Romeo,' but I'm looking at Monica.

'Romeo?' he says and takes another drink. 'Monica and
Romeo. That sounds very romantic. You've come to the right
place, you know, the sun and the beach and the quiet nights.'
He stops to drink down the rest of his pot of beer. 'How
have you been, Monica?'

'Good,' she says.

'The sun makes me too thirsty,' he goes on. 'I usually
work in an office with air-conditioning.'

Our new friend abruptly goes to the bar and comes back
with a jug and puts it down shakily. He tops up his glass and
Monica's glass and my glass as well, which doesn't need
topping up at all. He's as nervous as hell and I have the
feeling he's always on the verge of saying something portentous but just can't get the words out.

'Those are the most beautiful colours in your wrap,

Monica,' our friend says as he hefts another pot down the
elongated stem of his gullet. This portentous thing he's got
to say but can't definitely involves Monica. 'The most beautiful colours,' he says again and looks a litle closer at Monica,
and I know he's not seeing those colours at all but Monica
standing on the beach, in the sun, nude. 'What did you think
of the hail?' he says and his smile is actually a leer and now
I don't like him at all and would like to kick him in the face.

'Yeah, it was really good,' I say.

Monica drinks her beer and as she does her glassy eyes
study this fellow, Bill Shoemaker. She looks funny next to
him, she is so delicate and he is so dorkish, but it's not that
which makes her seem funny next to him and this puzzles
me too and no matter how I look at them I just cannot work
this peculiar thing out.

'Did you find you had leaks in your roof?' he says.
'Wally's not the most practical of men, I think.'

'Well, yes, we had to—' Monica starts.

'I think maybe I'll be running along,' he says, completely
cutting Monica off. 'I like to tuck the children in before they
go to sleep. The rest of the jug's on me,' he says, 'enjoy it.'

He stares so long and hard at Monica I think his tongue
is going to come out and lick his white lips. He gets up and
puts his arm around Monica's shoulder and then I understand
it, this weird thing between them. Bill Shoemaker is as arid
as a twig and Monica is as full as a fresh rose, and as for me,
well, the fact is that he already knows Monica has turned my
heart to a smelly shit of mistrust.

'Goodbye, Monica and Romeo,' he says. 'It's so good to
be so young.'

And then he's off and he trips over a bar stool and a
light fitting bounces off his skull and he misses the first step

out of the public bar and we see him in the night heading
off in a direction that seems wrong to us and he seems to
discover this too for he turns around and heads off in the
other direction and as he passes our window he gives us a
wave and a silly smile and I have never, ever, in my life seen
someone quite so anxious and quite so clumsy.

'Well,' Monica says.

'Fuckin' pissed all right,' the greaser says as he collects
glasses around us. He itches at his pock-marked face and forms
a row of empties right up one arm. ''e was in here when the
hail came and you know what, he just sat over there and stared
into space. Get some fuckin' idiots in here all right.' The greaser
goes away with his armload of beer glasses.

We sit and think for a few minutes.

I say to Monica, 'I can't believe you've been here with
Johnny.' Monica looks at me but she doesn't say anything.
'Well, how many times did you come here with Johnny,
Monica?'

'Does it matter? Twice.'

'Twice,' I say, and love seems no different to me than
fruit left too long in the sun. 'Twice. With his parents, or
just you and Johnny?'

'Just me and Johnny.'

'Christ, you're a fucking bitch.'

Monica stares at me. 'I'm not sorry for coming here with
him. What's the matter with you, Romeo? You want some
silly Sicilian virgin?'

'He's supposed to be my friend, Monica. Being here is
supposed to be special to *us*.'

Monica just looks more and more distant.

I drink some beer and my eyes and arms feel heavy. 'Do
you love Johnny?'

'If I was would I be here with you?'

'How the fuck should I know?'

'Uh huh. So I'm a succubus where men are concerned?'

'What's that word mean?'

'Oh, forget it.' Monica tops up her glass. 'I don't love Johnny at all. But there's something about him that—I don't know. There's just something about him. And now I'm kind of stuck with him.' Monica's hand grips my shirt. 'I told you we had all the time in the world.' She offers me some beer. 'Do we have to talk about it now?'

'I don't want any more beer.'

'I do. It must be the sun.'

Monica is quiet and her eyes are watery. In spite of myself I take Monica's arm and squeeze it and then give it a kiss. What happened to that church of lovelessness I was building in my heart? It's just too hard. I've thrown my dice, I've already told myself I'd take whatever bits of Monica's heart were left over from Johnny. Still, she seems as troubled as I should be, and this look comes over her face, and then she just turns her head and spews up so violently she almost comes off the bar stool. The most foul-smelling pile splatters the public bar's beer-soaked carpet and I grab Monica and she says, 'Oh my God' and brings it all up again.

The greaser's on to us in a second. 'What the fuck are you two doing?' and his tone says we are about an inch away from having our brains beaten in.

'*Fuck off*,' I tell him, and I can see how he doesn't like this and how he would like to take things a little further, but poor Monica throws up again, this time just a little less violently, and I pick her up in my arms and her head lolls and she smells awful, and as I quickly carry her out of the public bar and into the fresh night the greaser shouts after us, 'You're not leavin' me to clean up this shit!'

A spotlight illuminates the brilliant green grass in front of the public bar so I put Monica down where it's nice and dark and where the breeze smells of oceans and salt and not of beer taps and meat pies. The stars are out and the ocean is black. Monica breathes deeply and I hold her steady. Now she pulls her knees up close to her chest. I hold her hair away from her face.

'I'm sorry,' she says.

'How do you feel?'

'Awful.'

'We'll just sit still for a while.'

'Okay.'

'You've had too much sun,' I say.

'I made a mess,' she says.

'Don't think about it. But it was very colourful.'

'Yes. And I haven't eaten carrots for weeks, but there they seemed to be.'

It does me good to hear Monica's still got it in her to joke. I put my arm around her shoulders even though she smells of spew, and she turns her face to me and gives me a smile, and even though she looks awful it still is the sweetest smile, and then I can't help it and I don't know why but I start to cry like a baby and so does Monica and she ends up holding me very tightly with her hands over mine.

The sea breeze picks up and it looks like it might be a blowy night all right, and from inside the public bar the greaser hollers for me to fuckin' get back in there and clean up the fuckin' mess my stupid little fuckin' girlfriend made.

I wipe my eyes and turn around and look at all the ruddy,

sweaty half-pissed faces looking out at us from the public bar. I see the greaser's pock-marked face and it's twisted with anger, then beside him I see the face of Johnny Armstrong, but this can't be so, it's just for a second, and then Johnny's face or whoever's face or whatever's face has melted away and I wonder if somehow Monica has sent me just a little bit cuckoo.

Monica says, 'Look,' and so I look, and there is nothing but the black ocean, and then I see what she has seen, that all the red lights of all the trawlers have gone.

In the morning both the porthole and the front door are open but the sheets are crumpled around the bed and we're both sweating. Monica's face is pale and her skin is bad. I move outside and let her sleep.

Even this early morning sunshine rakes my skin. I've overdone my exposure to indolent beach life. There has been a gale during the night and fallen branches litter the scrubby ground. White ghost gums have been flayed, bark lying in tatters like the shedding skin of a very big snake. Lying amongst a pile of dead branches and dead weeds is a kook-aburra that's got nothing to laugh about any more.

Over and down the scrubby hillocks and sand dunes to the beach; the ocean is pounding. High tide. At least here my spirits lift. The long-legged family man's umbrella is nowhere to be seen but many other people are out. The breeze carries a drifting scent of coconut oil. A radio or a tape is playing. It's close to Christmas and all the world's budget holidaymakers are either here or on their way.

Past the breakers the sea is flat. The dolphins must have chosen another beach for their games. And their absence is like one more little knife in my heart. I stand on a dune and squint out to sea and hope to find their fins cutting through the waves.

'Good morning, Romeo,' Monica says because she's silently followed me down. She puts her arms around me and leans her head on my shoulder. She is in her sarong and it's as shapeless as a sack.

'Hi,' I say.

'It's already ten. Why didn't you wake me?'

'Look at the water. Do you want to go in?'

'No, I'm hungry. Where are the dolphins?'

'Maybe they'll come by in the afternoon.'

'I'm really hungry.'

'Okay. I'm glad you're better,' I say.

'Oh I'm better, I just need to eat. Come back with me?'

'I'll go for a swim first.'

Monica heads over a dune into the shade of the scrub and gums, and I think what a long walk that was just to tell me she is hungry. And that's all she's going to tell me, but it doesn't matter, I've figured it all out already. I'm a donkey all right. I should have seen it sooner. Monica and Johnny, him screaming out in the night, her bad skin and lethargy. All of it adding up to the same prize. There isn't a single bone inside me that's made of anything you'd call noble.

I'm just glad it's not mine.

I go down the sand and throw myself into the cold waves. A kid with a board tumbles over me. Another kid catches a wave right at me, his toboggan thrusting like a battering ram. Both of them shout abuse, pretty masterful abuse. I strike out for empty waters but there are lots of girls swimming today. Three teenage girls in particular take my eye. In colourful bikinis their boobs are big and buoyant so I dawdle around while their boyfriends give me their big bad looks. I don't give a stuff, I'm in the mood for a fight. They're all talking about maybe getting to see a dolphin, and I rinse my mouth with seawater and spit and rinse again, contemptuous in the knowledge that they can search all they like but they won't see anything like the dolphin-play Monica and I were treated to yesterday.

When I get back I think about burying the kookaburra before it ripens, but there is the invigorating smell of cooking instead. Monica passes in front of the porthole and she looks naked. I go to the wide-open door and stand there. The cabin is stinking hot from the gas bottle stove. And Monica has the porthole open, and is moving around with that sarong wrapped loosely around her hips and nowhere else. Her breasts are pink and fat, and her hair is tied back from her face. Anyone could waltz right in and have her.

I'm shaking.

'What the fuck are you doing?' I bellow. Monica's face snaps around. She has prepared breakfast and it looks like all our rations have gone into it, tea, toast, pancakes and marmalade. I come into the cabin.

'What the fuck are you doing walking around like that?' and I throw a pot across the room. 'Do you want to be attacked?' and I overturn a chair. 'Is that what you want, you stupid bitch!' and Monica stares at me, completely shocked.

Then she flings down her tea-towel and she screams back at me, 'YOU FUCKING BASTARD!' and she steps away from me, thinks about it, and comes back and lands me right in the belly. She's no slouch. I'm just about winded because she knows how to get her weight right behind a punch. Lucky she's not a bigger girl. But then the worst thing is she sits

down on a broken-backed wooden chair, looks at her hands,
and starts to weep.

'Shit Monica—'

Nothing will make her raise her head, neither tenderness
nor sorrow. I pour her a cup of the tea she has made, and
apologise. Monica will not look at me. I pull the chair I have
overturned close to hers and sit with her, next to her, but
she weeps alone and will not be touched.

When Monica finally gets herself together she says very
coldly, 'Well I guess you might be right, Romeo. Will you
get me that shirt over there?'

I would get her a shirt from Bangladesh or Babylon.

Monica pulls it on. She wants to speak but I think she
doesn't know what to say. Her lips are dry and the hard
pimple on her cheek is angry and red. Sometime while I was
out swimming she has tried to squeeze away one or two of
the smaller pimples and only made matters worse.

'What's going on with you, Romeo?' she says. Monica
gives me a long minute but I don't answer. How can there
be anything going on with me? It's her, her, her. 'All right,'
she says, 'I'm not here to rescue you. Are you waiting for
someone to rescue you?'

'I don't need to be rescued.'

'Uh huh. Listen. You ran away from home and you met
me and I think you expect me to make your life good. And
if I don't, if I can't do that, you're going to hurt me as much
as you can. Forget it, Romeo, I won't let you.' Monica stops
a moment and looks at me and then rubs her knuckles as if
they are sore.

'So,' she starts again, 'just get it into your skull that
you're never going to speak like that to me again.' Monica
wipes perspiration from her forehead. 'You've got the worst

temper I've ever seen and I don't know where it comes from but you better know I won't put up with it. And that voice. Jesus. You should be in the opera.' Monica tugs at the shirt, which already clings to her chest. I see her hands shake as she wipes perspiration from the side of her jaw. 'It's hot in here.'

And in a minute we're sitting at the table, sweating, drinking tea, eating a breakfast that should be delicious but which to me has all the flavour of dirt. For once I don't eat much. Monica helps herself to my share and finishes off a green salad she has made. We are not looking at each other. I mostly stare out the window. The perspiration is beaded on my forehead and running into my eyes. I'm too self-conscious to wipe it away. Monica cleans her plate with a crust of toast.

Someone is walking outside.

Our neighbour the dork sticks his ugly head on its ugly stalk in through the open front door. 'Monica. Romeo. See, I remember your names.' He comes in. 'Mind if I come in?'

Monica says, 'Have a cup of tea.'

'Oh no thanks,' he says. 'It's very hot.'

'We've got bulk pancakes.'

'Thanks, but my wife and I have been up since dawn. That's what having kids does for you. We had brekkie hours ago. Geez it's hot in here.'

'It's from the cooking,' Monica says.

'I won't stay,' he says, resplendent in full dorkarama. 'Are you interested in the darts tournament up at the pub tonight?'

Monica says, 'Oh.'

'Yes,' he says. 'They're very serious about it. It's a good laugh and it's very social. Everyone comes around for it. The beer is half price. We'd love to have you. My wife is very competitive. Will I put your names down?'

'All right,' Monica says.

'Well, good. You know you have a dead kookaburra outside? I'll take him now and bury him for you. What a wind last night. This time of year it's always the same,' he says and looks at me as if expecting me to say something. 'Well goodbye,' he says.

'Goodbye,' Monica says.

'Leave the kookaburra,' I say.

'No problem. Poor bugger, leave him to me. I'll make sure to give him a decent burial.'

And he's gone.

I turn to Monica. 'Why did you say we'd go and play darts with a bunch of fuckwits?'

Monica says, 'What did I tell you about your temper? And did you say "no" when he asked? Did you bother to say anything? *Leave the kookaburra*,' she mimics. 'Bloody hell.'

She goes outside and lies on a towel and gets engrossed in writings a century old. In its original it was Russian. It looks like she plans to spend the whole day under a tree reading about dead Russians in St Petersburg.

So I don't say a word. I just fuck off.

The beaches on this side of the island go on forever, huge sandwich bites taken out of a coastline you can follow into eternity in your search for that final, perfect beach. I climb peninsulas and promontories and swim at different places and don't give a stuff how many layers of skin the sun will eventually burn off me. I go exploring beach after beach, then high sandy cliffs and the scrub behind, and come across a rock pool that makes my skin sizzle when I lower myself in.

Further along I find a huge sandy hill that is so steep and so white as to be like a ski slope. Many kids my age are sliding down the slopes on sheets of cardboard, timber, whatever. So I climb the hill and join in the fun and watch girls sliding all the way down to the bottom.

I have a few turns, then one of the girls says, 'Are you a local?' and I think her sunburnt skin and freckles would look like magic in the dark. That's what I need, magic in the dark, not Monica's shit.

'Oh yeah,' I say.

'What do you do?' she says, and she's smiling at me. I like that smile, the fringe of blonde hair, her yellow bikini.

'I'm a poet,' I say.

'A poet?' She looks back to her friends, who egg her on. 'What do you do, like, for entertainment?'

'Well, we've got a darts tournament up at the pub tonight.'

'A darts tournament?' she repeats, and laughs. Her smile tells me that her sunburnt skin and freckles and little blonde fringe could be mine if I play my cards right—or maybe my darts. She trots back to her friends and I don't know why I do this, why I follow her up the hill, why I push her down the slope and why I roll in hot sand with her.

But I want Monica. Or anything. Or nothing.

It doesn't matter. In a little while the girl in the yellow bikini, who doesn't have a name, gives me a secret smile and takes me by the hand and then she leads me into the scrub behind the big sand dunes. The grass is long enough to reach your hips. The cicadas are singing. She leans against a tree with one knee up and holds both my hands.

'So you're a man in love,' Johnny Armstrong says while I'm getting closer to the girl in the yellow bikini.

Johnny's sitting in the crook of this twisted old tree
and he is swinging a leg. I look up at him. The girl in
the yellow bikini moves away and dusts herself off and grins
up at Johnny as she leaves. One day I'll be led by the dick
straight into hell. The bush and scrub crowds in but overhead the sky is absolutely clear. I can smell eucalyptus and
salt, and with his tanned face Johnny's eyes are bluer than
they've ever been.

'How long have you been here, Johnny?'

'About a week,' he says, and that's why he's so brown.
He drops down from the branches and lands gracefully, like
a leopard. 'We've got a house at Wategoes Beach and we're
splitting the rent five ways. Hardly anything at all. Want to
come over one night?'

'Not this time.'

'Looks like you could have a thing with Libby.'

'Get fucked,' I say.

'You too, Romeo.' Johnny toys with the tall blades of
grass and there is a swishing sound as he prowls around, still
like a leopard.

I say, 'Why didn't you tell me you were still seeing
Monica?'

'I didn't want to hurt you.'

'Thanks.'

'I thought it wouldn't last too long. It wasn't that
serious. Then . . . ' his voice trails off and Johnny looks at
me. 'It got serious. You used to say some real shit about
her, Romeo. You acted like you didn't give a fuck about
Monica.'

'I was wrong.'

'If you'd tried just a bit maybe I wouldn't have hung
around.'

'Yeah—maybe.'

'Okay.' He picks at a blade of grass and then chews it. 'Enjoying your holiday? Sorry the cabin leaks.'

'Jesus, Johnny, what the fuck do you want?'

'Hasn't Monica told you?'

I look at him, my heart thumping. 'Of course she has.'

Johnny grins but it's not real. I recognise his expression from that night by his ute. There's something in his face that is hurt and tired and broken. He's wearing tiny green Speedos with a red stripe. Johnny can't help looking lean and golden, but his tanned face seems like it's been stepped on. Unfortunately he's also got bad breath, maybe he's been eating himself up inside, or maybe he's just been overdoing it in the past week, who knows?

He says, 'Why don't you just finish it with Monica, Romeo? It's my problem, even if Monica hasn't decided what to do. How can she know what to do? The best way you can help her and help yourself is to just walk away.'

I say, 'It could be mine.'

Johnny steps in quickly, 'Yeah? It's not yours. Monica knows that at least. You want it to be yours? I don't think you want that, Romeo.'

'Why not?'

'Because you're a selfish little prick, Romeo.'

I push Johnny over and he falls into the long grass. I run out of the scrub and down the big sandy slope with all the kids laughing and sliding around me, and I run onto the hot beach and over slippery rocks, and I go as far as I can, who knows how far, just not far enough, my legs pounding until my chest and my throat are on fire, and then the ocean is liquid silver but it won't swallow me up the way I want it to swallow me up, and the curling waves just keep crashing down on my head, and I can't for the life of me get those stupid fucking words of Johnny's out of my mind.

By the time I get back to the cabin evening is falling. Monica sees me coming and she gets up from where she has been outside lying on her beach towel. She has put a dent in Chekhov but it also looks as if she has been sleeping. I arrive carrying wildflowers. We go inside. Monica looks at the wildflowers and looks at me and has to fit them into three different cracked water bottles on the table.

Monica says, 'Let's get ready for the pub.'

'Darts?'

'Well?'

She takes her one-piece off right in front of me, though this is unavoidable because the cabin is so small. I have to gawk at her. Nipples, breasts, belly. Here in the cabin there are no real rooms, only a place that is a kitchen, a corner where there is a bed, and a slight timber-partitioned annexe that is the bathroom. When you sit on the toilet in this rudimentary bathroom you have to squeeze and hold on to your guts in order to be polite. If your companion is polite they will go outside. It is best to avoid curries. Monica steps into the cramped shower cubicle and the water starts to run.

I stand beside the shower and search around for some words. 'You're going to need some moisturiser or you'll peel.'

Monica lathers her hair. Her eyes are scrunched up and she says without opening them, 'Why don't you get in?'

I get in.

She rinses the suds out and says, 'Do you know what the word ''trust'' means?' Monica squeezes shampoo out of her eyes. She is looking straight at me. 'I want you to trust me. Do you think you love me?'

'Oh fuck yeah.'

We kiss under the running water. The water is cold and I can't tell if it is her lips or my own that are just as cold. When we dry ourselves with towels damp and gritty from the beach I pull Monica onto the bed; she is on her belly and I rub moisturiser into her sunburn. Her back is strong but my hands are stronger. Sand has found a way between the sheets. I pick the sand grain by grain from her skin, and then kiss the small of her back. Monica rolls over and I kiss her below the belly button and between the legs.

She makes me stop and I lie beside her.

'Johnny's here,' I say, and from the way Monica looks at me I can see she didn't have a clue.

'You saw him?'

'Yeah. He's staying here. He called it Wate-something-or-other Beach. He's with some friends. I saw him a little while ago.'

'Wategoes Beach,' Monica says, 'It doesn't have anything to do with us. I want you to trust me.'

I say, after thinking about it some more, 'Monica, what are you going to do about the baby?'

Monica sighs and clenches her teeth and sighs again. 'I haven't decided what I'll do yet. I want to go to university. I want to travel. I don't want to be pregnant. Some things are right and some things are wrong. I don't know which.'

I say, 'All right.'

Monica says, 'What else did Johnny tell you?'

'He didn't have to tell me.'

'Right.'

'Monica, couldn't you have told me rather than just left me to figure it out?'

'Trust,' Monica says. 'I wanted you to trust that I would work things out with Johnny.'

'Yeah okay,' I say. 'I can see it's working out great. You're doing a great job.' I push myself out of the bed. 'Now I feel like a drink.'

'So do I.'

'Should you be drinking?'

'I'm not sure.'

Monica lies on the bed looking up at me, cheap and sticky moisturiser soothing her burned skin, cheap and sticky emotions pushing us apart. More sand from the sheets will be sticking to her back. She can pick the grains out herself. The sea has been taking the rich black dye out of Monica's tangled hair and the more natural shades of brown show. For some reason there is a hint of a smile, a hint of the real person, and after Monica watches me dress she ends up putting on identical clothes. Faded jeans, white t-shirt, brown shoes. There's a weeping in my heart at the sight of her dressed like me. Monica comes and hugs me but I go to the door, ready, and hold it open.

Monica says, 'I do care what you think, Romeo,' so I take her hand and lead the way.

The greaser with the pock-marked face and the big arms serves me two beers. The pub is rowdy. There is music in the beer garden and a multitude have turned up for the public bar's darts tournament.

The greaser says, 'Tell your girlfriend the first fuckin' sign of trouble you're both fuckin' out.' His ducktail is primmed perfect and his belly looks as if it's been treated to a huge feed of beer and prawns.

There are the unmistakable smells of trawlers and heavy machinery and burnt rubber. Grimy faces, grimy singlets, grimy hands. The men are mostly fishermen or sand miners. The wives or girlfriends smoke Alpine cigarettes and wear skirts that show off bad legs. People drink beer or rum and coke. A few games of darts are already in progress and an unpopular horse is winning a televised race. The second television shows Loony Tunes cartoons. The tournament prize is a hamper of canned food and chocolates, and it's displayed prominently.

I put Monica's glass in front of her. 'Are you going to play?' she asks, and I shake my head.

The long-legged dork is sitting on a bar stool in a far corner, and who should be sitting with him but Johnny and three very sunburnt girls. The dork's wife is tossing darts at a board and people yell encouragement as if she's the local champion.

Someone calls out, reading from a long sheet of names, 'Monica! Have we got a MONICA here?'

Monica has a wry grin as she gets up. She pushes through the crowd and is handed three darts. She pegs them at the board against the wall. Two hit the wall and one hits a toilet door. A crowd gathers around her and they make her do it again. There are moans and catcalls. Monica extricates herself, her face flushed and embarrassed.

'Jesus,' she says. 'Maybe I should have a few drinks first.'

'Romeo!' the guy calls out, and everyone laughs. 'Have we got a ROMEO in the house?' Of course a few comedians claim the name. Others yell out that there are plenty of

Romeos in the place. Their girlfriends and wives push and prod them into shutting up.

I won't be playing this round.

The dork sits over there with Johnny and even in a dark corner of a crowded public bar he stands out like a tree amongst knee-high scrub. I can't remember his name. He waves at me. Johnny also raises his hand but the place is packed and I don't have to pretend to be civilised. I'm not sure that Monica has seen either of them. My heart goes out to her so much, I can't even pretend to understand what she must be feeling or thinking. In her faded jeans and white t-shirt and brown shoes she really does look like that thing people say, *my better half*. So we stay together and watch the games a while. Mrs Dork has a firm wrist and a mind like a steel trap. She's beating everybody. Whenever she gets her three throws you can bank on three cheers. The heat of battle brings everyone closer and beer does the rest. Holidaymakers gather in from the beer garden. They look so alien amongst the regulars they might as well be from another planet.

'The music's better outside,' I finally say to Monica.

'All right,' she says, and picks up her beer and follows me out.

In the sultry night we stand and listen to a four-piece band murder some old standards that could do with a bit of murdering. We're in the midst of a beery crowd of revellers and I wish I could see the ocean, or at least some stars. By Sunday it'll be Christmas, for God's sake. I put my arm around Monica and she puts an arm around my waist. We drink and sway a little to the bad music and I'm never going to let her go, not tonight, not ever, no matter what.

'Monica,' I say.

'Yes?'

'What does it feel like?'

Monica smiles a little and she says, 'I do get a little sick in the morning. It's not like I always have to throw up, it's a bit like waking up as if you've been on a bumpy boat ride. And I've got this really funny fascination for white bread and salad at the moment. Any kind of salad just sounds so beautiful to me.'

I look at her in complete wonder. 'Bean salad?'

'Uh huh.'

'Tuna salad?'

'Uh huh.'

This is such a revelation. 'Anything else?'

'No, not really. Just that nausea every now and then. I think it could be worse. Overall I feel—good. Sometimes my breasts hurt. I don't worry too much. I feel different, but really good. Mum says she was always sick.'

'Yeah?'

'You know I told her.'

'Bullshit, Monica.'

'No. I told Mum. She's got her own ideas about what I should do, but anyway, look, I'm fine. I just don't want to give up my dreams. The first trimester is supposed to be the worst.' Monica holds my hand and of course she knows what I'm thinking. 'The doctor said I was about seven weeks. That's how I'm certain who the father is.'

Simple arithmetic. It was never to be. Seven weeks ago I was free as a bird. It's so easy and I'm off a hook I was never on.

'Oh,' I say. 'Johnny was right.' I'm cheated and frustrated, but more than anything I'm just relieved. But the weight of the world has not left my shoulders. 'What does Johnny say?'

'He wants to get married.'

'*Johnny?*'

The band changes tempo and it's an old Bachmann Turner Overdrive song I've always hated. The crowd love it. The Marshall amps have known better days. The sound is thin and overamplified but people pogo around like fuckwits. The beer gets knocked out of my hand. The next thing to go is Monica. My head hurts and I want to run away, that's what I'm good at, running away. *Johnny* wants to get married?

Monica is going back into the public bar. Maybe she's going in to get me another beer. Maybe she thinks she has said enough. Maybe she doesn't want to have to deal with me on top of everything else. *Trust*, she'd said to me. My God, what a word to impose on someone.

Over the amplified mess I can hear the guy inside with his white sheet of names calling, 'Monica! Where has that Monica gone?'

I go inside to see how she does.

The dork, somehow able to tear himself away from the cut and thrust of darts, descends on me like a vulture.

'Here,' he says, and fills my glass from his jug. Tonight he isn't even pretending to use a glass. He drinks from the lip of the jug, pouring it down his gullet, and wipes at his loose mouth with his sleeve. His temples run with sweat. 'Have you stopped to wonder why the ghost gums are dying around our place?'

'Are they dying?'

'Of course they're dying.'

There is a cheer from the crowd. Monica has put a dart through a framed photograph of the Queen. The dork glances back and loses his balance, then his loose lips widen at me.

'My wife is winning. My wife is amazing. Her name is Fiona. Fiona knows words that would leave you speechless. Fiona loves to read but she's smarter than anything she reads. Fiona is a clinical psychologist.'

'Monica likes to read. Maybe she'll be a clinical psychologist too.'

'But how smart is she?'

'Pretty smart.'

'Pretty smart. And pretty. I have the feeling you're smart. I have the feeling you're a very smart boy. I wonder whether a smart boy like you has asked himself why the ghost gums have to die?'

'Yeah,' I say. 'It's been on my mind. I couldn't sleep last night because I was worrying about it.'

'Little deadshit,' he says.

'Yeah,' I say, and we fall silent. I can't see Johnny anywhere.

Now both televisions are playing Loony Tune cartoons. It must be a bad night for football or the track. Pepe le Pew is trying to fuck a gorgeous white-breasted pussycat. Pepe is full of Gallic charm. He makes love like a real Casanova. The gorgeous pussycat is rubber-limbed in his arms, trying to push him away, slinking to be released, yet our hero Pepe is so randy he doesn't realise his skunk odour and Gallic ardour repulse this beautiful object of his desire. The more the feline pushes him away the harder Pepe pushes himself onto her. The feline struggles. Pepe insists and babbles loving non sequiturs.

I say to the dork, 'I thought you were so keen to play darts.'

The dork says, 'Oh, have a beer.'

The black pussycat escapes, brains Pepe with a lamp post,

but Pepe keeps coming, his head circled by little yellow chirping budgies.

'Where are your kids?' I ask.

'Neighbours have them for the night. We all look out for one another here. We visit and we watch that each of us is all right. Fiona and me, the Armstrongs when they come down. Johnny too, he's a good young fellow. He's my friend. He's going to go far but he's got things to work out and you won't let him work them out. You. You realise that, Romeo? Maybe I can help you see what you're doing.' The dork drinks some more and looks out a window into the black. '*We're* the ones killing the ghost gums.'

'So you don't like trees,' I say, wishing he would go away.

'Little deadshit,' he says again, and drinks. 'It's not deliberate. The ground isn't used to the salts and residues we pump out of our homes, especially in the holiday season. We upset the natural balance. Our shit leaches into the water table and builds up toxic residues that poison the vegetation. Gums aren't as hardy as they look. We should move our cabins away.'

'That's on the cards.'

'Exactly my point, Romeo. We're loving the place to death. None of us has the guts to let go. So we spoil everything. Do you follow me? It's human nature to not want to do what's clearly the best and only thing to do. Letting go. It's not easy.'

I finish my beer and watch a bead of sweat run from his hairline down into a wispy eyebrow.

'Jesus Christ,' I say to him, and push myself away. I go over to the jukebox and while I study the song selections I am not alone. Standing by my side is Johnny. I wonder if, along with the dork he has advice for me too. He does.

'Try ZZ Top or some Doobie Brothers, Romeo.'

As if.

I go away and buy myself another pot of beer. Johnny buys a jug and brings it over to the dork. Or should I call him a geek? I wonder what qualities differentiate the two. Then Monica walks away from the darts tournament, a loser again, sees them sitting there, looks lost for a second, and goes and sits with them. Through the crowd I see her face turning this way and that, searching me out. But then Johnny is leaning toward her and speaking intently, and the dork-geek is nodding, nodding, nodding, and I wonder if anyone on this planet can have trust enough to let their loved one work their own life out.

'Romeo! Will Romeo have a turn now? Don't put your name down if you won't play! Ro-me-o!'

The blood whispers through my veins. Is Monica conscious of me? She drinks and listens to Johnny but isn't looking at Mr Dork, who nonetheless keeps up his nodding at everything Johnny has to say. There's something about the heartfelt expression on Johnny's face that reminds me of Pepe Le Pew and makes me want to laugh. Almost. Monica is leaning away and I wonder if Johnny's still got his bad breath. The way Johnny pleads with Monica proves what the dork was trying to say to me—that you can't have love without greed, and Johnny and I are two greedy little boys indeed.

I finish my beer and its kick has coupled with my malice to create something new. I've always known a night like this would arrive. The dart-lovers move aside for me.

'Here I am,' I say to that loud prick of a tournament convener.

The prick gives me a sour look and hands me three darts and pushes me to the marked spot on the floor where you

stand to have your throw. The crowd like my name. They
are pissed. They chant Ro-me-o, Ro-me-o, Ro-me-o, Ro-
me-o, Ro-me-o and I stare at the dartboard and in one beautiful, fluid, slow-motion movement take my first throw and
it's a dead-set bull's eye, so suck on that you fuckwits.

The noise they make is deafening. You'd think I'd shot
a prime minister or started a religion. Someone slaps my
back, and then someone again. Cigarette smoke is in my eyes
and beer slops the floor and someone has dropped a coin on
a very crappy jukebox hit. I'm inside a mass of drunken flesh
and I don't like it one bit. I look around to see how Monica
is doing with those two creeps, and I shouldn't be away from
her, I should be with her, just forget what she has said to
me about trust, and I see that Johnny has had such an effect
on her that she is weeping, really weeping, crying into her
forearms and with Johnny's arm around her and him talking
and Mr Dork nodding, nodding, nodding.

And then it comes to me. I raise my arm, and three
bikies in leather get the fuck clear, heavy boots slithering in
beer, and I peg a dart at Johnny, right into his face, but he's
lucky that I've lost my beautiful, fluid, slow-motion movement because it doesn't go anywhere near his face but it does
go straight into his knee.

I go over and Monica looks at me with an ugly and loving
face. The dork gets up from his stool and he says something
that I can't understand. He smells of sweat and beer and the
vomit of babies, and he's like a gangly spider-shadow, and I
crush him, one blow, so that he falls down and takes a jug
of beer with him.

I reach for Monica but Johnny, poor Johnny, straining
and grunting, grabs my t-shirt and looks at me and I want
to hit him but he has been crying too and it makes me angry

and wild that I can't understand those tears on his face. Why are they there? Why does he say to Monica that he will marry her? I don't hit him and I don't even *want* to hit him any more, and I'm even sorry for the dart that looks so funny sticking out of his knee. All I want is Monica, and I want to cry out *Oh Monica, come on, let's run away now!* but they all grab hold of me and they carry me outside where the fat white moon is high over the white crests and is reflected in the black sheet of the sea.

I remember Monica's lines, written when she was a four-teen-year-old Juliet, sung to me in her sweet husky voice, *to swim out to the breakers and die, under the waves and sky.*

The greaser's so excited his ugly mug is barely recognisable. Behind him tall and ancient palm trees move to and fro, to and fro, waving slowly against a moon whose light doesn't reach the dark corner they've dragged me to. There is the humming of a diesel engine and the stench of gas and garbage. The greaser is screaming at me, really screaming at me, but I see I've still got plenty in me and it just has to come out. They drag me some more but what they can't know is that I'm no longer in this world. I am in the world of angels and devils and wolves. I get myself free of the arms that hold me and I charge at the greaser and knock him backwards, and the others stink of trawlers and oil, of sulphur and burning flesh, but I don't even feel their blows and it's only when I am pushed down and boots kick at my sides and at the back of my head and I feel my nose dig in the dirt that the pain starts to flood and I am under the waves and under the sky and, as my Monica would sing, mercifully drowned.

Johnny comes to the cabin the next day to see how we are. I'm not too good but Monica is worse. Monica has spent

most of the morning staying close to the toilet and, despite
this, wanted a bean salad for breakfast and I had to make it.
She needed last night like a hole in the head. I'm full of
remorse but that can't help much. It doesn't stop her
spewing. I went up to the nearest telephone booth and rang
the local doctor. Monica will be seeing him in a few hours
just to make sure she's all right.

Anyway, Johnny's limping around outside and he wears
a bandage that big his knee might as well have been blown
apart by a cannonball. And what should he be carrying in his
arms but a big bunch of wildflowers.

He comes inside and sees all the wildflowers I picked the
day before, and the way they stand in the three cracked water
bottles, and he gives a wry grin and just sets his bunch down
on the table. I've never seen him looking so much like an
invisible man.

'I guess you could use a few more,' he says.

Monica pulls out a chair for him. 'Sit down, Johnny,'
and the three of us sit there like invalids and have a cup of
tea. We don't say much.

When I've had enough I pick up my bag and say, 'We
need a minute, Johnny,' and I walk outside and Monica
follows me.

It's breezy in the scrub. The dead kookaburra has been
buried and our friend the dork has fashioned a little crucifix
of twigs. Monica and I hold hands as we head over a couple
of dunes to the beach. The sun glitters off the sea. Waves
pound the shoreline and if there are dolphins playing out
past the breakers the terrific glare makes them impossible
to see. The white sand of the beach swarms with holidaymakers. Babies, boobs, beach balls. Even Mr and Mrs Dork

are out with their two bratlings, I can see the umbrella, it's the biggest and best of all.

Monica and I sit on a dune and my bag is beside me.

Monica holds me and she puts her head on my shoulder. We talk for a little while about nothing in particular and stay like that until more holidaymakers come and start setting up camp around these very dunes. There are transistor radios and furled nets and screw supports for beach volleyball. We watch as things get set up for a game.

I say eventually, because it's as good as goodbye, 'Monica, just tell me you forgive me. You know how sorry I am.'

Monica holds me closer. She cuddles into me. She whispers in my ear, 'I love you, Romeo,' and she kisses me with a greater tenderness than a heart like mine can take. Then she says, 'Just tell me, Romeo, I need to know. What would you have done?'

It's what I don't want to admit, but I know the answer all right. So what's the point in lying to Monica? I'm fucked anyway. 'I guess I would have chickened out. I guess I would have run for the hills.'

She nods, trembling. She knew. My heart is no mystery to her. 'What about my *life*?' she asks. 'What if I won't go through with it? What if the best I can do is run away?'

So I say, 'Monica, whatever happens from here is okay. You're smart.' I look at her flushed cheeks. 'Monica, I trust you.'

Monica nods again and brings her face up to look at me. Maybe my heart *was* a mystery to her, because she looks really, really disappointed. More than that. The expression in her face is heartbreaking. I have never seen such desolation. I feel like I'm already a ghost in her life. Monica gets up and stands before the ocean a minute, and then I watch her loose skirt sway in the breeze as she goes away.

I don't want to sit there any longer. The holidaymakers make me sick. There's no point in having a last swim, it would hurt my bruises and my bones too much.

They're starting to play volleyball down there, they're laughing, all those kids, and they look pretty good. The way they run and dive around makes a mess of this perfect patch of beach. Well, we've all got a right to make our little messes. This isn't my place anyway. I'm heading back to Sydney and when Monica's ready, well she knows I'll be easy to find. Of course I might have forgotten about her by then, but my heart tells me no, when Monica comes calling for big dumb Romeo he'll be ready and waiting, no matter how long it takes.

It's a long hitchhike to the Dunwich car ferry. It's an even longer hitchhike south. The day is too fucking hot. Maybe I will have a swim before I go, and maybe I'll sit on the dunes and cool my heels a bit longer, but when I've gone there won't be the slightest trace to say I was here. If some things don't change that's how my life will turn out, when I've gone from this world there won't be the smallest mark left to say I hoped and slaved and cried here.

Christmas come Sunday. Fucking fantastic. Monica and Johnny will be spending it together.

EIGHT

Blue's Moon

I n a funny way it was good to see Nigel again, even though he was a naughty kid hiding from the law on the front verandah of Johnny Armstrong's house. He wasn't sitting on the outdoor chairs or at the round breakfast table where you could catch the sun, but down on the spongy timber floor-boards. His back was against the wooden rails so that you couldn't see him from the street. When he heard Aquila and me come in the front gate he peered through the wooden slats of the railing and ducked down again. He made me smile, which wasn't so easy at that juncture. Then Nigel got his courage up and rose to his feet, but he kept close to the

French doors so that he couldn't be seen from the street. That was when he got a load of Aquila.

'Bloody hell, Romeo,' he said, and then softly, as if he assumed Aquila was deaf, 'Where'd you get the zombie?'

Aquila tried to straighten his question mark shape but he stayed pretty much a living query. In his torn and dusty brown suit I guess you could be forgiven for thinking he'd just been exhumed. Aquila stuck his claw in Blue's collar to keep him away. Or maybe to set him onto Nigel, I wasn't sure. Blue wouldn't budge anyway.

Aquila said to me in Sicilian, *'But who's this black boy, and why is he shaking like that?'*

I dug out my keys.

Nigel's face was beaded with perspiration and the soft overnight bag he carried spilled a fat electrical cable.

'You want to come in?'

'Oh yeah.' Nigel looked up at the street and back at me. He didn't have any qualms about confessing. 'Silent house alarm. We thought we cut it off but you know, the best laid plans of mice and men. Police arrived while we were at work. We took off in different directions. But you know, Romeo, it'd probably be good to lie low a few days. I'm getting a bit too famous where I live. What do you think?'

As if I cared. I didn't see why Nigel should be so nervous anyway. No police officer would know to come here—but what did things like this matter at all, Monica was gone and my hopes with her.

Nigel said, 'No one's talking about freeloading, you understand that. I'm not a bludger. And I got a few things for you, matey. I was really hoping I could stay.' He started bouncing from foot to foot. 'Can we go inside?'

So I opened the front door and we all went in.

There was a message on the answer machine and it went like this: 'Romeo. Have you met Mary? You probably have. Look, you big dumb dickhead, Lufthansa just landed me in Perth. I cut short my trip. I've had time to think, and I don't know if she's said anything to you, but I guess I probably have to work a few things out with that girl. Ahm, that's all I can say. I have to find a domestic flight to get back to Brisbane. I should be home tomorrow. Fuck the snow was good this year. Too bad. There's always next year. Maybe you'll be able to look after the place for me then. Bye.'

Nigel's eyes were big and round. 'Does that mean I have to go?'

'Nigel,' I said, 'why should it?'

The answer machine was clicking off and I thought how crowded the house was going to be come this time tomorrow. Still, nothing at all mattered. I wanted to lie down and I wanted to sleep. It was getting on toward evening. Soon it would be dark and Mary would arrive home and I would have to somehow hold on to my temper. I was the walking wounded, shell shocked, nothing seemed real. Old Aquila didn't want to relive what had happened to Monica, not yet anyway. As if I was ready to hear about it. Now Aquila sat on the living room's big couch with Nigel beside him. They looked a funny pair.

Aquila said, 'In the country where I come from, the Sicilian is the black man of Italy. They no like us, you know that, always we get the broken end of the stick. For hundreds of years is the same. We are the donkeys and the slaves who do the work. Until Benito Mussolini he come along, and even then was no so good. We the black man of our country, and we proud of it. That mean you, me, we are like the brothers.'

Being inside the house made Nigel more of the laid-back disco boy I knew. He sat in the big couch with his long legs straight out in front of him, his bag by one foot, Blue panting up at him by the other.

'Yeah?' Nigel grinned uncertainly. 'Brothers?' He thought about this a moment, then said, 'Want a joint, brother?'

Aquila said, 'Joint?'

'Yeah.' Nigel dug in his bag and pulled out his booty. I went and sat down with them. 'Here,' Nigel said to me. 'This is for you,' and he passed me a Walkman. 'It plays CDs.'

'Really?' I'd never had one. It was shiny.

'Yeah. Here's a few CDs. Here's a few more. I'd like you to have them.'

'Thanks,' I said. 'I always wanted one of these.'

'Jesus, what a day.' Nigel pulled out a plastic bag of marijuana and started rolling a fat joint. 'I told you I don't expect to freeload. I believe in paying my way. The house we went into was humungous. They'll be insured to buggery. They'll get everything back. Except maybe for this.' He waggled the bag of dope and then went back to his rolling. 'Pity the police came. There was so much lovely stuff in that place. Oh I forgot, here're a few shirts.'

'You keep them,' I said. 'I'm okay for shirts.'

Nigel looked at Aquila. 'Silk,' he prompted.

Aquila felt the fine fabric and his eyes glittered with greed. 'Oh, I want.'

'You want?' Nigel pushed the beautiful shirts at him. 'You have!'

We all shared the joint and when that was finished we started on another. I wondered if Aquila knew what he was smoking. He didn't seem to mind at all. Blue lay down and went to sleep and the dark crept into the house. It was quiet and wonderful. I lay back on the floor and the world didn't seem such a bad place. Somehow Monica wasn't gone. She walked between the dark spaces of the rooms and I felt that if I turned my head just right I would catch sight of her silhouette. My heart started beating faster and I had to go to the toilet. In the bathroom mirror my face looked funny and my eyes looked funny too. The door was shut. I was alone in the bathroom and Monica was at my shoulder and I could hear her telling me she loved me, just as she did that last time I saw her on the beach. I wanted to ask her what she wanted but I was scared a question like that might frighten her away, and I didn't want her to go away. A breeze came in the window and grazed my cheek. That was Monica. I started to cry. I sat on the toilet with my trousers down and I cried and cried. Monica's head rested on my shoulder. At least I wasn't alone.

When I was done I came out of the bathroom.

Aquila said in a dopey voice, 'Oh Romeo, I very hungry. I tink we all want the dinner.'

I stood in front of him. 'What happened to Monica? Why won't you tell me? Don't you think you have to tell me?' and Aquila hid behind Nigel's shoulder.

I watched him cowering and the strength ran out of me. He was right anyway, we were all hungry.

So I went into the kitchen to prepare a last supper, for with Johnny coming home to his daughter none of us would be together like this again. And of course she was his daughter, not his lover. She was Monica's little girl and she worked at Il Vulcano with her grandmother and she was dealing with some awful schism with Johnny. It all finally made sense. I understood why it was that whenever Mary was in my arms, so was Monica.

I opened a bottle of South Australian cabernet, drank two glasses down like water, and threw the corkscrew at the wall. If I hadn't been such a fool all those years ago Mary could have been my very own flesh. I could have had a daughter. Long ago I'd been relieved; I wasn't relieved any more. Who was ever going to love me if not Mary? Who was ever going to see past the muscle and the anger to find the real me? I cracked a lot of garlic and finely chopped it and cut my finger too. I blanched a ton of spinach then stir-fried it in olive oil and garlic and a little sugar. I was sick to my soul. By the time I was chopping pine nuts to sprinkle over the top of the spinach Mary came home. She was in great spirits. For some reason a Sunday's work in the restaurant had agreed with her.

Nigel and Aquila were watching '60 Minutes' on the television. Aquila was silly as a wheel. I heard Aquila say in a joky tone, 'Mrs Romeo, this is the brother of mine, the poor black man of his country.'

'I'm Mary.'

'I'm Nigel. I stayed over the other night.'

'Oh,' Mary said. 'Can I smell cooking?' and left them and came into the kitchen, followed by Blue. She said to me, 'What a dynamic duo.'

I said, 'Could you get your mutt out of the fucking kitchen?'

Mary took Blue out and when she returned she put her arms around my neck and gave my face a hundred good-spirited kisses. 'I missed you,' she said. 'I really missed you.'

'Johnny called. He'll be home tomorrow.'

That got rid of Mary's good spirits. She stood in the

middle of the kitchen's parquet floor as if I'd slapped her, and though I didn't want to hurt her, though I thought there'd been enough hurt all around, I drank some more of the red and didn't have the ghost of a chance of controlling my temper.

So I said, 'How's our Mrs fucking Henderson? Was it chardonnay or chablis or champagne for her today?'

'How much do you know?' Mary asked.

'How much is there?'

Mary poured herself a glass of wine. When she gave me a little more I saw her hand was shaking. I was shredding parsley and marinated chillies, then frying onions and tomatoes. My finger was bleeding. What was interesting was that Monica lived in the wafting steam *and* in my whispering blood. How could I continue to be angry and resentful when the drifting aromas of cumin and pepper and blood were all my Monica? I put some pasta on to boil.

Mary said, 'Well, I *was* going to study nursing, but I dropped out of my first semester. I hated it. I prefer working in the restaurant with my family. There is a Mrs Henderson. She does our flower arrangements.'

I said, 'Oh yeah,' and kept on cooking. 'What I can't understand is you've been here in this house with your own father. No wonder he ran away.'

Mary stared at me and it took her a minute to get the gist of what I was saying. She looked shocked. 'How can you say such a disgusting thing?'

I turned on her. 'How? How about you, how many more lies have you got? How long can you keep it up? What's the matter with you?'

'Can you blame me?' she said. 'Gloria brought me up but she never let me know about my father. I had to find

out by myself. And then Dr Johnny Armstrong wanted a
daughter like he wanted a hole in the head. That trip away
was my last try, and of course he fucked off on me.'

'Why couldn't you at least have told me about Monica?'

'Monica? Isn't there anything else for you? Can't you see
you're obsessed? Can't you see that?' Mary drank her wine
and poured more. There wasn't too much left in the bottle.
She went soft and had to lean against a bench. 'I didn't want
to scare you away. I wanted you to stay.' She looked at me.
'Nanna Gloria told me Monica was too young. She was seventeen. You were there, Romeo, you knew all about it.
Nanna told me all about your disgusting little threesome.
Nanna told me she used to like you—until then. Nanna told
me all about how the three of you went berserk on Stradbroke Island.'

'We didn't go berserk.'

'Oh yeah? Family folklore says you're an incredibly
violent man.'

'I'm not violent,' I said, and then I understood why every
Christmas that I'd rung Mrs Aquila had kept me away from
Monica. It was my fault, again. 'I'm not like that.'

'Huh. And then you ran away.'

'That's not how it was.'

'Monica did a good job of running away too. It's your
generation's greatest attribute. Monica went to every obscure
part of Europe she could think of. Nice, huh? How do you
like that? That's the bitch you're in love with. My father
washed his hands of me too. All right? Are you satisfied?'

I found another bottle of red and uncorked it. I looked
at Mary. The fragrant steam of my cooking seemed to hang
around her long hair. I licked my bleeding finger. Monica
had taught me about herbs and about cooking, about wine,

about the way you can take a little piece of love and turn it
into a big piece of shit.

'Did you ever know Monica?'

'Are you deaf? I told you she went away. And then she
died. It wouldn't have mattered anyway. I was four.'

So I knew Monica better than her own daughter did. I
breathed in all the aromas of Monica and held them as long
as I could. Cumin and pepper and parsley. Steam. Chopped
garlic and red chillies. With those aromas we'd filled our
senses, the old red brick mausoleum in New Farm, the little
cabin at Stradbroke Island, and it had all been for nothing.

'Come here,' I said, but Mary wouldn't move. She
looked as if a hand had gripped her heart too hard. The hand
was mine. I put my arms around her. I didn't want her to
be sad, even if she was a liar; when was I made the patron
saint of truth anyway?

There was something I'd never told Monica, so I said it
to her daughter.

Mary listened and looked dubious. She was as smart as
her mother.

Sunday night, and it was getting on. Maybe it was high
time to just let go. Mary looked out the window. The palm
trees were silhouetted against the white moon. I turned back
to the cooking but loopy Aquila was standing right there in
the kitchen doorway. Mary turned around. Who could help
but like the way Aquila looked at her? He'd heard enough
to give his piercing blue eyes the glow of everything he'd
ever won and lost. He straightened his question mark, then
slowly and with tenderness, he held Mary's face and kissed
her full on the lips.

Behind him Nigel said, 'Hey, what's going on?'

*   *   *

When we all sat down at the table Aquila had to sit next to
Mary. He had to keep holding her hand. Every now and then
his bottom lip trembled. Every now and then he murmured
something that sounded a lot like, '*Mia cara.*' His eyes would
stay on Mary for long minutes. He said once, and then again,
'I see you mother,' and his bottom lip trembled some more.

Mary let herself be stared at. She said, 'Mr Aquila, in
the excitement I forgot I had something for you.'

Aquila pointed a trembling finger into her face. 'Is time
you call me *nonno.*'

'*Nonno,*' Mary said.

Nigel was heaping pasta and spinach onto his plate. 'It's
good to be around a family,' he said. 'I like families. Nuclear,
extended, either sounds really good to me. If I had a family I
wouldn't be in trouble. This looks good, Romeo. One day
you'll make a wonderful wife. You can start your own family.'

Aquila said, 'He too late.'

Mary went to her purse, opened it, and handed Aquila
a parcel wrapped in pink tissues. Like a kid with an interesting Christmas present Aquila made a production of peeling
back the layers of tissues. And then in his shaky palm he held
a full and very startling set of teeth. Aquila's eyes glowed
with greed again.

'Jesus,' Nigel said. So Aquila grinned and pushed them
into Nigel's face. 'Get them the fuck away from me!' and
Nigel jumped out of his chair.

Next Aquila held them up to my face, always with that
mischievous grin. I said, 'Nice set.'

Mary said, 'I hope one size fits all.'

'I don't think so,' I said.

'They're sterilised. I did it myself,' Mary went on. I
thought of her eucalyptus disinfectant and wondered whether

Aquila would be poisoned when he stuck those teeth in his mouth.

Aquila held the teeth in his palm and studied them from every angle. In a minute he took a deep and decisive breath. He turned his head to the side and very delicately but without ceremony plucked from his upper gum that last gravestone of his. It came away easily, just with a little sucking noise. Then Aquila's means of disinfection were as homey as Mary's for he poured a glass of wine and swilled and sucked it around his mouth and then spat it out the window. He put the yellow tooth with its little flecks of blood into his pocket, and then he tried the dentures.

'They good,' Aquila said, but his voice was a little muffled. 'They a bit tight.'

Nigel said, 'Gee, you look good. A hundred years younger.'

'Maybe they'll do until I can get you fitted with a proper set.' Mary took a compact mirror from her handbag and passed it to Aquila. 'What do you think?'

Aquila grinned this way and that. He clacked his teeth together, over and over. 'Oh, I like. I like!' He kept showing me. 'Look Romeo, I like!'

This went on for quite a while and the food was getting cold. I finally convinced everyone to eat. Aquila took out his new teeth and set them on a napkin by his plate. As we dug in that full set of dentures grinned around at all of us.

I was tired. Too much of a day, together with wine and Nigel's marijuana. I would sleep like the dead. Off in the nether world it seemed Monica had already made up her bed and gone to sleep. Everyone ate a lot and there was hardly any conversation. I wanted voices, not this silence.

So like a dickhead I said to Mary, 'Where did you find those on a Sunday?'

'Oh, just around.'

'Really? Isn't everything shut?'

'Well, I kind of borrowed them.'

Nigel said, 'That's not a sin. People get their dentures insured with their house contents. Pass the parmesan.'

Mary said, 'I took them from my grandfather.'

Aquila's head went up and my heart went down. 'Mister Jimmy Blake,' he spat.

'That's right.'

Aquila hurrumphed. He said to me, 'Tomorrow we go.'

'What?'

'We go tomorrow. We settle tings. You, Romeo, you strong! You throw them all out, but we keep Gloria. She stay with us.'

'*This* is your plan?'

'Yes!'

'Tell me one thing, why would Gloria stay?'

Aquila had to think a minute. He looked down into his pasta and spinach, he looked at his waiting dentures, then he looked at Mary's face. You could see he expected guile and cunning to save the day for him; Aquila knew what his end result was supposed to be but he didn't have the slightest clue about the means of achieving it.

'Because Gloria my wife.'

'What about her new husband?'

Aquila said, 'Him? We put him in the river. Down to the bottom. He never come up again.'

I said, at first very gently, 'Look, Mr Aquila, I think you should forget all about this. Think about what you've got instead. You've been re-united with a grand-daughter, and look—you've even got a new set of teeth. Maybe that should be enough for now. What do you want a big place like that restaurant for? It can't work, Mr Aquila. My advice is that you give it up. I can't help you.'

Aquila stared at me. 'Oh no,' and he giggled and started to bounce in his seat. 'You no say this. You make promise to me, Romeo. You cannot break.'

'Mr Aquila, we don't have a clue how to go about this. If you think I'm going to hurt anyone—'

'Don't matter! Is promise. In *Sicilia*, this something you cannot break. Oh no, you promise. Oh no. No break promise. No break. No break.'

And he would have gone on with his stupid giggling and bouncing unless I did break. He was just fucking crazy and I'd had more than enough. Why had I ever felt pity for him?

'What are you talking about, you stupid old man! Is this Sicily? Does this look like Sicily to you? Isn't this Brisbane?' I threw my napkin down. 'Don't you see it's hopeless? What are you hanging on for? Your wife is married and your daughter is dead and that restaurant business has nothing to do with you. Your wife is happy! Leave her the fuck alone. Nobody wants you. You don't have a family any more. *You* fucked your family up, not some "angel". What can you see? You and Gloria standing at the front door welcoming the prime minister to lunch? You're a toothless old man. Can't you see how stupid you are?'

Aquila breathed out through his nose. He jammed his new dentures into his mouth, click-clacked them, and stood up. He glared at me, then he made his creeping way away from the table. Nigel looked at us as if we'd gone nuts, and then he cleared his throat and kind of slunk away himself.

He went into the living room and sat on the big couch and
nervously started rolling a joint. I leaned my head on my
hand, picked up my napkin and threw it down again. Mary
was beside me. I tried to lean against her shoulder.

'That was disgusting, Romeo,' she said, and noisily
cleared away the dinner plates.

'But he's mad,' I said after her, yet it sounded half-
hearted even to me.

'How can you talk to an old man like that?' Mary called
from the kitchen sink. She ran water for the washing up.
'Shame on you.'

'Fuck!'

I pushed myself away from my last supper and wandered
around the house. I sat with Nigel and blew a few puffs with
him, wandered around some more, and then went into Aquila's room—the one that was Mary's until she'd come into
my bed. No wonder she'd been at home in there, that was
where she had slept whenever she tried to get to know her
unknowable father, Johnny Armstrong. Now it was Aquila
sitting on a corner of the futon. Blue was at his feet and
Aquila's shoulders were shaking.

'Look, I'm sorry, Mr Aquila.'

'Go away,' Aquila said. I came into the room and he said
it again, 'Go away.'

Mary came in. She sat down with him and soothed him.
She ran her long white hand over his long white hair and
started to redo his plait. Mary said, 'It's all right, *Nonno*, at
least you've got me. I'll look after you.'

Aquila said, 'Thank you, Maria, but you just no enough.'

Nice. Maybe it was genetic. The two of them wanted so
much their need was too great to be filled. Inwardly and
bitterly I welcomed Mary to our werewolf ranks.

I went into the living room. Nigel was glassy-eyed, staring at a wall.

He said, 'I like families, Romeo, but boy do they give you shit. The only thing is, you should respect your elders. I've never heard anyone talk so badly to an old man.'

'Oh, shut up.'

I sat down. Even Blue's loyalties were divided. He came and sat with us a while, went into Aquila's room, came back. He didn't like the atmosphere anywhere so he went out and lay alone on the verandah.

'Have you got any more stuff left?'

'Romeo old mate, there's enough to last us a month. Here, let me roll you another one.'

Nigel got to work. He might have been a little plastered but his fingers were swift and sure. It struck me we weren't so different. To bring comfort to myself and others I liked to crack garlic and cook lots of food; to do the same Nigel liked to roll joints. It made me appreciate Nigel more. He caught me smiling sadly at him.

Nigel said, 'Romeo, you're like one hundred per cent sure you're not a moof?'

I said, 'Yeah, pretty sure.'

He said, 'You'd probably really get off on eccy. It'd get rid of that temper. You'd love everyone to death.'

Mary joined us and though we all smoked together it wasn't the world's most convivial trio.

'What's Aquila doing?'

'Lying down. He's very tired.'

Maybe he heard us mention his name. Aquila came out of his room and went as fast as he could into the bathroom. We heard the sound of his retching and gagging. Mary tried to get up but I made her stay.

'It was the dinner,' I said. 'He can't hold anything down that isn't booze. How does he get nourishment? He must be slowly starving to death.'

Mary said, 'He's just upset. It's understandable,' and she gave me her dirty look.

We heard the toilet flushing and then Aquila edged toward his room again. He was wiping his face and his eyes with the backs of his hands. Neither Mary nor I could sit still any longer. We both went to help him. She took him by one arm and I took him by the other and we lay him down over his sheets.

Mary said, '*Nonno*, where are your teeth?'

Aquila's hand felt at his mouth. 'Oh no!' he moaned. 'Oh no!'

I went and checked in the toilet but the dentures had gone. Aquila was inconsolable. Mary kept telling him she would take him to a proper dentist tomorrow and get him his own teeth made up, but Aquila moaned about signs and I understood all about this now, and I knew as well as he did that his life was nearly over.

We sat with Aquila for a long time but he wouldn't go to sleep or even try to close his eyes. Maybe he believed that if he drifted off he would never come back.

Aquila said to me, 'I wish I never have met you again, Romeo. You are liar. A liar,' yet as he said it he kept holding my hand and sometimes he squeezed it. Then he said to Mary, 'You a good girl. You like you mother. You deserve better.'

Finally Mary and I were both too tired to keep up what was a fruitless vigil. When we left Aquila's room we found Nigel asleep in the fold-out bunk, comfortable as you please. I left Blue to sleep on the verandah and I staggered around, closing doors and switching out lights. Nigel's fat joints had hit me harder than I realised. In Johnny's room Mary took off her clothes and climbed under the covers, and when I came into the bed she opened her legs wide. I was dreamy and the room was glowing. Mary was dreamy too. The marijuana made us come forever and then we fell asleep together, but I was afraid and the darkness couldn't hold me because *sea breeze comes through the hippy-salvaged porthole and the branches of some dying ghost gums rustle to the rhythm of the sea wind and in my semi-sleep I feel something crawl across my cheek. There was a bad dream but I have already forgotten what it was that was so bad and now all I can feel is the blustering gale outside and this finger of death on my cheek. I hear a voice as well, it seems to whisper sweet and soft and warm in my ear, then the thudding of my heart calms as I realise it is Monica who is touching my cheek and it is Monica who is whispering in my ear and the sea wind is doing nothing but going about its business of shaking trees and carrying the living perfume of salt and sand and distant oceans. Monica's voice says my name over and over but now my heart truly does thump faster for she is curled away from me in the bed, she is fast asleep, and the moonlight illuminates her sharply and makes a glow-girl of her. This moonlight has become so piercing as to be a searchlight, or is this only a trick of my sleep-deadened brain? There seems no privacy in the cabin. It seems we're pets in a cage spotlighted by wardens and spectators with lousy senses of humour. Why has Monica become this glow-girl? Why can I still hear her voice whispering my name in my ear? Why can I still feel her fingers across my cheek? Outside, it's as if the trees are shaking themselves apart. It's cold. The winds are so high that I cannot hear the sea. I pull the insane asylum sheets over Monica and even this simple act, touching these sheets that once knew such agonies, is dreadful. It's like covering Monica with love and death, with good and evil, with the end of the world. I get out of the bed and go to the porthole. My knees creak and my spine cracks. The cabin's floor should be gritty with the dirt and sand our feet have carried back and forth from the beach, but no, it's warm carpet. When I look out through the porthole I don't see scrub or sand dunes or the distant beach, what I do see is a beautiful garden bathed in moonlight, palm trees and a huge jacaranda tree, an immense subtropical paradise. When I turn around and look at the bed I don't see a broken little cabin but a big bedroom, Monica like a glow-girl in the big bed, and a donkey of a man lying well apart from her, naked and sated and snoring. The floor seems to be tilting and the rush of the wind is like the hammering of great engines. I have to hang on to the round edge of the porthole. I can't remember who I am at all. I'm just a lost teenager in a room of strangers, but I do know Monica, of course I do, even if her hair is now long and brown, and I do know she is the person I love, so I rush across this tilting floor and under the sheet it's as if she still glows, not from the moonlight but from her own spirit. I turn this way and that and want to shout formless words into the night. Where there should be darkness there is Monica's incandescence. The floor careens. I crawl under the covers and crush myself to my glow-girl but the donkey of a man awakens and sits bolt upright and stares at me, his eyes full of hell and magic and pain, and we finally meet, across so many years, we are finally the one being, and I'm not afraid any more.*

Mary mumbled something like, 'Romeo, what is it?' and I saw I had my hand on her shoulder and I was shaking her. I took my hand away and lay staring at the ceiling, then I got up to dress. All over, my skin was oily. Mary moved in the bed. 'What are you doing?'

'Nothing, go back to sleep.'

'Oh God, I'm buggered. Are you getting dressed?'

'Go back to sleep.' I did up the buttons of my shirt and laced my running shoes.

Mary rolled onto her back. I saw her stretch this way and that. She sighed, 'Come on, Romeo. Can't you sleep?'

'I have to go out.'

'Now?' Mary snapped on the bedside lamp. It filled the room with the sort of soft glow that made me want to tremble. I had to get that dream off me. 'What's gotten into you?' Mary said. 'Why were you shaking me?'

'Put the light out, Monica.'

'My name is Mary.'

I ran my cold fingers through my hair.

'Where are you going? What are you doing?'

Mary looked at me in a strange way. She could sense something she didn't like. Either that or the marijuana made her more paranoid than usual.

I said, 'What does it matter? Get back to sleep. Why do you have to make such a big production?'

'You're leaving, aren't you?'

'Don't be stupid.'

Mary got out of the bed and tried to hold me. 'Don't go.'

I opened the bedroom door. Motionless shadows filled the house. Shadows, and the lingering scents of garlic and cumin. 'I just have to go out for a while,' I said, and Mary followed me around the house as I found my wallet and watch. She turned lights on as she went. Blue barked from out on the verandah and Nigel sat up in the fold-out bed.

'Hey, what's the commotion?' he said. 'The police aren't here?'

And then even Aquila, who thought he was dying, who was supposed to be dying, came out of his room. He stayed

by Mary, who stayed by me. I found the keys to the bashed
up green Volkswagen.

Mary said, 'What makes you think you can just take my
car?'

Nigel sat up in the living room's fold-out bed, staring as
we trooped by. I went outside and shut the verandah door.
Mary looked out at me as if I was a man about to go and
commit murder in her name. Behind the glass of the French
doors Aquila stood by Mary's shoulder. Through the square
panes Aquila watched me, thinking. Then he looked at his
grand-daughter's breasts. Mary raised her hands and covered
her chest and went away.

The night was dark and cold. I went up the front garden
steps. Blue wanted to come with me so I opened the Volkswagen's passenger door and let him jump aboard. He gave a
throaty howl. The engine gave a throaty rattle. I'd never
driven a Volkswagen. It was too loud. I didn't like it but
Blue sure did, his one eye staring lovingly at me.

Down by the Brisbane River the last Sunday ferry was calling
at its jetties. Some of the restaurant's lights dimmed. It was
only half an hour or so before the last of Il Vulcano Ristorante's patrons paid their way out. I sat on the green bench
by the bicycle path. Blue nosed along the river bank but never
went too far away. It was dark and lonely and I had a wonderful view of the restaurant. Through walls of smoky glass
I saw barmen washing glasses and lovingly polishing the
lovingly polished timber of their bar tops. Waiters and waitresses in Mary's black and white arranged tablecloths and
rearranged chairs. Music wafted over the currents and park-
lands. I hoped it was Caruso, but no, that would have asked
too much. It was Pavarotti or Domingo or some other world

star. I hadn't kept up with who the best aria-belters were.

The outdoor decks were empty and then who should come out for a breath of fresh air but Tony Aquila. He was followed by two young waiters. While Tony got his air the other two started moving tables and chairs inside so they could close up. It was so easy to pick Tony. He was dressed all in black and even from a distance he looked swarthy and handsome. I had to smile. It was like seeing an old friend, but he was no friend of mine. One of the young waiters was having a problem rolling back one of the deck's shade awnings. I heard Tony yell at him, 'The fuck you doing? Get it the fuck up!' as if his entire education was based on movies about New York's Little Italy. Well that was Tony Aquila all right. Mrs Aquila came out onto the deck. Tony stopped his yelling and went to lend a hand with the awning. Soon they had it rolled back, and all the outdoor furniture moved indoors, and Mrs Aquila was alone above the river, sweeping the smooth timber of the wide, encircling deck.

I told Blue to stay, and I went down to the river's edge. In the darkness I moved from rock to rock, then climbed some crossbars and supports and hoisted myself up over the rail. I was in shadows and Mrs Aquila was under a set of lamps, sweeping away as if it was her own living room floor. She felt movement and looked around.

I said, 'Hello, Mrs Aquila.'

To Mrs Aquila I was probably a silhouette without substance. Her face was sweet and lined and peaceful. A string of pearls glittered around her neck. She said, 'That hasn't been my name for many years. I'm Gloria Blake.' She took a step forward and peered into the shadows. 'Who is that?'

I liked that her English had improved. I liked that she wasn't frightened. I walked into the light and said, 'Do you remember me, Mrs Aquila? I'm Romeo Costanzo.'

Mrs Aquila put her broom aside and put a hand on her heart. 'Oh, Romeo,' she said, and I thought she was about to give me a stanza of Shakespeare's play. 'Oh, Romeo,' she said again.

'It's hard not to call you Mrs Aquila.'

'Romeo. You better call me Gloria.' She was smiling now, sweetly, the way Monica would have done if it had been possible for us to meet after so long. Mrs Aquila had put on a little weight and her chest was chunkier and her chin just a little lower, but she looked great. She was still a romantic, you could see it in the way she smiled at me. 'What are you doing here?' She came a little closer. '*Madonna santa*. How have you been, Romeo?'

'Fine,' I said, and it was as if this was a perfectly natural thing, to come visiting Mrs Aquila on this deck, to not come through the front doors but to climb struts and supports the way a lover would. Hadn't the real Romeo climbed an orchard wall to see his Juliet? 'I've been wondering about Monica, Mrs Aquila.'

She came over and stood by the rail. The murky river lapped at the deck's pylons and a few lights went out in the restaurant. Soon her husband and her son would come for her. The wind blew her hair and blew the tenor's rich voice out into the dark. Mrs Aquila looked at me then back at the river.

'Monica passed away, Romeo. It's been nearly fourteen years now. Didn't you know that?'

'I've been wondering about Mary.'

Mrs Aquila just couldn't help it. She had to touch me. She moved closer and with an expression of wonder and of joy she felt my face. I saw all the lines around her eyes and

around her mouth and I knew her life hadn't been so
untroubled.

'You've grown up to be a handsome man, Romeo.'

'I want to know about Monica and Mary.'

'Monica and Mary—what do you want to know about a
mother and her daughter? But why are you here so late?'
Mrs Aquila took her hand away from me and she must have
remembered my famous temper. 'My husband and my three
boys are inside. They're all grown men.'

'I didn't know you had three sons.'

'After I remarried two boys came along to be brothers
to Tony.'

'I'm not here to make any trouble, Mrs Aquila.'

She thought about this for a moment then she said,
'Please don't call me by that name.'

'All right.'

Mrs Aquila said, 'Isn't it time you were over Monica?'

'Yes, a lot of time has gone by.'

Mrs Aquila smiled knowingly. 'Mmm,' and that was all
she had to say on the subject. She shook her hair. 'This isn't
the time to visit, Romeo. Come to the house, tomorrow if
you like. I've had a hard day.'

I made Mrs Aquila look at me. 'Mary and Mr Aquila are
with me in Johnny Armstrong's house. I think Mr Aquila is
very sick.'

'Then send Mary home to me. I don't like the way she
chooses to live. That bastard Johnny never wanted to know
her. Why should she try to know *him*? What good does it
do? My husband and I and my three sons have been her whole
family since she was little.'

'What about Mr Aquila?'

'Romeo, how can you even ask me that? He hasn't been

my problem for a lifetime. God knows what he is now.'

'Could you come and see him?'

'No.'

'I think he's dying, Mrs Aquila.'

'Good.'

All the lines in Mrs Aquila's face had become deeply etched. It was as if sweetness hid only pain. I don't know why I did it, despite what she said I took her hand. I held her hand. We stayed at the railing and looked at the river. The tenor's voice was rich and slow. I thought of Mrs Aquila pouring wine over her lips and telling a poor dumb country boy to drink deeply, I thought of Mrs Aquila dancing slowly to a Dean Martin record and making some cheap television personality touch her here, on her breasts, and here, between her legs. She was Monica's mother and now the mother of Mary, and she hated Aquila. But I stood on that deck and held her sweet small hand and thought my craven thoughts— and they were to lift her dress and make love to her there, over the river, in the name of Monica and in the name of Romeo Costanzo and in the name of all the years I'd wanted her.

Mrs Aquila let me put my hand in her hair. I kissed her throat and her cheek and her eyes. It was like kissing Monica and Mary all at once. Mrs Aquila sighed and crushed my lips with hers.

I whispered in her ear, because I had to, 'Why do you have to hate Mr Aquila?'

Mrs Aquila's hands were trembling. She was afraid of me now but she held my face away and looked straight in my eyes. She said, 'That man killed his own daughter, Romeo,' and before I could even begin to understand the conjugation of words we weren't alone any more.

Tony Aquila cried, 'Ma! Who's that?'

Mrs Aquila turned around but she kept holding my hand.
'Tony, this is Romeo Costanzo. You remember Romeo. He's
come to see us again.'

Tony came forward. He was in his thirties, muscular and
mean. He said, 'Romeo who?'

I said, 'How are the Fiats going?'

He said, 'Fiats? What the fuck are you talking about
Fiats?' Then he stopped and looked at me closely, as if
inspecting something really despicable. The years had given
his mouth a sneer that couldn't be taken away. 'Bloody hell.
Aren't you that stupid prick from——where was it——Sydney,
Melbourne?'

Mrs Aquila said, 'That's enough, Tony.'

There was an older man in a good suit.

He said, 'Go inside Tony,' and he looked at me and took
off his horn-rimmed glasses and handled them and put them
on again. His teeth were perfectly straight and perfectly white
and perfectly fake. Tony didn't move so he said again, 'Go
inside.'

Mrs Aquila let go of my hand and Tony went away.

Mr Jimmy Blake looked at me and came closer. He said,
'I don't know who you are or how you got here but I'll give
you a minute and then I'm calling the police.'

I said, 'I'm a friend of Mrs Aquila's.'

He said, 'Yes, I saw that. Her name is Mrs Gloria Blake.'
We both looked at Mrs Gloria Blake and her cheeks were
burning. Then she walked away to a corner of the rail and
she turned her shoulders to us. Mr Jimmy Blake stood aside
and said, 'Goodbye, young man.'

I walked from the outside decks into the restaurant. It
was too cool inside, as if the air-conditioning had been turned

up too high. The place looked expensive and vast and the
river's currents reflected in all the smoky glass walls. The
kitschy framed photographs of famous people hung everywhere. Pity I'd never eat or dance there. I followed a marble
pathway lined with palms in terracotta pots. Tony was
waiting at the front doors. I walked straight past but he
couldn't help but shove one of my shoulders. I stopped and
looked him straight in the face. He didn't move and then for
a second I thought he looked scared. Then I walked outside
and the night air was a relief and none of them inside were
important at all.

As I walked down the dark bicycle path the restaurant
diminished behind me. Some volcano. It was just a mire of
perplexing human mistakes. I was glad to be out. The river
lapped against the polished rocks of its banks. There was a
breeze and a strong current. Wind kept blowing in my face
but I couldn't say it was Monica. Mrs Aquila's kisses too—
they were unreal, without substance, like the touch of
shadows. All that was real was what she had said, and I hoped
it was a lie.

Blue sat faithfully by the green bench. He turned to me
with a trusting eye. I wondered if in the dark he had been
chasing geckos. Leaves scuttled down the pathway, and a bit
of old wood floated like a body in the dark currents. Beside
Blue there was a real ghost. Aquila in his brown suit, perfectly shaved and with his tresses cut short, and under his
coat he wore one of Nigel's stolen silk shirts. He looked like
the ghost of a neat old man who liked to go out late for a
walk with his dog.

Aquila said, 'I know you come here, Romeo.'

'I thought you were dying.' My legs were actually

shaking. Was what Mrs Aquila said true or not true? I sat beside Aquila and said, 'Is that aftershave?'

'Is yours I tink. After you go nobody wants to sleep. I make Mary cut the hair and shave my face and call me taxi. She very good with the razor and with the scissors. My brother the black boy put on music and it like a party. But I come here to be with you. How I look?'

'Not bad at all. Pity you don't still have those teeth.'

'Eh.'

'How do you feel?'

Aquila said, and his voice was soft and throaty, a little the way I remembered Monica's to be, 'Feel pretty good.' He looked over toward Il Vulcano. 'Tummy feel better.' His short hair and clean face, his profile too, his longing, all of it almost made him the man I remembered from so many years ago. 'I have one last story to tell, Romeo.'

'Okay,' I said. 'I'm listening, Mr Aquila.'

And this was the last story Aquila had to tell.

When Monica came to see me in the boarding house, Romeo, she'd already been away years. She had a pizza and a bottle of wine and expected to tell a thousand exotic tales, but after she sat in that room with me for five minutes she couldn't bring herself to tell a single one. Monica kept staring at me and I kept staring at her.

'I made you this pizza myself, Papà. With lots of anchovies and olives, just the way you like. I'm staying in the spare room at the restaurant. I feel funny at home. It's better on my own, at least for now. Tonight after they closed I looked at the oven and I thought I'd make you something special. It's not too late, is it? Do you like my pizza?'

I ate a piece and drank a glass of wine and Monica did the same. I told her it was a good pizza but the anchovies were too salty. I told her the wine was good. I told her she looked well.

'I went to see Mary today. You know she's four now, Papà? She's got so much energy. Ma's been looking after her. Mary loves Ma. And Antonio's like a father to her. You should see them together, they're like a big brother and a little sister.'

'And that man, Jimmy Blake, is he like a father to your child as well?'

Monica looked down at the filthy carpet. She moved this way and that in her chair and colour came into her face. She put her greasy hands on the dresser and then she took them away. There wasn't enough light in the room, there was never enough light, and men were arguing in the corridors or snoring in their rooms.

'But he's a good man, Papà.'

I tried another piece but the pizza was beginning to stick in my throat. Monica poured me another glass of wine and she took one herself. The pizza went down a little better. Ah, Monica looked so beautiful, Romeo, she looked so fresh. Especially when the colour came into her cheeks. She looked like she hadn't left her baby behind so that she could go and parade like a slut in every European city you could think of. In four years, in cities with names I can't pronounce, she studied and worked and married some fool and divorced him—now here she was with a glowing smile and a pizza and a bottle of wine, all as if butter would not melt in her mouth.

'You know Ma's expecting, Papà?'

I put down my glass and wiped my mouth and we looked at each other.

'Don't say another word, Monica.'

'Yes, Papà.'

I made Monica sit there in front of me and I ate the rest of

the pizza. I picked out the salty anchovies and set them aside.
Monica kept her eyes on the floor. I wanted her to be ashamed.
With every minute that ticked by Monica grew more and more
ashamed. I wanted her to think about her abandoned child and I
wanted her to think about her mother in another man's bed, and I
wanted her to realise that it was her own bawling when she was a
baby that had let that filthy slut of an angel find me after so long,
and ruin all our lives. Monica knew what she'd done. I could see
her shame, as only a father can. She looked up at me just once and
in her eyes I understood there was fear and regret.

But she said, 'I'm glad Ma left you. Ma couldn't have stayed
with a man like you. I'm glad Ma married Mr Blake.'

'Lower your eyes, Monica.'

Monica lowered her eyes. I made her sit still while I drank the
rest of the wine, and when I finished the wine I said, 'I want you
to go away, Monica.'

'Papà, you need help.'

'Yes, you're right. I need help to get me what I want. But
you've helped enough. You and that whore have helped more than
enough. One day you and that whore will burn in all the fires of
hell. And on that day I'll be dancing, Monica, the whole world will
be dancing and you and that whore will be burning.'

'Papà,' Monica said. And that was all. Monica stood and then
she walked to the door of that dark little room I'd been living in
for years, and she didn't turn around and she didn't say goodbye
and I knew it wasn't Monica at all—but her, that whore of an
angel, or her kind, in the flesh.

'What did you do to her?' I shouted. The river was quiet.

'What did you do to your daughter?'

The wings were beating louder than ever. It was like the sound at the end of the world. It was as if all the friends and all the family I ever knew were talking to me at once. To comfort myself I went on my knees and kissed Monica's hand prints on the dresser, for the memory of my true daughter, wherever she'd been stolen away to. I couldn't sleep. The angel came into my room. She lay with me and she squeezed my cock and she turned herself over. And then she opened her mouth wide to eat my heart. In the rooms of that filthy boarding house the drunk and broken old men who had already been seduced by that angel did terrible things with each other. I had to run to save my life. I went out onto the street and I heard voices calling me and wings beating above me, and all the devils of hell were at my heels all the way to that wicked place on Petrie Terrace. I stood outside looking up at its darkened windows and locked doors, catching my breath but full of lunatic despair. I knew how to get in, so in I went, and I didn't have to switch on a single light because I knew the way around that place as well as I knew the way around the agonies of my heart.

I could even smell the pizza Monica made me.

And there she was too, this thing that wasn't Monica, that was where she had returned. Oh, but she was full of too much shame to go to her own child and to her own mother's house, and so there she sat in the darkness with an ashtray and a packet of French cigarettes and a bottle of whisky. Her head was on her arm and she was at a table and the angel came in and started to laugh because what truer end could she have envisioned for me? The angel folded her wings and sat in a corner and crossed her legs, and watched.

This thing that wasn't Monica looked up, but what did she see? Did she hear that laughter too? Was she sorry she had sold her soul and delivered me to the world of evil? If there was anything left in her at all, if there was a bit of Monica left to save, there was only one way to do that, to save my little girl, or what was left of her, and when she raised her drooping drunk eyes she smiled sweetly at

me and she said, 'Oh, I want to hold Mary now,' and I poured the
whisky and lit a match and the angel's screaming joy followed me
all the way onto the street and didn't stop until I was howling like
a wolf on my knees, and fire spewed from the mouth of the volcano,
and all the evil in the world burned and died as one in that belly,
except of course for me.

'You bastard. My God, you bastard. You killed my Monica.'

The horror would never get out of my head. We were
in the dark and the dog was nosing along the river bank and
some fat tenor was singing an aria over the currents. There
was a rustling in the bushes and the sky was black and my
Monica had been killed by this crazy piece of shit. The only
time the world has ever made sense was when I was with
Monica, and this Sicilian bastard had taken her life away
because of some endless cycle of Sicilian fantasy.

I covered my face and cried, 'How did you get away
with it? Why didn't they lock you up? Why didn't they
fucking kill you?'

Aquila looked at me strangely.

'I no get away with, Romeo. The police they come and
they put me in jail and the money Mr Jimmy Blake pay me
for Il Vulcano gets eaten by lawyers and barristers. They
plead arson and accidental killing. They say I no know my
daughter inside. They say I a sick man. The court cannot
prove otherwise. What I care? All I know is I very happy.
They can plead whatever they want. I get fourteen year and
I get out in eight. No one come to visit me in eight year,
only the priest and the social worker and the psychologist.'

'You should have found a way to open your veins in your
cell.'

'Ah. For long time I share cell with a good man who kill

his own brother. He talk to me a lot about the forgiveness
and love, and in the jail for a job they make me a sweeper
and pay me fifteen dollar a week. And then one day in my
cell all the voices I no want to hear stop talking and the good
man he has hung himself with his socks. I look at him a long
time and I see a waste of a good life, a waste of a good man
who know a lot about the forgiveness and love, and then in
my heart I see my Monica and I see what I done. My hair it
go grey and white in one night. My teeth they start to rot
and fall out and my belly it burns and I cannot eat ever again.
All I can swallow are cockroaches and nails and any bit of
rubbish from the ground. I want to die but I no die. And
then my time is up and they let me out so the only thing I
can do is drink, and I drink all I can. I drink until the world
is crazy, and then I do die.'

'What's that supposed to mean?'

'In hospital. Royal Brisbane Hospital. Someone find me
in the street and ambulance come and I wake up once and I
see the pretty nurses and a young doctor and things they
stick in my arm and come out the other. I know I dying and
I don't care. I close my eyes and I feel the spirit it slowly
go up into the sky. All I wish is I no come back to this place.
I find a beautiful stream and I know what it is, is the stream
from outside Piedimonte, and at first is very pretty but very
lonely. But then there are people, and they are friends. I
recognise faces. They smile at me and they clap their hands
because they happy to see me. I keep walking along this
stream and I see all the people from the old times, the people
from the village. The boys and girls, the good ones and the
bad, all the ones who live in Piedimonte with me. And then
there is black faces and yellow faces and is all the people of
the world and they like me and I glad, very glad to be there

with them. But then I find Monica, and my father and mother, my brother and my sister. Monica she take hold of my hand and she kiss it and she say, 'Come back later, Papà. Is no you time. I wait for you.' And I slowly go away and when I wake up the little nurse get a shock to see my eyes they open. She look scared, and the young doctor he come and he tell me my heart it stop but now it go again.' Aquila shrugged. 'I prefer to be far away by that stream with Monica but that the way it go. Eh.'

'You just can't stop with your bullshit, can you?'

'I go back in the old boarding house, Romeo. I see that life is a gift. I see that life is beautiful. After so many year I remember what it means to be alive, to have the wife and children. I start to tink maybe I can have life again. Maybe my wife, maybe my son, maybe my business. But now I know there is no use to be dreaming about such tings. I have my chance but my chance is gone. I very glad we met again here in Brisbane, Romeo. You right, this I see, no one they want me. I no get away with murder. No penance she can be enough. My penance she is to stay lonely and to slow-slow fade away from the memory until there is nothing left of Michele Aquila. Maybe that why Monica tell me my time is no ready. I have to suffer for longer. Here—until I fade away. Eh. That my story.'

I uncovered my face. I'd never hated a man more.

'Where is this fucking angel of yours these days?'

Aquila looked at me strangely again. 'There no angel, Romeo. My father he was wrong and I very wrong to believe the tings he believe. There is no such ting as sin and evil, there only the tings you do and some are right and some are wrong, and you know very well which is which. Sometimes you must pay for what you do but most times probably not.

Sometimes luck she comes along too, so there is really no sense you can make, the only sense you can make is to keep do what you tink is okay and hope for the best, and if that make you life good then fine, and if not, oh well.'

'You learned all this a bit late, didn't you?'

Aquila's answer was to shiver all the way through to his brittle bones.

'What do you want now?'

'I tink I go and speak to my wife.'

'They're all in there. Don't you think they'll kill you? Don't you think they'll eat you alive?'

Mr Aquila adjusted the collar of his new silk shirt. He ran a gnarled hand through his newly cropped hair and he wiped his wet eyes and his wet nose.

'You know something I wish, Romeo? I wish the little Mary she did know me and she did come to the jail to visit with me. Then it would be like Monica she not gone. Maybe that why you like the girl. You no want her. You want Monica. You still very hungry man, Romeo. But doesn't matter, the hope of the future is no with me and is no with you. Is with Mary.' Aquila stood and straightened his suit a bit. He looked down on me. 'If I say I sorry is not enough so I say nothing.' He whistled for Blue to come over and he bent painfully and rubbed the dog's head. 'Romeo, you look after my ugly little friend, eh?'

And then he was walking down the dusky bicycle path, dry winter leaves blowing around him. In a way I didn't want him to go. He shuffled along because he was an old man who had eaten himself up from inside. But what did I care about Aquila? What did I care that he had weighed up his life? What did I care that he believed Monica forgave him? I rubbed Blue's fur and I felt like I was going mad.

When I looked up Aquila was at the restaurant, he was bent and frail, he was a question mark walking into a volcano.

When I drove the old Volkswagen to the front of Johnny Armstrong's house I turned off the rattling engine and leaned my head down on the steering wheel. My hands were damp and so was my forehead.

Blue cocked an ear. I heard it too. From the street you could hear thumping music. My watch had stopped around midnight. Hadn't Aquila said Nigel made things like a party? Blue scratched at the passenger door. He was keen to investigate. I let him out and climbed out too. It was late. The sky was dark and the air was fresh, but I couldn't seem to gulp enough of that air into my lungs. The flowers I'd loved into life in the front garden made the air sweet. Blue led the way to the verandah and the doors were shut. Through the cracks in the French doors came the seeping, bitter scent of a lot of marijuana. Through the little square panes I saw Mary and Nigel dancing in the living room, the fold-out bed pushed aside. Most of the lights were out but you could still tell how good they looked together. The music was wild. Mary and Nigel's eyes were closed and the thumping beat made them deaf to our arrival.

Nigel was a dance superstar and Mary wasn't too bad herself. If they fell in love they could make clubbing their life's vocation. Boy, did they look good together.

I said, 'Come on, fella,' and Blue followed me around the house and down, down, down, to the deep and dark back garden. For some reason it seemed a little warmer. You could hear night creatures scuttling over the terraces. You could smell all the flowers I'd given new life. You could hear

the music coming down from the house. It was good to be
in a place that was so alive. My eyes adjusted to the dark,
and it was really dark for there were no stars and no moon,
and I walked over to the hammock perpetually strung
between the trunks of those two ancient palm trees. No one
had slept in it for a long time. The fabric was damp with
night dew. Still, when I climbed in and made myself comfortable it felt fine, and for a few moments it swung like a
baby's cradle in empty space. When Blue leapt aboard it
swung more. He didn't smell very good and he licked my
face to reassure himself that everything was okay. He was
heavy too but we found a way to arrange ourselves.

I knew the music that was playing. It was clear, even
down in the back garden. Now a song that wasn't so wild
but more melodic. The neighbours wouldn't need to complain anyway. The good thing about Johnny's place was that
it was so big and the other houses were so far away. I closed
my eyes and saw Mary and Nigel dancing. Nigel was playing
one of his stolen CDs. I hadn't listened to it but I knew this
particular song from the radio. A girl's voice wafted around
Johnny's little rainforest paradise, around the branches of the
jacaranda and palm trees.

> Run your life energy through me
> Keep me hot and alive
> I crave you until it consumes me
> I want you to crystallise.

Heavy wings were beating up in the trees. They belonged to
fat fruit bats. Now even Aquila knew there was no such thing
as that filthy whore of an angel. If I kept Monica in my mind
she would stay hot and alive and would never fade away. I

went to sleep with wings beating loudly and those bats squawking for fruit and the odd plump possum blundering off a branch and falling to the ground with a thud and a growl that sounded a lot like a fart. Blue coughed. The breeze was against my face. It was peaceful. I was peaceful. That breeze was still all Monica.

In the morning a scrub turkey was looking at me. I swung the hammock and Blue dropped out of it and went and urinated over a bush. The big colourful bird didn't move. Over days and weeks it had made a deep mound of rotting twigs and had laid its eggs in there. Days earlier I'd found two the size of nice easter eggs and had carefully replaced them. As the vegetation rotted the temperature inside the mound went up and that helped the eggs to come along.

We hadn't met face to face before. I rubbed the sleep from my eyes. The scrub turkey took its time and decided I was a friend. It picked its way around a bit and then stuck its head into the mound to check the temperature. When it pulled its head out it came a little closer to the hammock and looked at me some more.

Blue left the scrub turkey alone.

I went up to the house and used my key to get in. Mary and Nigel were already awake. They were drinking fresh black coffee and you couldn't tell which beds had been slept in and which hadn't. They both looked tired but they both must have been used to getting up early. Aquila wasn't around. My back and neck were stiff and I smelled like Blue. I went to have a shower and while I was under the strong hot spray I thought I heard the telephone ringing. I came out, wrapped in a towel. I still felt lousy.

Mary met me in the corridor. She didn't look happy.

She said, 'I have to go and pick Johnny up from the airport.'

I said, 'Let him catch a taxi. Why should you jump just because he's decided to call?'

Mary looked unhappier still. She left the house. I dressed and started packing my suitcase but I lost interest and went and poured myself a coffee. Nigel had some more. I sat down at the table with him and neither of us really looked at the other.

I said, 'Do you like Mary, Nigel?'

Nigel stood straight up and stretched. His joints popped. He said, 'Romeo, I can't believe how big this house is. I think I'm going to have a good look around outside.'

So Nigel left his coffee and went outside. I stayed at the table and finished mine. I wanted divine intervention because I couldn't work anything out for myself. Nigel took his time inspecting the house. When I went back to the bedroom I threw everything out of my suitcase and sorted through my clothes. I only wanted a few items. Then I found a little backpack that belonged to Mary. I stuffed it with my things and went and waited with it on the verandah. It could be a while. Johnny would have to get through customs, or maybe he had already, maybe that was when he'd called Mary.

When Nigel came back to the verandah he said, 'This is an unreal house. I'd love to get stuck into it. What about you, Romeo? We could do it together, you and me. A good paint job would just lift the place. You and me, three weeks if it doesn't rain, all done.'

I said, 'That's a good idea, Nigel. You should put it to the man of the house.'

And the man of the house arrived. Mary climbed out of

the Volkswagen and collected his bags. As she hefted those bags her royal passenger started to emerge. It took a while. At first I thought there was some mistake or some joke, that this was a friend of Johnny's and Johnny was coming later. But no, if you looked closely enough you could see Johnny in the folds of fat. He had a great belly and a nasty, twisted mouth, and he was bald save for a few wisps of hair across his sunburnt scalp. It was a pity he hadn't been allowed to keep that nice Elvis Presley hair, but at least his eyes were still a clear blue. The years hadn't been kind to him, or he hadn't been kind to himself. Maybe in his own way, like Aquila, Johnny had eaten himself up from the inside. Except that, unlike Aquila, he was too fattening.

Johnny waddled through the front gate, led by Mary. I have to admit I was in awe of his bulk. Mary was smiling. She was happy. I wondered what they'd said to each other. It only made me angrier. Mary just about swung those fucking bags she was so happy. Johnny was smiling too. He puffed and blew as he came up to the verandah. Boy was he big. Where was that waistline, that sexy black hair, that twinkle in the eye that always got him his way? Maybe if I'd been him I wouldn't have kept too many of my past and present photographs around the house either. The comparison would be just too depressing.

'Romeo!' Dr Johnny Armstrong said, and he grabbed me by the shoulders. 'You big dumb shit-for-brains! How are you?'

I let myself be shaken up by him but then I remembered my own doctor, Dr Kolner, and the money I'd spent on his advice. It was time for an affirmation. 'Johnny. You know what? You fucking call me that one more fucking time and I'll fucking break your neck.'

Johnny gave me a look and stepped away. He cleared his throat and said to Nigel, 'Who are you?'

Mary said, 'That's my friend. His name is Nigel. He's going to stay a while.'

Johnny said, 'Is he?'

Mary said, 'Yes. And there's one more to come,' and she went inside with the bags.

Johnny looked at me and said, 'One more? How many people have you moved into my house?'

Nigel took his leave and went after Mary. Johnny and I looked at each other, then Johnny went to the fresh garden but he didn't seem to notice any of my handiwork.

I couldn't think of a thing to say to him, so I said, 'Good flight? Jet-lagged?'

He said, 'Romeo, I'm scared to Christ about being a father.'

'You weren't so scared all those years ago.'

'That was because I wanted Monica. When Monica didn't want me, well, I just sort of lost interest.'

'I don't think you'll have to do too much. Maybe just know her a little. Mary's a big girl. Have you experienced her thumb-hold?'

'Thumb-what?' Johnny didn't have a clue what I was talking about. He wiped his broad face. 'I'm still scared. But I swear, I'm gonna love that girl.'

'Johnny, you got me up here to try and make me fall in love with Mary, didn't you?'

'It was worth a try. I knew you always kept up that thing for Monica. Mary's all Monica.'

'No, she isn't.'

'She is. I was hoping you'd see her in Mary. I was hoping you'd take her off my hands. Mary was so demanding and so scary I couldn't even think straight. The best I could do was *disappear*. I was in Wengen when it slowly started to dawn on me. I'm a father and my child needs me. Then I was working a downhill run and it hit me like a thunderbolt. I'm Mary's *father*. You know, Romeo, maybe there isn't a better thing to be. Anyway, that thunderbolt hit me and I nearly went over a precipice of the fucking Jungfrau.' Johnny started working himself up. 'I'm her father. I'm gonna love that girl.'

Well, things change all right.

I was glad that Blue came along at that moment. Johnny said, 'Hey, my mate!' and in the garden they had their reunion.

I took the opportunity to go inside. Mary and Nigel were talking low and terse in the big bedroom. Nigel had that hang-doggy, moony kind of look young men get on their faces when they're in love and they're about to get their nuts kicked in. When Mary saw me she went and busied herself with Johnny's things. My stuff had no place in there now. It had been pushed aside and replaced by Johnny's strong suitcases.

I said, 'Nigel, I just need a minute.'

Nigel, sad-eyed and already in love, said for some reason, 'Don't do anything silly, Romeo. Mary's a top girl.'

'I know,' I said, and before Nigel left the room I gave him a strong hug and he looked at me as if I was weird.

Mary straightened from Johnny's suitcases and she smiled at me. She came and kissed me on the neck. I held her close and her breasts pressed into me. She was very excited. Mary said, 'I don't want you to do anything. I don't want you to go and I don't want you to stay.'

I touched her long hair. I said, 'Mary, I love you.'

'You told me that last night, Romeo. What exactly does it mean?'

'It means I can't stand to be alone any more. It means you're in my heart, Mary, and I never want you to leave. It means I see the good in you and I want you to see the good in me. I want you to come with me. I'm going back to my home. I know you've got what you want with Johnny, and a real grandfather too, but I still want you to come with me. I'm not thinking of Monica, I'm thinking of you.'

Mary said very kindly, 'Don't you think maybe we don't know each other well enough?'

'We've got all the time in the world. What's important is we're in each other's hearts, and that doesn't happen every day. You can't push that aside. It's wrong to do that, that's the worst thing you can do. We'll get to know each other better.'

Mary shook her head. She said, 'No.'

So I let out all my breath and wondered if Mary and I really were strangers. My head was spinning. What could I do? I went for second best.

I said, 'Maybe one day you can come and visit me. If you still remember me.'

'Maybe.' Mary looked at the floor and then looked at me. 'I shouldn't say this, Romeo. Maybe after my grandfather dies I'll come to see you.'

I thought that was good. It was kind of funny. Why shouldn't my happiness be predicated on old Aquila kicking the bucket?

Mary came outside with me and I thought how neat I was, leaving when I wasn't needed any more. At least I wasn't throwing things or smashing chairs. It felt like those days were over. I'd made this type of exit once before with Johnny, walking out of the picture, leaving he and Monica on the island when I became superfluous. And look where it got us. But I couldn't think of another way.

Nigel was inside with fat Johnny, already telling him about what they could do with the house, the two of them, three weeks if it didn't rain, all done. He didn't sound like he was pleading. Nigel was a good kid. We should have gone dancing in the Underworld just one more time.

Mary came to the front fence. Her dress swayed in the breeze and her long hair blew across her face. She was radiant and it was easy to love her. I hefted her little backpack and she didn't comment on me taking it.

Mary wiped the straggly hair away from her mouth and she said, 'I love you,' but she still went back to Johnny's verandah.

Blue trotted out of the front garden and came up to the weedy footpath. I started walking and he came with me, tail wagging.

Mary called out loudly, 'Hey, what are you doing with that dog? Send him home.'

I called back, 'Why? Why the fuck should Johnny get everything? *Fuck him*!' and walked faster up Raintree Avenue.

'Blue!' Mary sang out. 'Blue! Come home, boy!'

But Blue stayed by my side no matter how much I picked up the pace. The day was sunny and Blue's claws clicked along the footpath.

I was beginning to like that dog.

It took us forever to get to Sydney. We hitched our way along but people don't like to stop for a man and a dog. At least interstate truck drivers seemed to like us. A few nights Blue and I slept in spooky, open parks on our own, and during the day the heels of my shoes wore down on hot

bitumen and dusty roadsides. There was a lot of walking. I
still preferred walking and hitching to flying. Once bitten and
everything, but it was more than that. I had to think about
Aquila and Monica. And I did, only it was impossible to
resolve anything. I wondered how Mrs Aquila and her new
family received Aquila that night. I wondered if he made his
way back to Mary and if he lived in Johnny's house, where
as interesting a nuclear family as ever there's been was
born—especially with Nigel thrown in. I wondered how
thrilled Johnny was to have that old bastard Aquila there.
But most times when I thought of Aquila I just couldn't think
straight. Other times I felt sorry for him. That was where
Monica came into the picture. Whenever I indulged my hate
she was nowhere around, but whenever I softened she was
close at hand. Monica made me calm. She liked to tell me
about the surprising twistings and turnings of people's lives,
the lies and the truths they live with, and she liked to talk
about blind luck too. Sometimes I heard her voice and other
times there was just some big truck's tyres whirring along
the highway. Sometimes Monica was singing in my ear and
sometimes it was some happy, pilled-up truckie in a blue
singlet warbling a Slim Dusty or a Willie Nelson tune. Whenever I knew the tune I'd join in just so the poor guy didn't
feel stupid.

One time Monica said, *But you shouldn't hate him, Romeo*,
and I couldn't reply. Then I woke one night in an open
football field, Armidale I think, and Monica was standing
there with her arms open and her sweet smile just for me.
She said *Are you all right?* and I said *I think, therefore I am* and
then she let me sleep again.

Blue and I arrived in Sydney and it was a miracle to be
home again. We made it to Bondi Beach without succumbing

to a bus or a taxi, all by hitching. Now that really was magic. By the time we were there it was 1 a.m.

Blue sensed the change in me. He yapped at the moon. He trotted down from the busy streets and strips and rolled around in the sands like a puppy. He dashed to the waterline and jumped over the wavelets and had a good old time of it. While Blue played I walked along to see my apartment block. It was all dark. My lodgers were out or asleep. My little Pepita and her squabbling brood were probably all asleep too.

If we could get away with it, Blue and I would sleep in the sand. We were getting used to the open air, all right.

There was music from the cafés and lots of people walking along the streets and the dark beaches. All the stars were out and a fat yellow moon hung low. No wonder Blue liked to yap at it. The night traffic hummed and drunks swayed under neon signs. That's the way Bondi nights should always be. An ocean breeze was whipping up. It felt good and wild on my face. I ran after Blue, down to the dark beach, and tackled the little fucker.

We wrestled and growled in the sand and Blue nipped at me but he wouldn't hurt me, and then we sat watching the black waves come into shore. It felt good to be alive. My heart was thumping. Monica kissed my face and I touched my face and held her kiss there. She said something nice but the cold breeze blew over me and drowned out her words. Breakers crashed. Somewhere on a forgotten little beach at Stradbroke Island Monica's feet had left their imprint at the waterline. In her heart there had been a wish to disappear beneath the breakers, to fade away under cold waves, under a blue sky. It wasn't death, it was the letting go that comes to all of us.

Now, here, shadows walked along in twos and there

were some quiet shadows that stood alone. They didn't look so bad, those solitary shadows, but the ones in twos were better. I looked down the eternal tract of sand and thought how beautiful it was, and wished for God's help to make me a better man, and when I looked back to the waterline Blue let out a moan and my Monica was gone.